"I'll go with y[ou,]"

Summer said.

"Summer—"

"I can't just let you do it all. It's bad enough I turned your life upside down, without sitting back doing nothing while you do all the investigating."

Lady, you turned my life upside down years ago. "I'm not doing much yet. Just walking, talking, feeling out the street. You can't help with that."

"I could talk to some people. Those small-business owners you talked about, the ones Sherwood was trying to shake down for protection money, maybe they've seen the shooter around again."

"Maybe. We'll talk about it tomorrow. Right now, you need to get to bed."

And I need to climb right in after you. Colter shuddered at the thought of lying beside her in that big four-poster, of, at last, turning his hands free to roam over her slender body, to caress that silken skin, of skimming the shimmering white satin she wore off her, of cupping her breasts in his hands....

"You, too," she said, and his heart slammed to a stop.

Dear Reader,

When two people fall in love, the world is suddenly new and exciting, and it's that same excitement we bring to you in Silhouette Intimate Moments. These are stories with scope and grandeur. The characters lead lives we all dream of, and everything they do reflects the wonder of being in love.

Longer and more sensuous than most romances, Silhouette Intimate Moments novels take you away from everyday life and let you share the magic of love. Adventure, glamour, drama, even suspense— these are the passwords that let you into a world where love has a power beyond the ordinary, where the best authors in the field today create stories of love and commitment that will stay with you always.

In coming months, look for novels by your favorite authors: Heather Graham Pozzessere, Emilie Richards and Kathleen Korbel, to name just a few. And whenever you buy books, look for all the Silhouette Intimate Moments, love stories for today's woman by today's woman.

Leslie J. Wainger
Senior Editor and Editorial Coordinator

JUSTINE DAVIS

Loose Ends

SILHOUETTE·INTIMATE·MOMENTS®

Published by Silhouette Books New York

America's Publisher of Contemporary Romance

SILHOUETTE BOOKS
300 East 42nd St., New York, N.Y. 10017

LOOSE ENDS

ISBN: 0-373-07391-7

First Silhouette Books printing July 1991

Books by Justine Davis

Silhouette Intimate Moments

Hunter's Way #371
Loose Ends #391

JUSTINE DAVIS

lives in San Clemente, California. Her interests outside of writing are sailing, doing needlework, riding and driving her restored 1967 Corvette roadster—top down, of course.

A policewoman, Justine says that years ago, a young man she worked with encouraged her to try for a promotion to a position that was, at that time, occupied only by men. "I succeeded, became wrapped up in my new job, and that man moved away, never, I thought, to be heard from again. Ten years later, he appeared out of the woods of Washington state, saying he'd never forgotten me and would I please marry him? With that history, how could I write anything but romance?"

To Tom—even though he won't believe
it wouldn't have happened without him

Chapter 1

It was time to make the swim to Key West again.

He'd put it off, let himself get lazy, let himself become too fond of drowsing in the sun. He would do it today, he thought. Soon, before it began to get dark. A half mile each way, he could do it in half an hour. Maybe forty minutes, he amended wryly, flicking sand off one bare foot with the other. All the nothing he'd been doing lately was bound to have added to his time.

He shifted his position against the curved trunk of the palm tree. Any minute. Any minute, he'd get up and head for the turquoise water. And he'd make it in thirty minutes, he thought with sudden determination. Unless he decided to go ashore for a drink at the Conch before he started back. Sounded pretty good. A cold beer, maybe. Might even be worth a swim back in the dark, if he—

"Colter?"

He froze. He hadn't heard that name in over a year; people here used his first name, or just called him "el tur-quezo," a nickname coined by the Cuban locals for the color of his eyes. And he especially hadn't heard that name, or any other he answered to, in a ~~voice~~ like that. Not since—

No, not ever.

Slowly, he lifted an index finger and pushed the brim of his battered palm-frond hat back from his forehead. Making it seem an even greater effort than it was, he pried one eye open.

"It *is* you. I'd know those eyes..."

The figure that was only a silhouette against the south Florida sun bent, crouching beside him. In the shade of the tree, it changed from a dark, sun-haloed shadow to a slender yet curved feminine shape clad in a loose, lightweight cotton jumpsuit of a pale green print patterned with darker shades, belted snugly at a slender waist.

Her small feet were bare, and a pair of sandals dangled from one hand. The other clutched a small straw bag that matched the darkest green of the fabric. Beneath the wide brim of the green cloth hat that covered her hair, sunglasses with very dark lenses sat atop a small, straight nose, masking her eyes. They left him only a delicate yet determined looking chin and a soft, wide mouth to look at. And look he did. At least, he did until the realization of what she'd said came back to him.

"Now that we both know who I am, who the hell are you?"

His voice was more than a little blunt. He didn't care; he didn't like surprises in his new life, and people who dropped into this out-of-the-way paradise he'd found, unannounced and using a name rarely heard anymore, definitely fell into the surprise category.

"Has it really been that long?"

That voice, he thought again. Not only was it soft, husky and incredibly sexy, it was familiar. No, it couldn't be. He would never forget a voice like that, not a voice that made you think of cool silk drawn over hot, naked skin.

You idiot, he muttered inwardly. Maybe you need to stay in Key West for more than a drink if the first female voice you've heard in a month sets you off like this. He sat up beneath the tree, then, for the second time on this hot, tropical day, he froze.

She had pulled off the hat, exposing a short tousle of blond hair. It left bare neat little ears adorned with small gold hoops and covered her forehead in a thick fringe of bangs. The sunglasses had followed the hat, unveiling clear, light green eyes fringed with long, spiky lashes. He knew he was gaping at her, but he couldn't help it.

"Summer?" His voice was incredulous, stunned.

Her mouth bent into a soft smile, her full lower lip curving in that maddening way he'd never forgotten.

"Not that long, then," she said in that silken voice.

He pulled off his own hat, running a hand through shaggy, sandy brown hair that had been bleached to a golden streakiness by the sun of the Florida Keys. He shook his head as if he could dissolve the impossible vision that had materialized before him. She was still there, watching him with an almost amused expression.

"How...? What...?" He let out a short breath.

"Funny," she said dryly, "I don't remember you ever being speechless before."

He took a breath and tried again for coherent speech. "I've never had the last person in the world I ever expected to see show up in front of me almost thirty-five hundred miles from home before. You stick a pin in a map for a vacation spot or what?"

"No." She let out a breath as she sat down on the white sand. "I was looking for you."

"For...me?" She nodded. His eyebrows lowered. "And you found me. How?"

"Dave Stanley told me when he'd last heard from you, you were in Miami, heading for the Keys."

"That was over a year ago." He remembered the postcard he'd dropped in the mail on impulse, for a reason he still didn't quite understand.

"I know. But it was all I had. So I started in Key Largo and headed south. When I hit the Mile Zero marker in Key West, I had to backtrack a little, but here I am."

"Just like that?" He knew it had to have been more complicated than what she'd said, but she only shrugged. Then she grinned, the green eyes lighting in a way that sent an odd ripple of sensation down his spine.

"Yes, actually. You're rather...well-known around here, 'el turquezo.'"

That grin and the teasing note in her voice produced a re-action he hadn't had in years; he blushed. He lowered his eyes, trying desperately not to remember the last time it had happened.

It had been her words that had done it then, too, that morning they had all met at that all-night café—Summer, Terry, Dave and Joyce, and him. They had just gotten cof-fee when Summer had begun jokingly talking about setting him up with her girlfriend.

"Sure," he'd said dryly. "Just call her and tell her you know this broke, divorced—"

"Hunk, with a great body, a better smile and the most incredible eyes."

From her, that had been enough to send color racing to his cheeks. It had also been the first time he had begun to realize the power she had over him; there had been an un-dertone in her voice that belied the teasing note in her words, and it began a train of thoughts he didn't dare pursue.

"...do it right, don't you?"

He came back to the present with a start, grateful that she couldn't know where his thoughts had wandered. "What?"

"Why here?"

He shrugged. "It's as far as I could go and still be in the country."

"No kidding." She glanced around at what she could see of the small island. "Does anybody live here besides you?"

"Not for long. People come and go. No fresh water, so you have to bring it over." He shrugged again. "It doesn't matter."

"Does...anything?" she asked, her voice oddly intent.

He shrugged once more; it was a habit he only now real-ized had become chronic. "Not really. Who brought you over?"

"An enterprising young man named Enrique." She glanced at the stretch of water between them and Key West, then back at him. "He said el turquezo usually swims over. I got the impression he expected me to do the same."

He couldn't help smiling. "I hope you didn't tell him you could. It would destroy his macho belief in frail womanhood."

She looked at him, surprise showing in the light green eyes, as if she hadn't expected him to remember her affinity for the water. He smothered a wry laugh; he could have given her a long list of the things he remembered about her.

She was playing idly with the pristine white sand, letting it run through long, slender fingers. Ringless fingers, he noted. There was a long moment of silence, and uncertainty clouded her eyes when she raised them to his.

"I . . . Aren't you going to ask me why I'm here?"

He started to shrug, then caught himself and stopped the movement. "I've learned a lot of things since I came here. One of them is that people eventually get around to what they want."

She studied him for a moment, one side of her lower lip caught between white, even teeth in another gesture that was all too familiar. "You really have changed."

"It's what I came here for."

The uncertainty in her eyes changed to a doubt that was more specific somehow, as if she were wondering if she'd made a mistake. She lowered her head to stare at the graceful swirl of lines she'd created in the sand. He caught himself staring at the bare nape of her neck below the thick blond hair, thinking how incredibly fragile it looked, how fragile she looked. And remembering how fragile she'd been, once. He'd held her then, had felt her tremble, and had damned himself for wishing it had been for a different reason.

When she lifted her head, the fringe of bangs had fallen forward to her arched eyebrows, making her eyes look impossibly large and troubled. She looked tired, he realized suddenly. And from more than jet lag. He waited.

"Then maybe you won't care," she said at last, quietly. "Maybe it won't matter to you."

"What?"

The peridot eyes fixed on him steadily, unflinchingly.

"The man who killed Terry is back."

Every instinct, every bit of reflex and training he'd tried to bury these past five years leapt to the fore as if he'd been using them every day of those years. He came rigidly upright, and it took every ounce of his will to beat back the string of questions that rose instantly to his lips.

With a slowness that screamed of the control it took, he leaned back against the tree that had been his backrest most of the morning. This was what he'd come here to forget, he told himself sternly. He ordered suddenly taut muscles to unclench, to regain the state of relaxation they'd been in before. He waited for the spurt of adrenaline her words had caused to ebb, ordered his heart to return to the lazy, slow beat he'd attained since coming to this tropical wonderland. She watched every slight movement.

"I guess that answers my question, doesn't it?"

He heard the strange note in her voice, but forced himself not to respond to it.

"I'm not a cop anymore, Summer," he said mildly.

"And I'm not a cop's wife anymore."

He couldn't stop his wince. "Summer—"

"I didn't come here to talk to Colter the cop." It was unnerving, hearing her call him Colter, as she always had before. As Terry had. "I came here to talk to Terry's best friend."

He looked away from her. "You should be talking to The Department, Summer." His mouth twisted wryly; he'd never quite been able to break the old habit of referring to The Department as if both words were capitalized.

"Do you think I didn't?" Her lovely mouth twisted bitterly. "They don't care. And you know why. Just like you know it's all a lie."

"What I know is that there's nothing I can do."

"Nothing *does* matter to you anymore, does it?"

He lifted his head, meeting her eyes. "Not if I don't let it." His voice was flat, emotionless.

She looked at him steadily for a long moment. "Then who's really dead? Terry? Or you?"

She got up in one smooth, swift movement, then stood there, looking down at him. It took more effort than he'd expended on anything since he'd left five years ago, but he kept his face expressionless.

"Damn it, Colter!" Emotion, hot, vivid and angry, glowed suddenly in her eyes. "I thought you were different!"

Whoa, he thought, she's grown some claws. And they scratch, he added ruefully, shutting his eyes against the sting. When he opened them again, she was gone, as if she'd never been there. He sat up. He spotted her running toward the small dock where he could see Enrique's little skiff bobbing on the slight swell. She tossed the boy her purse and the other things she held, and pointed across the half mile of clear, aqua water.

Good, he thought, looking away. The last thing he needed was her disrupting his life again. She would go home now, and leave him to his peace. The peace he had worked so hard for. The peace, he thought wryly, that he hadn't realized was so fragile until a big-eyed vision from his past had arrived to shatter it. It wasn't true, anyway, what she'd said. He was alive and doing just fine, and he didn't need her messing things up. He'd come too close to it before, too close to messing up a lot of lives.

He heard the small outboard start and glanced up once more. And stared. Except for the slender Cuban boy in the stern, the little boat was empty.

He sat up. Something fluttered in the wind created by the skiff's passage, something pale and green that was on the seat. The jumpsuit she'd been wearing. He scrambled to his knees. She couldn't be. Could she?

She was. He spotted her now, a slender figure cutting cleanly through the crystal water. Her strokes were strong, regular and somehow furious.

"Damn, damn, damn!"

He spat it out as he leapt to his feet. He yanked off his shirt and raced down the beach. She didn't know this water, didn't know about that outcropping of coral that jutted from the point of the island. A cut from live coral could be dangerous. He hit the water in a smooth surface dive and came up swimming hard.

She was fast. He didn't know if she still swam regularly, but if she didn't, she still hadn't lost much speed. He had to push himself hard to catch her. With one last stretch, he passed her, then turned in front of her. She came up sputtering, glaring at him.

"What the hell do you think you're doing?" He was panting; the fact that she seemed to be breathing easily only made his words sharper.

"Blowing up a macho myth," she spat out, her tone leaving no doubt that blowing off steam was her real purpose. Her fury startled him; she'd always been so quiet. She moved to go around him. He grabbed her arms.

"Don't be an idiot," he snapped. "This isn't a damned swimming pool."

She twisted away, still glaring at him. "I know that."

"Do you have the slightest idea how coral can slice you up?" His voice was harsh, more from the little shock that had run through him the first instant he touched her than from anger. His muscles were tense as he tried to hang on to her while treading water. "Do you know that some kinds are even poisonous? And that there's a reef of it about five feet ahead of you?"

Her head snapped around, then she looked back at him suspiciously; the reflection of the blazing sun on the water made it impossible to see beneath the glittering surface.

"It's there, believe me," he said, reading her look.

"Then I'll go around it."

Her jaw was set, her eyes flashing. They were hotly, passionately angry, and he felt a sudden jab of an equally hot, equally passionate need to see them that way for another reason. This was a different Summer, just as lovely as she'd always been, but more vividly, cracklingly alive.

No, he thought. This couldn't be happening. She couldn't walk back into his life and make him revert as if the years since had never been. He'd fought too hard against the urges that had made him hate himself to give in now. He clamped down on the suddenly reawakened feelings that had lain dormant for so long.

"Summer, you can't—"

"I can't? The macho bit must be catching down here."

"I didn't say you couldn't do it! I just meant..."

"Meant what?"

"Come back to the beach, will you? We can talk there."

"I was under the impression we were through talking."

"Just come back."

He heard the outboard and looked up to see Enrique heading toward them, watching them with avid, dark-eyed curiosity. Colter gestured sharply with his thumb toward the dock. The boy nodded, blithely ignored Summer's instant protest and headed back.

"No wonder you like it here," she ground out.

"Summer, please."

The green eyes searched his face. The entreaty seemed to both surprise her and decide her, and after a long, silent moment, she turned and began to swim toward shore.

He followed her, pausing as soon as he could stand up to smooth his wet hair back from his forehead. He stopped in midmovement, his breath caught in his throat as he watched her walk out of the water.

She had obviously had the swimsuit on under the jumpsuit, and it revealed every lush curve the loose green fabric had concealed. He'd seen skimpier suits and bikinis that covered even less, and even, on occasion in this tropical setting, women who did away with the already minuscule tops altogether. Yet somehow, none of them were as striking, as alluring, as downright sexy as the simple one-piece suit she wore. The white background was glistening and pure, and the pale green of the leafy print exactly matched her eyes. The suit clung to her provocatively, molding each trim curve, and bared legs that were long, taut and beautifully shaped.

God, he'd forgotten. He'd made himself forget. But his body was responding as if he'd thought of her every day. He watched her walk slowly toward the big palm and the small cottage he called home, and it was a moment before he dared to walk the rest of the way out of the water.

Enrique—her things clutched in his hands—met him as she dropped down to sit in the sand. He took them, then tugged a wet, wrinkled five-dollar bill out of his wet, wrinkled shorts and handed it to the boy.

"Quedate aqui," he instructed.

"You bet!" Enrique nodded eagerly. "Five dollars, I wait here until night!"

Colter walked past Summer into the small, low bungalow. It looked as if a good breeze would send it flying, but it was sturdy enough for his needs. He crossed the one large, airy room, walked past the screened off sleeping area and into the small bathroom. He picked up two towels and walked back out. He handed her one, then sat beside her. She wiped off, then toweled her hair, but made no move to wrap the towel around her; the water and the air were both bathtub warm.

"Not exactly Puget Sound, is it?"

She looked up at him, one slender hand going to smooth a trickle of water from her cheek. A few strands of hair clung to her forehead, to the sides of her face. Lord, he thought, even soaking wet—especially soaking wet—she was gorgeous. And looked about eighteen, although he knew she was twenty-six. Or would be on June 21, not that he was keeping track.

He felt a sudden pang, realizing just how young she had been when life had risen up and slapped her down, barely more than a girl. But she was all woman now.

"No," she said slowly, "it's not." She glanced around at the green palms, the sparkling white sand, the clear, turquoise water. "It's not Puget Sound at all."

Her eyes came back to him. They flicked over his bare chest, still wet from the sea, then went rather hastily back to his face. "Do you ever...miss it?"

"No."

He said it flatly and much too quickly, and he saw by her eyes that she wasn't fooled.

"Even that's too much to admit?" she asked softly.

He winced inwardly. She saw right through him. It was amazing that she hadn't back then. He slung away the towel he'd been using. It slapped against the door, then fell on the small porch at the top of the two steps. He turned on her.

"What the hell do you want from me?"

She looked at him and he felt a shiver ripple through him at the coolness in the green eyes.

"Nothing that will interrupt your life. Nothing that will disturb your precious numbness. All I want from you is information."

One sandy eyebrow rose. "About what?"

"Sam Sherwood."

He went rigid. "No."

"Why? You know he's involved, you said yourself he's the only dealer in Seattle who pays the kind of money they found that night."

"No."

"Colter—"

"Damn it, Summer!"

She reached around him and grabbed the bundle of her things. She unrolled the jumpsuit and shook it out.

"Goodbye, Colter. I'll tell Dave hello for you."

Her words were inflectionless, as if she didn't find him worth her anger any longer. It stung more than the anger had. She stood and began to pull the jumpsuit on over the still-damp swimsuit.

"Summer, don't." He rubbed at his eyes. She waited. He let out a long, weary sigh. "Sit down. Please." She hesitated. "Tell me what happened."

After a moment, she slowly sank down to the sand once more. She didn't speak, just watched him, as if she wasn't sure he truly meant it. When he realized she wasn't going to speak, he knew it was up to him, no matter how much he hated it. He called up the string of questions he'd stifled before.

"Who saw him?"

"Mr. Webster."

Both sandy eyebrows rose this time. "The old man who saw the shooter?"

She nodded. "He saw him in the same area, near the waterfront."

"He's sure?"

"Yes."

"Did he call the police?" It still felt odd, he thought, to talk about the police as though they were something he had nothing to do with.

"Yes." She lowered her eyes. "They didn't believe him."

"Why?"

She sighed. "Same reason they didn't want to before. Except he's...gone downhill in the last couple of years. He has...bad spells where he's disoriented."

"Senility?"

"No! Most of the time he's fine, completely lucid. When he's..."

"Sober?"

She nodded, a short little lurching movement.

"And he was when he saw the shooter?"

"Yes. He was as rational, as coherent as anyone. And he still remembers that night. Clearly."

"But the police don't believe that."

She looked at him, for the first time a hint of a plea in her voice, in her face. "You know they don't want anything to do with opening this up again. They've got their scapegoat. Any excuse will do, so they call him a senile old drunk."

"Did you go to them?"

"Yes." The undertone of anger was impossible to miss.

"And?"

"Oh, they have another category for me. I'm crazy with grief. I never got over Terry's murder."

He looked at her for a long, silent moment before he asked softly, "Have you?" He wasn't sure why he asked it, nor was he sure why he wanted to know. Or if he really did.

"That's not your problem," she said coolly. "All you have to do is decide whether you'll tell me what I need to know."

"To do what?"

"To watch Sherwood and his people. To get proof that the man is back. You worked him long enough; you know how he thinks, how he moves, where—"

"If the shooter is back, what makes you think he'll go back to work for his old boss?"

"Why not?" she said acidly. "It's obvious the heat's off. Why shouldn't Sherwood take him back? If he ever stopped working for him at all."

"Okay, okay. What if he is back working for Sherwood? What then?"

"I'll figure that out when I find him."

"That," he said dryly, "is not the time to have to start improvising."

"Okay, I'll figure it out before then. But I will find him."

"Why?"

Her forehead creased. "What do you mean, why? He—"

"If you're after revenge, Summer, it won't work. It never does."

"I don't want revenge. I just want them to eat their words about Terry. I want proof of what you and I both know."

"And just how do you think you're going to get it?"

"I won't know that until I find him."

"Oh, sure. Why don't you just march up to Sam Sherwood's office and ask him nicely for a list of his employees? And the name of the one who shot a cop and then planted payoff money on him?"

She flushed, but she didn't look away. "Because you already did."

He chuckled; it was without humor. "Yeah. And all it got me was a departmental warning about harassment."

"I know."

He was surprised. He hadn't thought she remembered much of anything about the days after Terry's death. She read his look.

"I know what you did," she said softly. "How hard you tried to find the truth. And how much trouble you got into because of it."

He shrugged before he caught himself this time, then wondered why he was worried about it. Being a creature of habit wasn't going to get him killed here.

"It didn't do any good. Sherwood hid the guy so deep he might as well have dropped off the face of the earth. Then he called in every little favor anybody with any pull owed him. And the lid came down. Tight."

"If it…means anything to you, most of the people in the department…the real ones, I mean…admire you for having the guts to leave."

He let out a short, compressed breath. "That won't even buy me a coconut here."

She studied him for a moment. "And that's the way you like it?"

"That's the way I like it."

"No 'once a cop, always a cop'?"

"No."

"Even though you were one of the best?"

He snorted in derision. "Is that what they say, too? Amazing how things change, isn't it?"

"They do say it, but I already knew it."

"Yeah. Sure."

"Terry always said—"

"Listen to me, Summer," he said, his eyes narrowing suddenly, "don't get any idea that I left in some noble rage about what they did to Terry. That was part of it, but not all, not by a long shot."

She hesitated, and he had the strangest feeling that he knew exactly what she was thinking, that she was pondering whether to ask him what his other reasons had been. In the end, she didn't, and he breathed an inward sigh of relief that ended abruptly when she did speak.

"I never really...thanked you for everything. Afterward."

"You didn't have to," he said gruffly. "Terry was my partner and my friend." *And you, you were my nights, all the dreams that became nightmares of guilt.* He sighed heavily. "He wouldn't want this, you know. He wouldn't want you anywhere near that kind of scum. Let it rest, Summer. Let him rest."

"Rest? In peace?" The reflective softness had vanished from her strained voice. "How can he when the whole world thinks he was a crooked cop?"

"Nobody who knew him thinks he was."

"But that's what his record shows. My God, Colter, he died trying to protect the public from trash like Sherwood, but that public thinks he was on the take."

"Look, even if I do tell you what I know, most of which is probably useless by now, and even if whoever you hire does find him—"

"I'm not hiring anybody."

He stared at her. "What?"

"I said—"

"I heard you. What do you mean?"

"If you heard me, then you know what I mean."

"Wait a minute, here. Do you expect me to believe that you have some crazy idea of poking around into this yourself? Personally?"

"It's not crazy."

"Are you nuts? These guys play hardball—with people's heads!"

"I have no choice."

"What do you mean, no choice? You—"

"There isn't a private detective in Seattle who will touch it. None of them will say why, but one of them said he couldn't afford to have his license up for review. To me, that says the department wants this to stay buried."

"Get somebody from out of state, then."

"*I* can't afford that."

His eyes narrowed. He'd assumed that she was doing fine. She should have been, he'd checked before he left. "Why?"

Her cheeks turned pink. "Look, if you don't want to help, just say so and get it over with."

"I didn't say that."

"Then what—"

"Look, Summer, give me awhile, will you?" He gave her a wry half smile. "This hasn't exactly been an average day in paradise." He shook his head. "I've been vegetating for a long time—my brain's not ready to jump right back into the fast lane."

She looked at him for a long, silent moment. Slowly, her expression changed from irritation to a soft remorse.

"I'm sorry," she said. "I should have thought . . . but instead, I just drop in out of nowhere, dump this on you and expect instant help."

"It's all right. I—"

"No, it's not." She took in a deep breath. "You've been through enough of your own hell. You've earned whatever peace you've found here."

"God, Summer . . ." His voice had gone low, husky, and he didn't dare go on. There was something in her expreson, in her eyes, that made him think of that morning in the café when she had said those things about him.

"I'll go now. I'm staying at the Duval House tonight. If you…change your mind, I'll be there until my plane leaves at noon."

She began to rise, and without thinking, he reached out to touch her arm. That little jolt radiated through him again, and it was a moment before he could speak.

"And if I don't?"

She looked at him with that softness still in her eyes; it sent a shiver through him.

"Then it was nice to see you again," she said quietly.

This time, he let her go. He watched Enrique's little boat until it had reached Key West, watched her walk away from it, a tiny figure in the distance, her slender shoulders slumped, her head bowed in thought. Her hair had dried quickly in the heat, back into that tousled blond cap, and he could see it gleaming in the sun.

He watched that gleam until it disappeared. He sat unmoving for a long time, fighting against opening doors in his mind he'd kept closed and locked for five years. It was a battle he knew he was going to lose, but he kept fighting as long as he could. The final seaplane of the day, coming back from the seventy-mile trip to the Fort Jefferson Monument with its load of tourists somehow seemed to be the last straw.

When he'd first come here, he'd watched those planes and the other airliners come in and discharge their swarms of people, and he'd wondered what kind of futile lives they had temporarily escaped. On the few occasions when he had any contact with them, they looked at him enviously, seeing his life as an ideal they would never attain. He watched them come and go, affecting him as little as the surface ripples on the water, leaving his hard-won serenity undisturbed. Until today. He closed his eyes and the doors swung open.

It had been so stupid. Terry had been on a routine stake-out, watching one of the buildings along the waterfront that they were certain Sherwood used as a regular drop. They'd gotten word that there would be some action that night, but the snitch hadn't been the most reliable in the past, so they were only covering the base.

They had, at the last minute, traded the stakeout assignment. Terry had been set for the late shift, but he'd gotten a last-minute court subpoena for the next morning and he'd asked Colter to trade so he could get some sleep. Colter had agreed, thinking he might just as well sit around on the stakeout as at home.

He'd been on his way to relieve Terry when the call came on an officer-involved shooting. His heart had slammed into overdrive when he'd heard the location, and he'd broken every traffic law in existence getting there.

He was too late. The paramedic bending over Terry had shaken his head grimly, then moved aside. Already, the bright blue eyes had begun to glaze, fading even as they tried to focus on him.

"Hang on, Terry," he pleaded, even knowing as he knelt in a spreading puddle of blood that there was no hope. The rasping of Terry's breath through the hole in his chest confirmed it. Colter bent closer as his mortally wounded friend tried to talk.

It came out as a hard, choking sound, then, "...Sum..."

He knew then. Summer. "I'll take care of her, Terry. I promise."

Confusion showed for a moment in those dying eyes, then understanding. An understanding that seemed to go beyond a promise asked for and made. And then, incredibly, with the last of a fading strength, Terry nodded. And in that sinking, heart-stopping moment, Colter knew that Terry had known all along.

And then he was gone. The habitual light rain that was as natural to Seattle in the spring as the sun was to Key West fell unheeded in that dark, dreary alleyway. Colter sat in the water and blood, cradling the body that had once been his partner and his friend. The friend who had been Terrence Patrick O'Neil, a wiry, audacious Irishman with a leprechaun's twinkle in his bright blue eyes. The friend who would still be alive if Colter had been five minutes earlier.

The friend he'd betrayed. Not by not getting there in time to save him, but by a much more simple and elemental act.

That he'd never done anything about it, never even admitted it to himself, was no solace, not now, not here in this dark, wet place where Terry died in his arms.

He'd never in his life felt so lost, so utterly damned. He sat there, the rain mixing with the tears on his face, his entire being stripped away except for the elemental core; he wasn't Terry's partner, he wasn't Detective Colter, he wasn't Jack and Elizabeth's son, he wasn't even Katie's big brother, Shane. He was simply the bastard who had committed the unpardonable sin of falling in love with his best friend's wife.

Chapter 2

Summer O'Neil picked at the slice of key-lime pie, telling herself that she would never again be in the place where it had originated, so she should enjoy it. It did no good; she couldn't seem to taste anything, not even the luscious, fruity tang of the Caribbean dessert.

She soon gave up and left the restaurant to make her way on foot back to the small inn. Built in the 1880s as a house, it had been recently restored, and she liked the sense of history it had. Her room was small, but inexpensive, compared to some of the three- and four-star resorts on the island, and that was a priority these days.

She was glad she'd chosen to stay in the old section of town. As she walked down Duval Street with its open-air cafés and the bustle of visitors, it at least gave her the idea of what it would be like to come here for pleasure.

She blushed when she realized that the thought of coming here for pleasure led her mind straight back to Shane Colter. Lord, she'd forgotten how big he was. Terry had been at least six inches shorter, wiry and compact; Colter was just shy of six-three and solidly muscled. Where Terry had moved with a darting quickness, Colter moved with a smooth, easy grace that she'd always thought surprising for a man his size. It still was, even though she'd forgotten that, too. But one look at him in that pair of wet, clinging shorts, striding out of the clear Florida water had reminded her in a hurry.

He'd lost that pale, Seattle skin with a vengeance, she thought, then regretted it as she tried to divert her mind from the memory of crystal drops of water beading upon the bronzed skin of his bare chest.

She bit her lip. She hadn't expected this. She'd come here for help in laying the past to rest. Her mind had been so full of what she would have to say to convince Terry's old partner to help her that there had been no room for the defenses she'd always made certain were in place around him. And it had been so long, she'd almost forgotten the need for them.

She hadn't expected to feel guilty, either. He'd found a haven here, a place where he could forget. Perhaps, he even had forgotten until she arrived to drag it all out again. She sighed as she slipped beneath the covers and settled down for what she feared would be a restless night. Maybe he was right. Maybe she was crazy. Maybe she should just forget it.

But she couldn't. She owed it to Terry, to his memory. He hadn't deserved to die at twenty-five, not like that, with his name left as dirty as the alley he'd died in. The brash, young Irishman she'd married at eighteen and been widowed by at twenty-one had been many things: boisterous, sometimes rude, even unkind, and now and then, a little free with his favorite whiskey, but he had been honest to the core. And somehow, she would prove it; she owed him at least that much.

Summer sat quietly, staring at the milling people waiting to board the plane. She wished now she had taken the time this morning to at least go to the Hemingway Home and Museum; she'd never have the chance again. But she hadn't. She had delayed checking out until the last possible minute, until she finally had to crush her last hope and zip up her single suitcase.

She couldn't blame him. He had every right to be left alone. And he'd done quite enough for her already; if it hadn't been for the strong, supporting presence of Shane Colter, she would never have survived the horrible days after Terry's death. Every time she had needed him, he'd been there. She'd known it had really been for Terry, but that did nothing to lessen her gratitude.

He had cooked for her, made her eat and cleaned up the mess afterward. He had forced her to go outside, to find what comfort she could in the beautiful evergreen country she loved so much. He had listened to her talk and held her when she cried. He'd slept on the couch in the living room of her house every night for a month, just to be there when she woke up screaming. She hadn't wondered until later, after he'd gone, if he'd ever woken up screaming himself.

At last, they called for boarding and she got to her feet wearily. The line moved slowly forward. She stared straight ahead, unseeingly, only aware enough to move forward when the line did. At first, the commotion behind her didn't register, then it penetrated even her dazed state and she turned to look. She saw the turned heads, like a trail of toppled dominoes, before she saw the cause.

Her head came up and her shoulders straightened as she stared. He was coming toward her, clad in a pair of worn, black jeans and a white shirt with the sleeves rolled up over tanned, muscular forearms. The shirt was loose above the waistband of the tight jeans, and the contrast made his slim-hipped grace even more evident. No wonder, she thought numbly, that most of those turned heads were female.

He kept coming. His blond-streaked hair fell forward over his brow where it was dry, and lay in damp, combed furrows over his ears where it wasn't. And his eyes, those extraordinary turquoise eyes that she had never forgotten, were fastened on her.

Joy leapt in her, and she told herself firmly it was only because he'd decided to talk to her after all, not merely at the sight of him. She was wondering if she could get a seat on a later plane when she noticed the big, battered leather knapsack that was slung over his shoulder. Her eyes widened in shock. When he came to a stop in front of her, she saw the boarding pass in his hand.

"No," she whispered, stunned.

His mouth twitched wryly. "I thought you wanted me to help."

"Yes," she breathed. "No," she corrected quickly, "not like this. I never expected you to come back."

"Does this mean I'm not welcome?"

"No!" She was coloring furiously as people who should have been moving ahead in the line were, instead, watching them with great interest. "I mean I—I don't want you to... Damn it, Colter, you walked away, you put it all behind you! You're free of it. I never meant for you to get involved again, to go back."

"I never meant to." He grinned crookedly. "I gave away every sweater I owned."

"Then why—"

"I left a lot of loose ends behind, Summer. But only one I regret." And a tangled loose end it is, he thought ruefully. Terry, the truth... and you. If nothing else, I owe it to him to see that you don't get hurt. "If this is a chance to put it to rest, I can't pass it up."

"No," she said again, barely hearing the call for the final boarding stage. "You can't do this, I only wanted—"

"Why are *you* doing it?"

"I—I owe it to Terry. He deserves better than to have that cloud over his name forever."

"Is that all?"

Colter knew he was pressing, but he had to know, he had to hear her say it was because she still loved her husband.

Summer stared at him, trying to understand what it was he wanted her to say. Finally, she let out a tired sigh.

"He's dead. He can't do it himself. I'm alive. I have to do it for him."

Something about the choppiness of her words and the note of exhaustion that underlay them tore at some raw spot deep inside him, some wound that had been hidden but never healed. He reached for her convulsively.

Summer was too surprised to react, to resist, and once she was in the haven of his arms, she didn't want to. For a moment, she gave in, she let herself lean on him as she had all those years ago.

And then, suddenly, it was different. She was different, no longer the devastated girl she had been. She was a woman now, a woman who was all too aware of the man who held her. She'd always been too aware of this man. And she was no longer thinking of his embrace as comforting but as tempting, and it frightened her. She pulled back.

When she looked up at him, she caught a glimpse of something hot and alive in the turquoise eyes before it swiftly disappeared, to be replaced with his usual unreadable mask. Yet that look stayed in her mind as if burned there by its own heat, and it made her voice shaky when she spoke.

"I don't . . . I can't ask you to do this."

"You didn't ask," he said softly.

"But—"

"I owe him, too, Summer. More than . . . you'll ever know." I owe him because he was my partner. Because he was my friend. And because he died thinking I would be making a move on his wife as soon as he was cold. But most of all, because, for a while, he was almost right.

He told himself all these things, over and over again. But glowing immutably in his mind was that brief, fleeting moment when she had hugged him back, not as mourner to comforter, not as friend to friend, but as woman to man.

They made the short flight to Miami in silence, the excited chatter of the rest of the plane's occupants more than filling the gap. At Miami International, he got a seat on her flight; she made no comment when he requested they change her seat to one adjacent to his. He glanced at her curiously when he found she'd been flying standby, but before he could speak, the flight was already boarding.

"Were your bags checked clear through to Seattle?"

He'd turned to her as he said it and nearly caught her staring at him. She'd been watching the way his slightly shaggy hair brushed the back of his neck and the way the lighter streaks were nearly as blond as her own hair, while the rest was the sandy brown she remembered.

"What?" she asked, startled and embarrassed.

He repeated the question, looking at her a little oddly again.

"No." She gestured to the single, small nylon suitcase he'd taken from her when they got on board in Key West. "That's it."

His eyebrows went up, one disappearing beneath the thick lock of hair that fell nearly to his right eye. She gave him a small smile.

"I don't have much in the way of Florida-type clothes."

He hadn't thought about that. "I suppose you don't," he said, then smiled ruefully. "Except for that swimsuit. You could stop traffic in Florida or anywhere in that thing."

She blushed. "I thought it was...pretty tame." Her brow furrowed suddenly. "It *is* pretty tame. I've seen suits here that I could make twelve of from mine."

"I know."

Of course, he knew, she thought. He'd lived here for nearly a year. "Then what—"

She broke off suddenly as something glittered in his eyes. It was gone in an instant, but she knew it had been there. Just as she knew it had been that same look she had surprised there earlier.

He'd meant her. Not the swimsuit. *Her.* Shane Colter thought Summer O'Neil could stop traffic? She whirled away from him, staring at the flight number and time posted at the gate as if they were the most fascinating things in the world.

Don't be an idiot, she ordered herself. He wouldn't— He didn't. And if you have any doubts, stupid, just remember all the gorgeous girls in those skimpy bikinis that populated this end of the world. And a man who looked like Shane Colter, who turned female heads in airports, could have his pick. One look from him and any one of them would fall into his hands like a ripe coconut.

And, she told herself as they walked down the gangway to the big jet, she was sure they did. When Terry, already exhilarated by his promotion to detective after only three years on the force, had found out he was going to be partnered with the man with the best reputation in the division, he had been anxious to find out all he could. He'd told her about the cases Colter had made, the big names he'd arrested and the commendations he'd received. She remembered it all vividly because Terry so rarely talked to her about his work.

And Terry had told her that, after the divorce that had come shortly after Terry had started on the force, Colter had gone through about a girl a week.

"Rumor only, you understand," he'd said one night soon after they'd begun to work together. "I've yet to see it, myself."

Nor had she seen it, she realized, now that she thought about it. She considered it as they found their seats and settled in. Whenever he had joined them for a meal or on an outing with other friends from the department, Colter had come alone. And then, after about a year of being Terry's partner, he'd stopped coming altogether.

She had wondered about that. They had always seemed to have such fun, whether it was just she and Terry and Colter or when they joined Dave Stanley and his wife on some lark, usually something Colter had thought up. Yet he had suddenly been always busy, although they never quite knew what he'd been doing. He and Terry still went out now and then or joined other officers at a local watering hole, but she had rarely seen him at all. Until the night Terry died.

"Will you be all right?"

She looked up quickly. There was nothing in the turquoise eyes except a warm concern, and with an effort, she convinced herself that that was all that had ever been there.

"All right?"

He nodded. "Flying, I mean."

She smiled. "Yes. I don't have Terry's aversion. I love flying."

He chuckled. "Aversion? He was a raving lunatic! I remember when we had to fly to Atlanta on an extradition, he wanted to go handcuff the pilot to his seat. 'I'm not trusting myself to any autopilot,' he kept saying."

"That sounds like him," she said softly.

"And he kept asking where the black box was. Said 'It always survives, so that's where I want to be.' The whole way back he—'' Colter broke off suddenly, looking at her in shocked remorse. "Summer, I'm sorry, I—''

"It's all right." He looked doubtful. "I mean it. I don't mind talking about him," she assured him. "In fact, I wish people weren't so careful around me."

"Careful?"

She nodded. "People don't talk about him because they're afraid it will upset me. It's like everyone's forgotten him. Sometimes it's like he . . . never existed."

She didn't seem upset. There was a sadness in her voice, but not the ripping sound of grief. He'd been right to leave when he had five years ago, he thought. She had come out okay, and surely better than she would have if he'd stayed. He was glad he'd gone, for her sake.

Right. You ran like a rabbit for your own sake, Colter.

He winced; his conscience hadn't jabbed him like that for a long time. And even though he had deeply and thoroughly buried it along with everything else five years ago, he knew it was right now. He'd run like hell.

It had been bad enough before, when Terry was still alive. He hadn't been able to stand being so near and yet so far. To be with her, yet not, to talk with her always among others. To watch her smile, to hear her laugh and then watch her leave. And he hadn't been able to stand the way it made him feel that she was leaving with his best friend.

Eventually, he'd had to start avoiding her. It had been tearing him apart and he'd had no choice. He couldn't even bring someone else as a shield; he'd known instinctively another woman would see through him in a minute.

But Summer never had. He wondered why, then even as he thought it, knew the answer. Terry had always said she had no idea how attractive she was. An innocent, he'd called her, and had laughed when he'd said that was why he'd grabbed her right out of the cradle, before the ugly world got its hands on her.

Well, the ugly world had gotten its hands on her in a big way, and through the very man who had wanted to keep her from it. And once that man was gone, Colter had had only the love and respect he'd felt for his partner as a barrier between them. And he'd run because he'd been afraid it wouldn't be enough. But it would be now. It had to be. He'd make sure of it.

"I never forgot him," he said softly. "I never will."

She jumped when he laid his hand over hers, almost as if she felt the same jolt he did whenever they touched. The light green eyes were wide and luminous as she stared at him, as if his avowal had brought the tears the memories had not.

Without warning, his mind flashed back to the night a month after the funeral when, after bearing up so incredibly under the horrible strain of Terry's death and the nasty accusations and aspersions that had followed, she had at last broken down.

Colter had held her that night, all night, first as she finally let loose the flood of tears, then as she slept. It had been a blessed release for her; for him, it had been a night of sheer torture. He had sat there, holding her, breathing in that scent that was so uniquely hers, that scent of rain-washed flowers. It had teased him, taunted him through that long night. The night that had convinced him he had to leave the house that had been Terry's.

He managed to resist the urge to do now as he had then, to pull her into his arms and soothe away the pain, the tears. He could beat it now, he thought. He could resist it, with five years of distance between them. He could do that, but he couldn't stop his fingers from curling around hers.

To his surprise, she didn't pull away. She looked away, rather hurriedly, but she left her hand beneath his on the armrest between them. And after a while, in a low, softly reminiscent voice, she spoke.

"Do you remember the time we all went sailing?"

Oh, Lord. "Yes."

"It was like magic. I've never forgotten it."

How odd, he thought, that she should remember that. It was a memory that had been seared indelibly into his mind, but he hadn't expected it to be that way for her.

It had been the last time they'd been together, the day he had finally admitted this was one battle he couldn't keep fighting. He'd joined her and Terry for a day with Dave and Joyce Stanley on their sailboat, on one of those crystal Pacific Northwest days that were so spectacular and all the more precious for being in limited supply.

Terry had been drinking a bit that day, growing more rowdy with every cold beer he downed, and Colter had seen Summer grow increasingly uncomfortable. When he announced he was going for a walk, she had scrambled to join him, leaving Terry to pop the first of another six-pack.

They had walked in silence until they were out of sight of the small cove they had anchored in, then she had stopped to take in a deep breath of the evergreen-scented air.

"Thank you," she'd said.

"For what?"

She eyed him wryly. "You just spent three weeks on a stakeout and twelve hours writing arrest reports. I don't think you really felt an undeniable urge to go for a walk."

What I feel, he thought, is an undeniable urge to grab you and race off into the woods. What I want is to find some nice, grassy spot to lay you down and ease this damned ache I can't get rid of.

What he did was mumble some faint, unintelligible disclaimer.

Summer sighed as they began to walk again. "He didn't used to be like this. The alcohol, I mean."

Colter's mouth twisted wryly. "Nobody starts out like that. But being a cop will do it damned quick if you've got the inclination."

"It hasn't done it to you."

"Just stubborn, I guess."

She smiled, a soft curving of her mouth that made that ever-present ache expand a notch. "I think it's more than that. You're—"

He couldn't bear to hear what she thought he was. He looked away from her rather wildly. Fate unexpectedly threw him a life preserver.

She broke off when he grabbed her arm. He was looking past her, and when he glanced back at her, there was an odd light in his eyes, an almost exultant expression on his face. He was trying to smother a grin when he took her shoulders and gently turned her around.

"Look," he whispered, standing close behind her as he pointed down to the open stretch of water below them.

She gave a little gasp of delight when she saw them. Sleek, glistening, polished creatures of stark, dramatic black and white, the killer whales frolicked in the blue water.

"Oh!" she exclaimed. "Four of them—no, five, look, there's a calf!" She glanced back over her shoulder at Colter, her face shining with excitement. "Aren't they wonderful?"

"Wonderful?" he teased. "I expected something a little more knowledgeable from a fledgling marine biologist."

"Orcinus Orca," she said promptly. "Length from twenty to thirty feet, average weight ten to eleven tons, swims up to twenty-five miles an hour, lives—"

A laugh broke from him and, before he was even aware of it, before he had a chance to fight it, he had let his arms go around her. He might have been able to pull away, but she leaned back against him as naturally as if she belonged there and he was unable to stop.

God, she felt so good! He tightened his arms, letting his chin come down to rest atop the golden silk of her hair. And there it was again, that sweet, clean scent. Honeysuckle, he thought, not sure how he knew. Honeysuckle after a night's soft rain. He took another deep breath, savoring it.

They had stood there for a long time, Summer close in his arms as they watched the huge mammals. She had exclaimed over the powerful beauty of the adults and laughed in guileless enchantment at the antics of the baby, trying so hard to imitate its elders.

She really was an innocent, he thought, aware of and fighting his body's immediate, fierce response to her closeness. She was innocent, but instead of making him feel old and somehow tainted by comparison, as he so often did when confronted by simple goodness after dealing with the underside of humanity for so long, she gave him hope, hope that some clean, unsullied part of him still existed somewhere deep inside, buried beneath the distasteful reality of his day-to-day life.

Only at the sound of someone coming through the trees behind them was the spell broken. And only then did Summer seem to realize how the scene they presented might be interpreted. She backed away, color tinging her cheeks. She cast one look at the whales he'd found, then turned away. Colter had stood there for a moment, missing her warmth, yet oddly pleased at her obvious intent not to show them to whoever was coming. It made it more special somehow, personal, as if she wanted to keep it a small, private secret between them.

He had known then he would never forget it; and now she had told him she never had, either. A little spark of pleasure warmed him, a faint echo of the pleasure holding her that day had given him. It joined with the feel of her hand beneath his now, and settled somewhere deep inside him, glowing and warm.

He didn't know when she actually slipped into sleep, he only knew he wasn't surprised. The weariness he had seen in her was that of days of too little sleep, not merely of jet lag. She was leaning awkwardly in the seat, her head twisted to one side, her long legs looking cramped where she had pulled them up beneath her.

He studied her for a moment, wondering why he was even bothering with this mental battle when he knew he was going to lose. At last, he gave it up and reached for the armrest between them and pulled it up out of the way. Gently, he reached for her. She murmured something sleepily, but didn't awaken as he settled her comfortably. She nestled against his shoulder, one hand beneath her cheek, the other resting on his thigh.

He stared at that hand, slender and delicate looking against the faded black of his jeans. It was impossible, he thought, that just looking at her hand on him could do this, could send heat rocketing through him in pulsing little spurts. But it did until it seemed all of that heat had settled in one low, swelling place. Until it was all he could do to hold still. Until he couldn't stop himself from imagining what it would feel like if she moved that hand a few critical inches....

He smothered a low, pained groan, and resolutely shut his eyes. He let his head loll back against the top of the seat and wondered how many seconds were in the minutes that were in the hours he would have to survive until they reached Seattle.

"Summer."

"Mmmph."

"Wake up. We're about to land."

She opened one eye sleepily. Land? Was something wrong? They'd just boarded, just taken off... hadn't they? They had—

Her rather muddled train of thought derailed when she realized that the wonderfully warm but somewhat resistant pillow she was nuzzling was Colter's leg, and that the back of her head was resting intimately against his hip. She sat up sharply, suddenly totally awake. She glanced out the window; the dark shapes of the tree-covered islands that dotted the Puget Sound told her unmistakably that they were, indeed, about to land.

Her gaze flickered to his face. Had she really slept all the way, even through the stop in Denver? And had she been using him as a pillow all that time? His face revealed nothing, but the way he stretched and shifted in the seat gave her the answer; he hadn't moved much, if at all, for a long time. Because of her. Her cheeks flamed.

"I—I'm sorry. I didn't mean to fall asleep." And I certainly didn't mean to fall asleep... like that, she added silently, her color deepening.

He shrugged. "You needed the rest."

She glanced out the window again, looking at the water sparkling in the summer sun, at the boats that dotted the water and the big ferry that was on its half-hour journey from Seattle to the little town of Winslow on Bainbridge Island. She watched it, able to hear in her mind the deep, powerful blast of the ferry's horn.

"You... haven't been back, have you?"

"No."

She turned to look at him then, hesitating before she spoke. "Have you thought about... where... I mean, you have to have a place..." She faltered again, then said in a rush, "My house is small, but I have a spare room and you're welcome to it, if you want."

His brow furrowed as he looked at her. "You moved?"

She looked down, fumbling with the seat belt she had just fastened in answer to the announcement from the flight crew.

"Yes. I . . . the old house was too big."

He stared at her for a moment. She'd loved that house. He knew that she'd spent hours fixing it up inside and more hours on the beautiful garden she'd created outside. She'd told him once she loved having space around her instead of being cramped up in some modern condominium or apartment, and that the near acre of land the house sat on was worth the work and price. And despite the price, the insurance from the department should have more than paid it off.

"Where to?" he asked at last.

"Near Federal Way. Just north of Tacoma."

The furrow deepened. "That's a hell of a lot farther from the Aquarium."

Her hands stilled on the metal buckle, but she didn't look up. "It . . . isn't a problem."

"But why—"

"If you'd rather not, just say so." She lifted her head then. He knew she was determinedly protecting her pride, but he didn't know where he'd gotten the impression it wasn't over asking him to stay. "I'm sure you have friends you'd rather stay with."

"No, I—"

"Or your family." Her expression changed then, to one of embarrassment. "I forgot they lived in town."

"They don't. My folks moved to Arizona a couple of years ago."

"Your mother's arthritis?"

As he nodded, he looked a little surprised that she had remembered.

"What about your little sister?"

More surprise showed as she asked about Kate, then he gave her a rueful grin. "Not so little anymore. She's married now. Lives in Portland." He shrugged. "Nobody in

Seattle anymore.'' Except you, he thought. The only tie left. And the strongest one he'd ever tried to break.

She lowered her eyes again. ''Then if you want to stay...''

No, his mind yelled. Not under the same roof with her. It had nearly killed him the last time, and it would be worse now. He couldn't. He just couldn't.

''Yes. Thank you.''

He stared past her out the window as they made the final turn and headed down the flight path to SeaTac Airport. The familiar land and waterscape tugged at him with a strength that surprised him.

Once, the town sprawled below him had been his. Most of the cops had thought of it that way, their town; any insult to it was an insult to them, and they took it personally. He'd worked, lived and breathed this town. He'd poured his soul into it. He'd given it everything, until there was nothing left. He hadn't expected to feel this way, hadn't thought, after all that had happened, it would still pull at him this way. Yet, as they landed and disembarked, he couldn't deny that it was happening.

They had just gotten off the tram that had carried them from the concourse to the main terminal when a feminine voice rang out behind them.

''Summer, hi!''

He stopped when she did to turn around and look behind her. A young, dark-haired woman in an airline uniform was hurrying toward them, waving.

''Hi, Jenny.''

''I heard you'd gotten on a flight to Miami, but I didn't believe it. You actually took a vacation?''

''Sort of.''

Summer smothered a smile as Jenny tried to hide her obvious interest in the tan, tall man beside her. She was about to make an introduction when a male voice called Jenny's name urgently.

''I've got to run,'' she said. ''See you next week?''

Summer barely had time to nod before Jenny whirled and hurried away. She glanced at Colter and shrugged. ''That's Jenny. Always in a hurry.''

"People in airports are usually either hurrying or waiting."

"Or working their heads off."

She sounded a bit vehement and he looked at her quizzically. "That, too," he said after a moment.

She glanced through the glass doors of the terminal, then back at him.

"I didn't want to leave my car here, so I took the bus," she said carefully.

"Never mind. I've got to rent a car anyway." He made the call, then they went outside to wait for the van from the rental agency.

The pull he'd felt as the plane came in over the city was even stronger when they stepped outside. There really was something in the air here, he thought. Something fresh and clean that was missing—baked out, maybe, he thought—from the heated tropical air of the Keys. Especially on days like today, when it was crystal pure and clear and you could look to the east and see the Cascade Mountains, to the west and see the Olympics, and the sun glittered on the water of the sound in between.

In less than an hour, Summer sat in the passenger seat of the coupe he'd rented as he maneuvered them out of the airport complex as easily as if he'd never left. He drove with careless expertise, but she wondered when he'd last been behind the wheel. She'd heard in the Keys that he rarely went anywhere; she supposed that four years of roaming across the country had cured any wanderlust he'd felt. Besides, as he'd said, he'd gone about as far as he could go.

As they neared the ramps of the freeway, he glanced over at her, seemed to hesitate, then spoke quietly. "Do you mind if I . . . take a look around first?"

"Of course not."

A while later, as they were traversing the city streets, she almost wished she'd said she did mind. It was gradual, a slow transformation, and she watched it happen with a growing dread. He drove a little slower, his head began to turn from one side to the other, his eyes flickering over everything, seeking, searching. She knew that rhythm too well, she'd seen it often enough before. He was driving, observing, acting like a cop. He was alert, aware, on edge, as if he was back on the job that had burned him out.

What did you expect? she asked herself acidly. He'd been a cop here for nearly ten years. Lord knew what horrible things he'd seen and had to do long before Terry had died, things she didn't know about, that had happened in the seven years before he and Terry had become partners. And then, when he finally walks away, leaves it all for the peace he'd worked so hard to give to others, you go and drag him back.

"I'm sorry, Colter."

He looked over at her at the soft words, his eyebrows rising at the contrite expression she wore.

"About what?"

"I . . . never thought about what it would do to you. To come back."

She could sense his withdrawal. "I'm fine."

She smiled, but it was a rather gloomy smile. "Then why are you driving like you're on patrol?"

He looked startled, then chagrined. "I was, wasn't I?"

She nodded. He gave a wry chuckle.

"Reflex, I guess. Used to be my beat, when I was on the street."

"I know. You won your medal on the Ballard Bridge."

He was genuinely startled. "How'd you know about that?"

"You're famous, Detective Colter. I read about you long before you and Terry started working together. Especially how you pulled that guy out of his burning car right in the middle of the bridge and almost went over the side into the canal."

He'd recovered now and only shrugged. "It wasn't as bad as they made it sound."

"Bad enough to win you a Medal of Valor."

He grimaced. "I didn't want it. I just happened to be there at the right time."

"And happened to be the right man."

He made a low, muffled sound that could have meant anything. The smile she gave him this time was sincere.

"Don't like being a legend?" she teased.

"Legend," he muttered. "Right."

"It's true. Dave says the stories get better every day."

"And further from the truth."

"When you're talking legend," she said lightly, "the truth is usually the first casualty."

Glancing at her, he started to speak, then shut his mouth. He looked away quickly, but not before he saw the realization in her eyes and knew that they were both thinking of another time when truth had been a casualty. With his jaw tight, he drove on.

Chapter 3

You're nuts, Colter, he thought. Absolutely nuts. You've been up twenty-two hours straight, you flew across the entire country, it's four in the morning, Florida time, and you're still wide awake. And likely to stay that way, he added to himself grimly. He had so many things chasing around in his mind, he couldn't seem to slow them down enough to sort them out, let alone sleep.

He rolled over again, to stare once more at the ceiling. He began to wonder about this house again, realizing even as he did it that it was an escape valve for a mind—and body—that was much too occupied with the knowledge that Summer lay sleeping a few feet down the hall.

It was barely half the size of the one she and Terry had lived in. And at least forty years old, he thought, although her knack for creating a cozy home hid much of the work that was necessary. But the place would need a roof soon; he'd noticed that when they'd arrived. A good scraping down and a coat of paint wouldn't hurt, either.

Why had she sold the other house, he'd wondered, the house she'd loved so much, to buy this old place? Had it been too painful, too full of memories of Terry? This place certainly wasn't, he'd thought when he'd first stepped inside, halting as she went to flip on a light.

He had watched her as she walked over to the phone, then stopped in the act of reaching for it. She turned away from it and met his questioning look.

"I was going to call my landlady," she explained, "but I forgot it's her day for bridge. She was watching the place for me since I didn't know for sure how long I'd be gone. I guess I'll call her later."

"You're renting this place?"

"Yes. It's small, but I like it." Her chin had come up, as if daring him to say anything derogatory about it.

"Summer—"

"I'll fix that steak now. The guest room is the first door on the left, if you want to unpack."

She turned on her heel and strode into the tiny kitchen, leaving him wondering what he had done to set her off. He stared after her, brow furrowed. He never remembered her being so touchy. Yet she had been that way at the small market they had stopped at after she'd told him she'd left behind an empty refrigerator.

He'd tried to pay the entire bill after she'd commented her budget didn't run to the top sirloin he'd picked out, but she'd coolly refused, only the two faint spots of color in her cheeks revealing her perturbation. In the end, she'd let him pay half, grudgingly.

None of this made any sense, he thought now as he stared into the darkness. She should have been able to afford anything she wanted. There should have been enough to pay off the house and her last year of school. She had even told him she planned to do just that. She sure as hell shouldn't be living here, riding buses, flying standby and not able to afford steak if she wanted it.

Like most cops, Terry had made certain his will was up to date, and he'd been well insured. The fact that he had been killed on duty would have increased even that sizable amount. Colter was sure of it; he'd checked it all out before he'd left. He hadn't lightly made that promise to see that she was taken care of, even if he hadn't been able to stay and do it himself.

He turned restlessly, kicking at the unfamiliar weight of covers; even in summer, the nights in Washington were a far cry from the balmy, sultry nights in the Keys. Again, he had to yank his mind back from where it had wandered: the room down the hall that held the big, four-poster bed that held Summer. Sleeping quietly, no doubt, he thought glumly; you're the one with terminal jet lag.

She had fixed the steak to perfection, but it had been a silent meal. She seemed withdrawn, and he wondered if she was regretting asking him to stay. Finally, when she looked at him with a flicker of surprise as he rose and began to gather the dishes and take them to the kitchen, he had asked.

"If my being here bothers you, I can find someplace else to stay." He almost wished she would say yes because it was certainly bothering him. Just being in the same room with her was enough to bother him, and in ways he didn't care to think about.

She'd looked a little startled. "No. It's not that. I just..." She hesitated, then sighed. "I was just thinking about... dragging it all out again."

He set the plates in the sink, then turned back to look at her steadily. "Do you want to drop it?"

"Part of me does. The part that remembers what it was like, those months after Terry was killed, when they said all those horrible things about him."

"They never proved any of it."

"Because they couldn't. But they didn't exonerate him, either. And all anybody remembers was that he had that money on him."

He studied her for a moment. He knew she would say yes, knew he didn't want to hear it, but couldn't seem to stop from asking, "It still hurts you, doesn't it?"

"No," she said, and he blinked in surprise. "It just makes me angry. Terry was a good cop, being a cop was his life, and he was not crooked."

Her voice had risen, and she slapped the silverware she'd brought in down on the Formica counter.

"I know that," he said quietly. "You don't have to convince me."

She sighed. "I know. I'm sorry. It just makes me so mad. He lived—damn it, he died for the department, and what do they give him? A noncommittal 'inconclusive evidence.'"

Colter turned the tap marked H, staring at the flow of water. In silence, he washed the plates, then the silverware, and placed them in the rack next to the sink to drain; a dishwasher was something else she apparently was doing without.

Methodically, he shut off the water and dried his hands. Then he just stood there, staring out the small window over the sink at the stand of trees across the small yard, his hands gripping the edge of the counter until his knuckles were white.

"Colter?"

"I should have stayed. I shouldn't have let it go at that, shouldn't have let them stop me from finding out what really happened."

Suddenly, unexpectedly, she grabbed his hands and pulled him around to face her.

"No. You did all you could, then. I know you did."

He tensed, staring at her hands around his. He couldn't seem to speak, couldn't think of anything except that she was touching him. After a moment, she dropped her hands. He leaned back against the front of the counter as if he were suddenly too tired to stand up. He let out a long breath as he slowly shook his head.

"Not enough. Everything dried up. It's always tough when it's a cop because everybody's scared we're going to shoot first and ask questions later."

We. There it was again, she thought. Perhaps it was true, despite his denial, that once a cop, always a cop. Or was it just her fault for bringing him here? Until now, nothing had seemed as important as vindicating Terry, but suddenly, she wasn't quite so certain.

"Nothing on the street. My best snitches went cold on me. Even when I went under, I couldn't turn up anything."

"I know, Colter. I'm sorry I didn't realize until afterward what you'd been doing."

"You weren't in any shape to worry about that."

"I still should have seen." She tried to lighten the sudden intensity. "I should have guessed by the hours you were keeping, not to mention that you suddenly forgot where your barber was and lost your razor and all your clothes, except those raggedy old jeans and that leather jacket."

He smiled rather sheepishly, and she didn't mention that she had also been aware of how, no matter how long he was gone during the day in that month he'd spent with her, he had always been back before she finally gave up the battle with the miserable daylight hours for the hellish hours of fitful sleep. He had always been there for her when the sleeping nightmare turned into the waking one.

"I should have known you'd gone under," she went on, "but I didn't put it all together until . . . after you left."

"Lot of good it did," he said sourly. "I didn't turn up a damned thing."

"But you kept trying. Until they came down on you." His eyebrows quirked upward. "I heard about your session with the brass."

His brow furrowed, then cleared. "Dave."

She nodded. "He said they told you to back off Sherwood or you'd be back on the street in a patrol car, working graveyard and facing insubordination charges." She smiled at his expression. "He also said he heard it all through closed doors and halfway across the room."

"Dave seems to have said a lot."

"He was good to me." She lowered her eyes. "He told me you asked him to . . . watch out for me."

He didn't say anything. He had no answer that wouldn't require the explanation of why he had gone, why the pressure had grown so great that he couldn't fight it anymore. He couldn't, wouldn't do that, so he said nothing. He looked back out at the trees, trying to occupy his mind with thoughts of how different it was here, staying light out late into what would have been evening in Florida.

"Do you want to go see Mr. Webster tomorrow?" she asked after a moment.

He nodded. "I want to go by the department first, and have Dave pull the file for me." Not that there was much chance he would ever forget a word of it, he thought. He'd read it until he knew it as well as he knew his own name.

"All right."

He looked at her then. "If you'd rather not, I'll come back for you."

"No, that's okay. I don't mind, if you don't mind if I don't go in."

He nodded in understanding. Then a weary sigh he couldn't quite stop escaped him, and she was suddenly brisk.

"You'd better get some rest. It's nearly midnight your time."

He started to protest, but thought better of it. That moment when she had touched him, had taken his hands of her own accord, had played havoc with his nerves, and the strain of being so close to her for so long was wearing down defenses he hadn't had to use in five years.

So he had gone to bed, expecting to be asleep in minutes. Instead, hours later, here he was, wide awake and tired of trying to smother the chaos of his whirling thoughts. With a low groan, he rolled over, burying his face in the pillow beneath his head.

They sat in the car, staring at the building that had once been the center of both their lives in different ways. Colter's hand was tight around the steering wheel, and he made no move to get out of the car.

"Do you miss it?"

Her voice was soft, gentle. She felt him tense, as if he was going to once more deny that he missed anything of what he'd left behind. She heard him take a deep breath, and then he relaxed, his hand unclamping from the wheel.

"Sometimes. When I remember the good things, the good busts. And most of the people." He shrugged. "But the bad caught up, outweighed the rest. It had a long time before I left."

"I—I'm glad it wasn't just Terry. I know you loved your work before, and I hated thinking that you'd left it just because of that."

He stared at her, opened his mouth, then shut it and looked away. After a moment, he tried again, his voice low.

"I didn't think you'd...think about me at all."

She didn't say anything right away, and he mentally kicked himself for sounding like a lost soul begging for recognition. Then she answered him in a soft, silky tone that sent ripples down his spine.

"Of course, I did." His heart leapt and his head snapped around as he looked at her. "You did so much for me...."

Right, he muttered silently. Down, Colter. She thinks she owes you or something. "I didn't do anything," he said shortly, and reached for the car door before she could speak. "I'll be back as soon as I can."

It took him longer than he'd thought it would. He hadn't expected to have to run a gauntlet of old, familiar faces, all of whom wanted to stop and talk, and several minutes passed before he at last stood in that familiar doorway. A powerful wash of memories swept him and for a second, it was as if he'd never been gone, as if he was just coming back from a long undercover assignment to the office that had been his. And Terry's.

Except that the poster of the leaping killer whale was gone from the wall. The poster that Summer had bought for Terry to bring in, the poster that Colter could never look at without remembering that golden day on the sailboat, the poster he could never look at without wondering if she had meant something by intending it to hang here, where he would see it every day. It had taken all the mental discipline he had ever possessed to stop himself from assuming she had.

No, the office looked different. The poster was gone, Terry's trophy from the department softball team was gone. The various plaques and degrees and pictures were gone, and he wondered vaguely where everything had wound up. Except for the picture of Summer that had been on Terry's desk; he knew where that was.

He hadn't thought she'd miss it, and he hadn't been able to resist taking it with him when he'd left. He'd tried, knowing he was only making it harder on himself. He'd even made it to the locker room to clean out his locker before he'd finally given up and raced back to the office to get it. It had gone with him on all his wanderings and now sat in the one drawer that existed in the hut on the tiny, nameless key he lived on. He rarely looked at it. He didn't have to; he knew it as well as he knew his own reflection in the mirror.

It had been taken just before he and Terry had become partners, the second year of Terry's marriage. It was the first time he'd ever seen Summer O'Neil. He had assumed it was a rather flattering portrait with some professional makeup and retouching; no one could really look like that every day. And no eyes could really be that color or that huge.

Then she had come to pick Terry up one day two weeks after his transfer, and Colter had had to eat all his ungallant thoughts. He'd wondered since if he'd been doomed from that moment, from the instant he'd found out that the reality more than matched the image, that the quiet charm and spirit of her made even that incredible photograph a pale imitation.

But it didn't matter now. Just as it didn't matter now that the office belonged to the man sitting at the desk, hunched over the stack of paperwork before him. Some things, Colter thought wryly, I don't miss at all.

"Hey, paper pusher, know where I could find a real cop in this place?"

Dave Stanley's dark head came up sharply, his brown eyes wide and startled.

"Son of a—" He stood up, a broad smile splitting his face beneath his bushy moustache. "Colter! What are you doing here?"

He held out his hand, and Colter took it in a firm handshake. "Slumming," he said with a grin.

"I guess! Sit down." Dave pointed to the chair beside the desk. "Unless, of course, you want your old chair back."

"No, thanks," Colter answered as he sat down. "I haven't been near a desk in five years, and I don't miss it."

"Don't make me jealous. That's one hell of a tan you've got there, buddy," Dave said, looking him up and down. "Doesn't look like all that lying in the sun has put any weight on you, though. What've you been doing?"

"Little of this, little of that."

"Sure. Working your way through the female population of Florida is more like it, I'll bet."

"Not me. I've been as pure as a monk since I got there." And damned near ever since I left here, he thought.

"The way women drool over you? Give me a break."

Colter shrugged. He hadn't expected Dave, or anyone else, for that matter, to believe it. He barely believed it himself, and he'd lived it.

"So, what gives? Get homesick or something?"

"Not exactly."

"Then why—" Dave's eyes narrowed. "She found you."

It wasn't a question, and both men knew an explanation of who the "she" was wasn't necessary.

"I talked to him when he called, Colter. And I went to see him. You know I wouldn't say no to her. But the old man's lost it. He was a shaky witness even then. Now he can barely remember who he is anymore, let alone recognize a guy he saw in a dark alley for a few seconds five years ago."

Colter just shrugged; he was finding it a useful habit, after all.

Dave studied him for a moment, then ran a hand over his short, wiry hair before he spoke. "Is that really why you came back? To dig all that up again?"

"Why else?"

"Summer."

Colter sat up straight, his eyes narrowing as he looked at his old friend. "Just what is that supposed to mean?"

Dave, apparently deciding that five years away had done nothing to warm the icy look Colter could turn on you, backpedaled hastily.

"Nothing. I just…nothing. What are you going to do?"

After a moment Colter relaxed. "Talk to Webster. Nose around a little, see if anything turns up." He paused, eyeing Dave carefully. "Read the file on the internal investigation again."

It took a moment for Dave to react; when he did, it was with a low groan. "Oh, no, man, I can't pull that thing! I'd have to explain to the Lieutenant—"

"So I'll ask Hartman myself."

Dave's mouth twisted into a sour smile. "It should be so easy. Hartman's in burglary now."

"Okay. Who do I have to beg?"

"You won't. I guarantee it."

Colter raised his eyebrows. "That bad? They put Kupner in, or what?"

"Worse."

"How could anything be—" Colter broke off, staring at Dave. "No," he said lowly, "not . . ."

"Yes. *Lieutenant* Grissom."

"Damn."

"Yeah. Good thing you left when you did. You two were like gasoline and matches."

"When did *that* happen?"

"He got the promotion six months after you left." Dave lifted one shoulder in a reluctant shrug. "I have to admit he made some good pops. Not big, but a lot of the smaller dealers. Enough to get him the lieutenant's bars, anyway."

Colter shook his head. "That's what he was always good at. Take off the little guy and blow the chance to get the bigger fish." He snorted in disgust. "Lieutenant. You're right, it's a good thing I left."

"I know. I don't care for him much, either, especially after the way he sold out Terry. But you see why I can't pull that file for you."

"Yeah." He sat silently for a moment. "Maybe I should have hung on to my old files instead of shipping them down to property storage."

Dave's eyes widened. "Your files?"

"Yeah."

"Don't tell me. You had a copy of the investigation?"

Colter smiled crookedly but didn't admit anything.

"Damn, Colter, what if Grissom had caught you with that? He'd have known you rifled his office."

"He didn't. He's not that smart." The smile became a grin. "Besides, I hid it where he'd never look."

"Oh, yeah?"

"Yeah. In my atta-boy file. As much as he hated me, I knew he'd never look in there."

Dave laughed. "No kidding. Reading all those commendations you got would turn him green." He became serious again. "What did you do with it when you left?"

"Left it there, with all the other files I tagged for the property room. I figured if he found it, he'd just burn the whole thing without looking at it anyway."

Dave's eyebrows rose. "You didn't even take your commendations with you?" Colter shook his head. "When you cut loose you don't mess around, do you?"

That, Colter thought, had been the easy part. The trappings of his life as a cop had been relatively simple to shed. The memory of a pair of clear green eyes had been the thing he hadn't been able to leave behind.

"Well," Dave was saying, "I might just be able to help you out, after all."

He got up and went to a small closet in the corner of the room. When it had been the office Colter had shared with Terry, it had contained a couple of changes of clothes that would suit a number of different covers, a sport coat, shirt and tie in case they ever had to unexpectedly go to court or see a judge, and Terry's rarely used golf clubs. Now it contained Dave's version of the same items, plus the stack of file boxes he was digging into.

Suddenly Colter realized what those boxes were and rose out of his chair just as Dave turned around, a thick manila folder in his hand and a sheepish smile on his face.

"I didn't think you'd mind. And I'll tell you, some of this stuff has been a lifesaver. More than once."

"I don't mind," Colter said, eyeing the folder. "There's a lot of stuff in there about some of the regulars."

He didn't add that a lot of it was stuff he hadn't put in the department's computer system; Dave had worked with him enough to know that. Those files held information from snitches, informers and various people he'd arrested over the years. Alone, it meant nothing and would have been useless to anyone but him, but often he'd found some little tidbit that broke a case for him.

"I know. I've made a few decent busts myself, thanks to what's in here." For a moment something both warm and sad glowed in Dave's eyes. "You really knew this town, Colter."

"I should have, after more than nine years." Impatience took over. "Is that it?"

Dave held the folder out to him. "Yeah." He grinned. "I kept it around to keep my ego under control. Whenever I started thinking I was God's gift to law enforcement, I just looked at the size of that stack of commendations."

Colter grinned back as he took the folder, searched inside for a moment, then extracted a stack of papers that reduced its thickness by about a third. "Most of it was this."

"Hardly," Dave said, looking at the still-sizable remainder. "But it's still there?"

"Yep. You got my file on Sherwood in there, too?"

Dave nodded and pulled out a file folder at least twice as thick as the first. Colter took it.

"Good. Now I don't have to burgle Grissom's office."

Colter was still grinning, but Dave was somehow not completely sure he was joking. He decided he was better off not knowing and quickly changed the subject.

"So, how long are you staying?"

"I don't know. Depends on how this goes."

"Do you have time to come over for dinner with us? Joyce would love to see you."

"Maybe. But I've got to go now. Summer's out in the car." He saw the flicker in Dave's eyes, and added quickly, "She's going to take me over to see Webster."

"I'll walk out with you and say hi, then."

Dave talked as they went, telling Colter of other changes in the department as they walked down the halls that had once been more of a home to Colter than his own apartment. When they reached the car Colter saw Summer had shifted over to the driver's seat, so he went around to the passenger side. As he got in, Dave leaned over to rest his forearms on the driver's door.

"Hi, kiddo. We missed you at dinner last week, but—" his eyes flicked to Colter and then back "—I guess your trip worked out."

Colter saw her thick lashes lower for a moment, then lift as she looked back at Dave.

"I got . . . more than I bargained for," she said softly.

Dave chuckled. "There are some guys in jail saying that same thing about him." He chuckled at Colter's sour expression, then went on. "You're going over to see Webster?"

She nodded. "I know you don't think he's—"

"Never mind, Summer. I hope I'm wrong. Good luck."

"Thank you. And tell Joyce I'll call her soon."

"I will. You going to see Mrs. O'Neil today?"

Summer hesitated. "I don't know."

"Say hello for me if you do."

"All right."

She reached for the ignition as Dave walked away, but stopped when Colter spoke.

"How is Terry's mother?"

"As well as could be expected, I guess." A flicker of pain shadowed the green eyes. "I try to see her as often as I can, but I missed her this week, being gone."

Reacting to the look in her eyes more than her words, he asked, "Do you want to go now? I'd like to see her, say hello."

Summer looked at him rather oddly. "Yes, I would. If you're sure you want to."

Colter's brow furrowed. "Why not?"

"She . . . gets confused sometimes. It's . . . hard to see her like that, in that place, even though it's very nice, for a rest home."

"A what?"

Colter was startled. Fiona O'Neil had been a vital, active woman, despite the fact that she was older than he had at first expected. She had been nearly forty when she'd had Terry, her first and only child—"a gift," she had laughingly called him. And more than once, Terry had laughed about not being able to keep up with his always-on-the-go mother.

"She was never quite the same after Terry's death," Summer explained, "but Sean was the real blow. She just couldn't seem to go on without him."

He was staring at her, his face suddenly pale. "Sean . . . Sean's dead? Terry's father?"

Realization dawned in her face. "You didn't know?"

Numbly, he shook his head. "When?"

"About three years ago. Suddenly, a heart attack." She gave a bitter little sigh. "Sean couldn't go on without his son, and Fiona can't seem to go on without her husband." Suddenly fervent, she said, "The shooter did more than just kill a cop that night. He killed an entire family."

Colter let out a long breath, rubbing at eyes that were weary from far too long with too little sleep.

"I'm sorry," she said softly. "If I'd realized you didn't know, I wouldn't have brought it up like that."

His hand dropped from his face and he stared at her. "Did you really think I could have known and not come back?"

Summer looked at him in surprise; he sounded almost hurt. And it was in his eyes, too, a pain she hadn't expected. Somewhat inanely, she noticed again how the Florida sun had lightened even the tips of his thick lashes to a glinting gold.

"I..." She tried again. "You were in such a hurry to leave, to get so far away, I didn't think you'd ever come back." He winced, and she went on hurriedly. "I didn't expect you to. I know you had your reasons...." She sighed. "I would have gone myself if I could have."

He looked at her quizzically. "You would have left here?" She'd been born here; he never would have thought she'd consider living anywhere else.

"I thought about it, but I couldn't leave Sean and Fiona, not then. They needed me after Terry was killed. And when Sean died, I couldn't leave Fiona. She was so lost...."

"What about what you need?"

She shrugged, as if it meant nothing that she had stayed, despite her own pain, her own needs, for their sake. "I love them both. They... were my family, too."

"Then let's go," he said softly.

She reached for the ignition again and started the car. She drove silently, not looking at him. After about fifteen minutes, they turned into the driveway of a beautifully restored Victorian home, its front yard dotted with lounge chairs and tables, each occupied by residents of varying ages and conditions. Several of them waved in greeting, a welcoming salute to a familiar visitor.

"You do come here a lot," he observed.

"I try to. It seems to perk Fiona up." Summer stopped the car, but before she got out, she turned to look at him. "Do you really want to see her?"

He hesitated. "Will she want to see me? Or will I just . . . remind her?"

Summer smiled, a soft, sad smile. "Probably not. She's shut out most of it. She might not even remember you."

He followed her up to the house, looking around with a morbid kind of interest. It seemed clean and well kept, a considerable improvement over some he'd seen and heard about.

"It's a nice place," she said as if she'd read his thoughts. "They take good care of her." She looked away. "I tried to keep her at home, but I was gone too much. She needs someone around all the time. Sometimes she walks at night. . . ."

"You did all you could." He didn't have to have been there to know it was true. He knew Summer; she could do no less.

She sighed as she pulled open the door. "I was glad to find this place. It's so much better than most of them, where they treat people like cattle or like little children."

She was greeted by a kindly looking middle-aged woman, who smiled cheerfully.

"Hello, dear. Are you looking for Fiona?"

"Yes, Mrs. Gordon."

"She's out on the terrace in back."

Summer thanked the woman and led the way. Colter waited hesitantly as Summer approached the woman sitting in a padded lounge chair, looking out at the flower garden that was still colorful with the last lingering blooms of spring hanging on in these first days of summer.

Fiona O'Neil had aged fifteen years in the past five. Gone was the animated, sprightly woman with only the slightest sprinkling of gray in her luxurious hair. In her place was a woman who looked eighty-five instead of seventy, her face crumpled with age, her hair a stark white.

"Fee?" Summer knelt beside the chair. "It's Summer. How are you?"

"Why, hello, dear. You're home early, aren't you?"

Colter's brow furrowed, but Summer just went on speaking softly, soothingly.

"Yes, it is early, but it's lovely, isn't it?"

"Yes, it is. But you shouldn't leave school early."

Colter winced, but Summer never faltered; it was clear she'd been through this before, and often.

"School's out, Fee, remember? It's summertime."

"Oh, yes, of course. Summer for Summer." The old face creased into a travesty of what had once been a vivid, lively smile. "We always call it that, don't we? But who's this with you, dear?"

It was just as well she didn't remember him, Colter thought as Summer introduced them as if they'd never met. It would only upset her. He pulled up an empty chair for Summer, then knelt beside it as she sat down.

"So, is this your young man, honey?"

Summer blushed. "Fiona—"

"I'm glad, dear, that you found someone of your own. I know you think you love Terry, but you two aren't really suited, you know. He's too much like his father, a little too fond of his drink and a little wearisome on a woman. You need a gentler hand, my girl."

Her attention suddenly switched to Colter. "You be good to this girl, young man. She's a precious, sweet child, and I love her as if she were my own. She's been my daughter since she was fifteen, and I don't want her hurt," she said sternly.

Colter was aware of Summer's flaming cheeks, and he answered as steadily as he could. "I don't want her hurt, either."

For a moment, the pale blue eyes that had been so clouded cleared, and Colter felt that in that instant Fiona saw right through to his soul. And when she spoke, he couldn't shake the feeling that her words were in answer to everything that she'd found there.

"I believe you. You'll do."

And then, abruptly, the vague look was back. She turned to Summer. "It's been lovely, dear, but I must go start dinner. Sean will be home anytime, and you know how that Irishman gets if his meal's not on the table, waiting."

Colter was amazed at how easily Summer handled it. She merely nodded, helped the woman to her feet, then let her go. After she had watched Fiona, whose once even stride had been reduced to a pained shuffling, make it safely into the house, she turned back to him. Her cheeks were still tinged with the pink of embarrassment, and she lowered her eyes as she spoke.

"Thank you for...going along with it. She seems...happy this way, so I don't try to make her remember."

"What did she mean about you being her daughter since you were fifteen?"

Summer looked up. "My parents were killed in an accident then. Fiona and Sean were their best friends, and they took me in. My only relative was an uncle in Cleveland who I'd never met, so the court let them become my legal guardians."

She said it simply, without self-pity, but he felt the tug of the sad facts just the same.

"I didn't realize you'd lived with them."

And Terry, he added to himself as they walked back to the car. No wonder she loved him so much; she'd been with him since she was fifteen. Remember that, idiot. She'll always love him.

"Yes, until Terry and I got married. But we'd always been close. We lived across the street from each other since I was born. When my parents were killed, Terry was already away at school. He was nineteen then, but he came home summers and at Christmas."

Great. She'd known him all her life. "And that's when you . . . fell in love with him?"

An odd look flashed in the green eyes. "We'd grown up together, played together, even when the older kids used to tease him about having a kid four years younger tagging along after him, and a girl at that. He was always getting in fights over it. You know what a scrapper he was, any excuse for a brawl."

As he opened the driver's door for her, Colter managed a smile. He walked around the car and slid into the passenger seat, saying, "Yeah, I know. That Irish temper of his almost got us both in trouble more than once."

"Anyway, it was never any big, romantic scene. We knew each other inside and out, and . . . well, it just seemed natural for us to get married. To us, at least." She glanced back toward the house as she started the car. "Fiona thought we were *too* close. Like brother and sister. She . . . well, you heard her."

Yes, he thought, I did. And what she'd said bothered him. He needed some time to think about this. Not romantic? How the hell could anyone have a chance with Summer O'Neil and not turn into a bumbling, romantic idiot? I'd shower her in roses—no, honeysuckle, he thought, remembering how she loved the sweet scent. I'd build her a house on as much land as she wanted, all the space she craved. I'd—

You'll never have the chance, he interrupted himself acidly, so quit daydreaming. You've got no business prying into what their relationship had or hadn't been. She loved Terry, he loved her, and now he's dead. There's no room there for you, not with your best friend's wife.

He was startled when he came out of his reverie to see where they were. A few blocks from the waterfront, what had once been a warehouse had been converted into a shelter of sorts, the sign in front proclaiming it rather grandly, Olympic House. He looked at Summer quizzically.

"I told you Webster had slipped a little," she said defensively. "He lost his apartment and was hanging around at the airport where he could stay warm and rest. He had to have a better place to stay."

"Okay, okay," he said as they went inside, "take it easy. I just wondered."

The place made him uncomfortable, images of his lazy life in Key West flitting through his head. He was glad when Summer spoke again.

"They do their best here, but he should be in a place like Fee's," she said with concern. "With trained people to look after him. But there's no money, and— There he is," she interrupted herself, pointing to one corner of the big room.

There'd been radical change here, too, and for a second, Colter wondered if he'd somehow lost track and been gone for much longer than five years and just didn't know it. The man who had been gray haired but spry and alert then was in an old, worn recliner, a blanket covering his thin frame despite the warmth. He was muttering angrily as the young volunteer tried to tuck the blanket around him.

"...leave a man in peace, will you? I didn't ask for your help!"

"I'm sorry, Mrs. O'Neil," the young man said as Summer approached. "It's been a difficult day."

"It's all right, Tim. I understand."

"He was so much better the last time you came to see him, I hoped we were making some progress."

"I know. We'll be all right."

"Look here, missy," Mr. Webster broke in, waving a thin hand, "don't you be talking over me like I was already dead! I'm still alive and kicking!"

"You're quite right, Mr. Webster," Summer agreed easily, "and I apologize."

She nodded to Tim, who smiled warmly and turned to go. Too warmly, Colter thought sourly. He knew the look in the young man's eyes. He'd seen it too often in his own, that hopeless, frustrated longing. Knock it off, he ordered himself. Pay attention here. This old guy is the whole reason you're here.

Sure he is.

Ignoring his own thought, he turned back to face the chair and dragged his attention back to what Summer was saying.

"...feeling better. I brought someone to see you."

"I don't want to see anyone," the old man said testily. "I don't even want to see you!" He looked her up and down. "As a matter of fact," he said, gray eyebrows lowering as he looked at her blankly, "who *are* you?"

Chapter 4

"Why don't you just say it?"

Summer paced back and forth across the small living room.

"Say what?" Colter asked tiredly, swinging his legs up and leaning back against the pillows of the window seat.

"What you're thinking." She stopped, whirling to face him. "That I'm a fool for believing the old man."

"I never thought that."

"How could you not?" She resumed pacing. "He didn't even recognize me today, let alone you."

"It's all right. I understand.'

"No," she said urgently, "you don't. He just has bad days, sometimes. This was one of them. He hadn't even been drinking."

Colter didn't answer, just turned his head to stare out the window. Once, he'd enjoyed the fact that the summer days here were so long, that it stayed light so late. Now he wondered if he could ever get used to it again.

He caught himself with a wry inner smile; he had no intention of ever getting used to it again. Not while she was here. If nothing else, the past three days had proven to him that it would be altogether too easy for him to fall right back into the pit he'd climbed out of when he'd left. She still had that incredible power over him, and if he didn't keep his guard up, he would succumb to it.

It had been a hellish afternoon. An hour spent with the crochety Mr. Webster had gotten them nothing but more frustration. Dave had been right, Colter had thought glumly. The old man had lost it. He couldn't have come up with a less credible witness if he'd tried. The man was as irrational as—

As Fiona. Pain laced through him. Watching Summer's eyes as the woman had chattered on as if her son were still alive, as if her husband were just in another room, as if Summer was the child she'd once been, was wrenching in a way he'd never felt before. Summer had been gentle and unfailingly kind to the older woman, with a patience that amazed him considering the pain he knew the rambling talk must have caused her.

And after they'd left the shelter, Summer had been quiet all the way back to her house. Lack of sleep was catching up with him, and he had smothered a weary sigh as he dropped down on the window seat. It was then that she had broken her silence, saying what she was sure he was thinking.

Summer watched him while she paced, studied him as he stared out the window. He agreed with Dave, she thought. That it was a wild-goose chase. He was trying, she was sure, to think of a way to let her down easily. She bit her lip.

"If you could only see him when he's himself," she said. "He's as rational as anyone. And he remembers every detail of that night. You could quiz him on it—"

"Summer—"

"He knows who the shooter was, Colter! I know he does."

"Summer, listen," he said softly, hating the distress in her face. "I know how you feel. Sometimes, you want something so badly—"

"Stop it!" She whirled on him again. "Do you think I haven't thought of that? Do you think I haven't told myself that even if he's right, I should let it go? Do you think I want to go through all this again?"

"No. I know you don't. But I also know how hard it is to leave something unfinished."

"Loose ends? Is that what it is to you?"

Her eyes were fastened on him fiercely, and despite the sting in her words, he held her gaze.

"You know it's more than that," he said evenly.

"I don't know anything anymore." She turned her back on him and began to walk away.

"Summer, wait."

When she turned back to look at him, her face was stiff, her eyes unreadable. When she spoke, her voice was chilly.

"I'm very sorry you came all the way here for nothing, but I didn't ask you to come. All I wanted was information. I still want it. But if you can't do that..." She shrugged, the stiffness of her shoulders evident in the gesture. "There's a flight back to Miami tomorrow at nine. You should be able to get on it."

"Damn it, Summer—"

"Just go, Colter. You did what you had to do five years ago. I'll do what I have to now. It's what I'd planned to do all along."

She turned away again, but this time, she ran to the small hallway and was out of sight before he could free himself from the enfolding pillows. He heard the slam of her bedroom door echoing down the narrow hallway and he sank back against the soft cushions.

Damn, he thought. He hadn't meant to do that. The last thing he wanted to do was make this harder on her. She wanted so badly to vindicate Terry. Hell, so did he. He'd come back to a place he'd sworn he'd left forever just on the chance he could do what he hadn't been able to do five years ago. And the discovery that that chance had never really existed was hard to accept. He stared out the window for a long time, watching the sky darken, the moon rise.

He picked up one of the pillows, pounding at it with a clenched hand. He stopped abruptly when he realized it was an exquisite needlepoint design that was obviously handmade. Summer?

His mind flashed back to Terry commenting that she seemed to always be working on something, almost as if he were complaining. Colter looked at the pattern of rich blues, turquoises and greens, at the intricate work, at the detail and care that had gone into it. He didn't know much about that kind of thing, but he couldn't understand how anybody could complain when this beautiful thing was the result.

This house had, as had the one she had lived in with Terry, that same feeling of care, that same flair for the blending of color. Combined with polished tables and other pieces of fine wood, the softly colored walls and the rich greens and blues of the Pacific Northwest brought indoors, it was a welcoming, warm place. Wherever she was, she seemed to take the knack for comfort with her.

And she took her level head, too, he thought. If he'd learned anything about her in those horrible days after Terry's murder, it was that. Her quiet, almost shy calm had concealed a core of steel he'd never expected. Even then, at only twenty-one, she hadn't overreacted or gotten hysterical, hadn't gone to pieces when it got rough.

She hadn't, he thought, gone to pieces at all until it had all become so horrible, he'd felt like crying himself. In fact, that night he'd spent holding her when at last she had broken down, he wasn't sure he hadn't cried right along with her.

It hit him then. She *didn't* overreact. Even when she had all the reason in the world, she didn't overreact. So she hadn't overreacted to this. If she believed Webster, she had good reason.

But the old man was practically senile, even when he wasn't drunk, Colter thought. He was hardly reliable. Yet she'd trusted what the old man had told her. So he must have seemed reliable, then. But he clearly wasn't now.

"Damn," Colter muttered. How could he start an investigation, especially after five years, with information from a witness he couldn't rely on?

He started to hit the pillow again in frustration, then made himself stop. He carefully set the pillow down, staring at it as if it held the answer to all his questions.

Use your head, Colter, he ordered himself. You do it the same way you build a case on information from a shaky snitch. You use it as a place to start. It hasn't been *that* long. You're just too tangled up with Summer to think straight.

A snitch, he thought again. Treat it like a tip from a snitch. It might be all true or all false, but the chances were good it fell somewhere in between. So you didn't stake your life on it, but you didn't turn your back on it, either.

He got up, reaching out to touch the needlepoint pillow once more. Then he crossed the now dark room and walked down the hall to her closed door. He stopped, took a short, steadying breath and tapped lightly.

"Summer?"

Nothing. He tapped again.

"Summer, please. We've got to talk."

Still nothing. Or was that a sound? He reached for the knob and eased the door open. The room was dark, but his eyes were already adjusted and he quickly spotted the huddled shape on the big four-poster bed he'd seen the one time he had risked a glance into her room. All he'd been able to think of then was his relief that it wasn't the bed she and Terry slept in, and his mind had recoiled so sharply from the realization of what that thought meant that he had sagged against the doorjamb for support.

"Summer?" he whispered, jerking his mind forcibly back to the present.

"...'way."

Her voice was muffled, but he gathered she'd said "Go away." He didn't. Slowly, he crossed the room and sat on the edge of the bed. Even in the dim light, he could see her tremble, and with a little shock, he realized that she was crying. It startled him; he'd thought she was angry. And it stunned him; he knew so very well what it took to make her cry.

"Summer," he whispered, reaching out to her.

"Go away." The words were clear this time, but her voice quivered.

"No."

She seemed surprised by his simple answer; he both sensed and saw her sudden stillness.

"We have to talk," he said again.

She took a gulping breath and he saw the wetness glistening on her cheeks. "We already did."

"Okay, I'll talk. You just listen." His voice was hoarse with his effort to control it. "Just don't cry anymore."

An odd, strangled sound broke from her, a tight little sound of both despair and anger. "I swore I'd cried my last tear over this a long time ago."

Convulsively, unable to stop himself, he swung his legs onto the bed and gathered her into his arms. He expected her to fight him, to pull away, but after she stiffened for a brief moment, she went limp against him, so close he could feel the little shudders that went through her as she tried to control her weeping.

He lifted a hand to smooth her hair back from her tear-stained face. "It's okay," he soothed, his voice low and tender. "Let it out." He held her for a long time before he said quietly, "It's not just that, you know. You had a hell of a day."

She murmured something he couldn't hear, but he knew as well as he'd ever known anything that it was a rejection of his rationale; Summer O'Neil had never been one for excuses.

"It must be hell seeing Fiona like that. But you just take it because she needs you."

"Because I love her."

"And nothing's too much for someone you love, is it?"

"What else do we have?"

A small, choked sound escaped him, and he tightened his arms around her. So simple. So true. And so damned hard. If he'd had her courage, her valiant heart, he never would have left. He would have stayed, would have taken care of her, no matter that it tortured him that he couldn't have her. But he didn't have them, so he'd run literally to the end of the earth.

He couldn't change that now. She'd needed a friend, and he'd let her down. Let her down because he wanted to be more to her than that. And the past three days had shown him he still couldn't stand being so near and yet so far, looking but not touching, and all the other tired clichés that described what he was feeling.

Spineless, he told himself bitterly, that's what you are. Jellyfish city. Shane Colter, resident invertebrate. Don't even have the guts to face the truth. You're just Terry's best friend to her. She doesn't want you, not like you want her....

The thoughts of how he wanted her, of all the ways he wanted her, of all the times he'd dreamed of having her rose up together to haunt him. They combined hotly with the fact that he was here with his arms around her, on her bed, and he scrambled desperately for a diversion.

"Tell me what happened. What Webster told you."

She went rigid, slowly lifting herself away from him so she could look at his face. He tried to ignore the fact that she was doing it by bracing one slender hand on his chest.

"Why?" Her voice was taut, tense. She reached out suddenly, turning on the bedside lamp as if she had to see his face when he answered.

He shrugged. "Got to start somewhere."

Her eyes widened. "You're...going to start?"

He swallowed tightly. He owed it to her, he thought, and made himself say it. "You're no fool, Summer. If you believed him, you had reason. I'll do what I can to check it out."

Summer stared at him, her lips parted as she drew in a quick breath. She'd thought it was over. She'd known that while she might try and dig up the truth, she had little chance of succeeding, especially after all this time. But Colter could do it, if it could be done at all. He had the knowledge, the background, the contacts, the instinct. He could do it, she knew he could.

She drew in another quick, harsh breath, then another, through parted lips. She wondered why she couldn't seem to get enough air. This was drying her mouth, her lips, and her tongue crept out to moisten them. Something that showed in his face when she did made her suddenly aware of their position, of the heat of his skin beneath her hand, and that they were intimately entwined on her bed.

With a jerky little movement, she straightened, drawing her legs up until she was sitting cross-legged, no longer touching him. He let out a small rush of air. A sigh of relief, no doubt, she thought. The last thing he wants is you hanging all over him. He had enough of that when he was consoling the grieving widow.

She didn't find it odd that she thought of the woman she'd been then as someone apart from who she was now. She'd been a child then, really. But the night Colter had come to her, blood on his clothes and hell in his turquoise eyes, she had begun to grow up.

"When did you find out?" Colter's gentle prompting sent the memories spinning away.

"Two weeks ago. Dave called me. Said Mr. Webster had called him." She bit her lip, took a breath and went on. "He told Dave that he'd been out walking, down on the waterfront, near Pike Place Market."

Colter froze, watching her intently. Terry had been killed barely a block away from the popular outdoor market.

"I know," she said. "I told you Webster saw him right back in the same area. Dave said he'd check it out, but not to expect anything. He just thought I should know."

Colter only nodded, not speaking, and Summer's eyes narrowed. Was he just pretending to take this seriously now? He certainly seemed to have done a sudden turn around. Was he just trying to placate her?

"I'm not patronizing you, Summer," he said quietly. "Tell me the rest."

She flushed at how easily he read her and lowered her eyes to her hands as she went on. "Mr. Webster said this big limo pulled up, a white one, and stopped at the intersection right in front of him."

"And the shooter was in it?" A skeptical look flitted across his face before he could stop it; fortunately, she was still looking downward and didn't see it.

"Not exactly. Webster couldn't see the passenger, the windows were tinted." She lifted her eyes to meet his then. "But the driver's window was lowered for a moment. Webster got a good look at him."

"He was driving it?" Summer nodded, and Colter's eyebrows came down. That, at least, made more sense. "Did the guy see Webster?"

"He didn't think so." She paused uncertainly.

"What?"

"Would it matter if he had? There was never a trial, so no one really saw Mr. Webster."

"It was in all the papers that there was a witness, along with the fact that he'd seen him well enough to do a sketch with the police artist. If the shooter did work for Sherwood, you can bet the boss made a point of making sure he couldn't be tied into it. He probably had a man on Webster the minute he found out he existed."

Her delicate brow furrowed. "Then why didn't he just . . . kill him?"

Colter shrugged. "Sherwood doesn't work that way." He smiled wryly. "He runs hookers, drugs and numbers, but he doesn't kill unless he has to."

"Scruples?"

"Not on your life. He just doesn't like the heat a murder would bring down on him."

"Especially a cop." Her tone was harsh but not pained.

"Yes. That's the last thing he'd want to do. So Terry must have stumbled into something they couldn't let him walk away from."

"And Mr. Webster?"

Colter shrugged again. "Sherwood obviously decided to wait. He knew he could get him if we got too close." His mouth twisted into a grimace. "Which means we never did."

"And now he doesn't have to worry at all," she said bitterly. "They barely believed Mr. Webster before. They surely won't now."

"Probably not," Colter said gently, "if they've only seen him like he was today."

"But he isn't always like that," she protested again. "I've seen him, I know. I know when he's drifting and when he's not." She stopped, biting her lip as she tried to control her frustration. "But they won't believe me, either."

"They don't know you or they would."

He said it simply, honestly, and the smile she gave him sent a ripple of heated sensation along nerves already strung tight by her closeness.

"I suppose I can understand," she admitted, "but they didn't have to be so vicious about it. A simple 'go away, lady' would have been sufficient."

He stared at her in disbelief. "Dave was—"

"Of course not! Dave would never do that. And he went out to talk to Mr. Webster right away. He was better that day than he was today, but Dave said it still wasn't much to go on. He did some checking, but it didn't come to anything. I think..." Her voice trailed off.

"What?"

"I think he was ordered to stop."

"What do you mean?"

She sighed. "I went to the station after Dave called me. I wanted to go with him, but he was already gone."

"What happened?"

She made a face. "Lieutenant Grissom."

"Ouch."

"Yes. And after what he said to me, I'm sure he wouldn't have let Dave spend any time on it."

"I can imagine." Colter shook his head. "What did Lieu—" He broke off, chuckling sourly. "I can't even say it. What did he tell you?"

"What didn't he? That I was, at best, a misled crusader, at worst, a fool. That I couldn't accept the fact that Terry had been dirty. That I was wasting his time and the department's, and that I should go away and forget it."

Colter muttered something unintelligible. Summer sighed and went on. "He wouldn't even talk about it. Said the case was closed and it was staying closed." She dropped her gaze to where she was picking at a loose thread on the thick comforter that covered the bed. "He said I should be glad I hadn't wound up in trouble myself."

"What?" Colter came abruptly, rigidly upright.

"He hinted, rather nastily, that there were those who still thought I was involved. That I'd helped hide the money."

"That son of a bitch," Colter ground out. "I swear I—"

"Colter, stop. It doesn't matter. I've been through it all before."

"That doesn't make it right," he snapped. "Any more than it was when Terry was killed. They had no right to pull you into that mess."

Had she once thought, only two days ago, that nothing mattered to this man anymore? "You fought for me then, too, didn't you?"

"What was I supposed to do while they dragged you through their damned investigation, calling you up in front of that damned group of vultures and accusing you of knowing all along? What they said about Terry was bad enough, but to do that to you when he wasn't even two weeks gone—"

"They did it to you, too. Do you think I've forgotten how they accused you of being in on it with him? Of, at the least, knowing about it and covering up for him?"

He shrugged in dismissal. "That's standard. They always pull that. I expected it."

"For you, but not for me?"

"You?" he snapped out. "All they had to do was open their eyes and look at you and they'd have known you'd never do anything like that!" He let out a compressed, angry breath.

Summer felt an odd warmth at his fervidness. A slow smile curved her mouth. "As I recall, you told them that. Loudly."

"They should have known," he said stubbornly.

"And got yourself kicked out of the hearing."

"I didn't get kicked out. I left."

"And got an official reprimand."

"That was nothing compared to what they were doing to you."

Funny, she thought, how it didn't sting anymore. She'd thought she would never recover from the humiliation of discovering that the department Terry had given his life for had been prying into her life, destroying her privacy, dragging her past, Terry's past, their families, even their rather lean bank account out in public, and all with Terry barely buried. But they had found nothing because there had been nothing to find.

"Remember that last Saint Patrick's Day?" she asked softly, not certain why that night had come back to her just now.

"Yeah," Colter answered, puzzlement mixed with remembrance on his face. "How could I forget? I don't think McRory's has ever been the same."

I haven't either. For a moment, she thought she'd said it aloud, but his expression didn't change and she knew that she hadn't.

"What made you think of that?"

"I—I'm not sure."

And she wasn't. Just that something about this night reminded her of that one. Perhaps because then, as now, Colter had been there for her. When Terry had gotten roaring drunk at the annual Saint Patrick's semi-controlled brawl at a favorite bar in Seattle, it had been Colter who had pulled him out before he started a fight that would have landed them all in hot water. It had been Colter who had smooth-talked the angry partyers who had wanted a piece of the drunken young Irishman; it had been Colter who had taken a wild, roundhouse punch from Terry when he took his keys away from him; and it had been Colter who had driven them home and carried Terry inside and put him to bed.

And it had been Colter with whom she had spent the remainder of a quiet March 17, sipping coffee in the warmth of the kitchen.

She had never forgotten those quiet, companionable hours. She'd told him of her studies, of how much she loved her part-time job at the Seattle Aquarium and how they had promised her a full-time job when she got her degree in marine biology. Colter had been genuinely interested, had encouraged her and had, oddly, almost seemed proud of her.

And he'd talked to her, this man everyone had always told her never let anyone get too close. He'd told her about his own days in college, and then the police academy, about his father, who had also been a cop, and about the things he loved and hated about the job. He'd told her things Terry never had, and after that night, she felt she understood the work better than she ever had.

She hadn't known on that night that when she saw him again, on the day they shared the whales, it would be for the last time before disaster struck. She had never dreamed, in those moments when they watched the huge sea mammals together, that the next time she would see him would be the night that would blast her world to pieces, the night that would change her and her life, forever.

"What?" he asked, and she realized she had been watching him intently as the memories unrolled in her mind. She felt suddenly uncomfortable and in an odd way, almost frightened, as she always had whenever she found herself thinking too much about him, as if she were a child playing with fire.

"Do you think there's any hope?" she asked quickly.

He met her gaze levelly. "I won't lie to you, Summer. I don't know. All I can do is try."

She realized, more now than before, how much he was taking on trust. Trust in her. He'd come clear across the country because of it. And even when it must have seemed to him that she'd been a fool, he had come around to her side. He had pushed aside his doubts and been there once more to support her.

She had missed him, she thought suddenly, unexpectedly. It had been different when he had just stopped coming around; she had still heard about him. But when he'd gone after the final, inconclusive decision in Terry's case had come down, it had been an abrupt and total break. He had come to the house to tell her and to say goodbye.

"I have to, Summer," he'd said at her bewildered look. "I can't . . . There are things I have to work out."

"Do you have to leave?"

He had looked at her with an intensity she hadn't understood. "I can't do it here."

"Where are you going?"

"I'm not sure yet."

"When?"

"In the morning."

She remembered dropping down weakly on the sofa. He'd been her only prop, her strength for these long, horrible weeks; she didn't know what she'd do without him.

"Is it . . . Terry?"

"Partly."

"How much time are they giving you?"

He took in a deep breath. "None. I quit."

She stared, stunned. "Quit? But you love your job!"

"I did. But there's too much of it I can't deal with any-more."

"But—"

"You'll be all right, Summer. The insurance will pay this place off, and you'll have money from—"

"I know that," she said quickly. "I know you took care of everything for me. I just . . . I never thought you would leave."

"I have to. I—"

He broke off and turned his back to her. He walked to the window that looked out over her vast garden and stared through it.

"I have to," he repeated, his voice sounding strangely thick, as if his throat was tight, and almost distant, as if he'd forgotten she was listening. "There's got to be someplace to get away from it. I just have to find it. Someplace where I can sleep at night."

She felt the awful tug of self-contempt. He'd been the only thing that had kept her together for nearly three months, and now that he wanted some peace for himself, she was begrudging him.

"I'm sorry, Colter. If you feel you have to go, then you have to. You've done more than enough for me, more than I had any right to expect."

He whirled on her. "Don't say that. You have the right to expect anything. More than I could ever do."

He was so unexpectedly vehement that she was taken aback. "You've done," she said carefully, "more than anyone has ever done for me. I will never forget it, and I love you for it."

He went strangely pale and took a step toward her, his hands raised as if to touch her.

"Summer, I—" He broke off, shaking his head fiercely. "No. No, I can't."

She had stared once more as he turned on his heel and walked to the door. He opened it, then looked back over his shoulder.

"Goodbye, Summer."

She had thought about him often after he'd gone, wondered where he was, how he was, if he'd found the peace he'd been after. And she'd wondered about how strained he had seemed that night and what it was that he had been going to say or do that he'd decided he couldn't. But she hadn't realized until now, when he was back in her life, how much she'd missed him.

"Summer..." His voice was low, oddly husky.

"What?" The softness of memory and of the realization she'd just arrived at echoed warmly in her voice. Colter groaned. "Don't look at me like that."

She looked startled. "Like what?"

"Like... Just don't."

He moved to the edge of the bed. When he got up, she did, too, looking at him a little warily.

"Do you want to go back and see Mr. Webster again tomorrow? Maybe he'll be better."

"Not yet. I'll go with what you told me for now. Maybe somebody else saw the guy, too."

Somebody else. As if he'd never doubted her or Mr. Webster at all. Oh, Colter, I knew you'd come through. Suddenly, unable to stop herself, she threw her arms around him and hugged him fiercely.

Colter was stunned into immobility for a moment. But what his mind couldn't deal with, his body was ready and able to react to and his arms went around her tightly. He could smell it, that sweet, honeysuckle scent, could feel the slender softness of her pressed against him, and his heart began to hammer in his chest.

Summer didn't understand. She had meant to thank him for his faith, had wanted to show him how much it meant to her that he would try even when everyone else had turned her away. But somehow, her impulsive hug had turned into something else.

How could she have forgotten? How could she possibly have forgotten what this man could do to her? He had always unsettled her, made her think things she'd had no business thinking. He'd made her wonder what it would be like to be held by somebody else, what it would be like to look up into a pair of vivid turquoise eyes glowing with heat instead of Terry's ever-present indulgence.

She had to stop this, had to move away. She couldn't stay like this, so close, with her head pressed so tight against his chest. But it felt so good to be held again. No, she corrected with her innate honesty, if felt so good to be held again by Colter. It had always felt good, even when it shouldn't have, even when it filled her with a gnawing guilt, when her conscience told her she shouldn't feel anything at all for this man who was her husband's friend and partner. And that he would be embarrassed if he knew.

She could hear his heart beneath her ear, thudding steadily and, she thought, oddly fast. His heat warmed her and somehow made it hard to breathe. Her mind was reeling. For one confused moment, she even thought she felt his lips pressed softly against her hair.

Stop. She had to stop. He'd only meant to comfort her, he'd never, she told herself firmly, in all the time she'd known him, meant to do anything more. A man like Shane Colter would have no interest in a mouse like her, not that way. She had to remember that. She found the strength to pull back, only to find it was useless against the greater strength of the arms that held her.

"God, Summer..."

It was low, harsh, and came from deep in his chest, somewhere beneath her ear. Something about the sound of it sent a little dart of heat along nerves she hadn't even known she had. His hands slid from her shoulders, down her back to her waist, to pull her even closer. She dragged in a breath as she tilted her head back.

"Colter..." she began.

Then she stopped, her voice lost somewhere in the shock of meeting his eyes and finding them glowing with the heat she'd only imagined, somewhere in the shock of realizing, as she leaned against him, that he was fully, hotly aroused.

At her stunned look, Colter suddenly released her. He took a step back, his chest rising and falling quickly as he stared at her, and Summer got the oddest impression that he was shaking. Then she dismissed it as ridiculous, an idea he swiftly enforced with his short, almost sharp good-night.

Then he was gone, leaving Summer swaying unsteadily. She sank down on the edge of the bed, her arms curling around herself as she tried to figure out what had just happened. She was awake long into the night.

Chapter 5

Summer woke from a short, fitful sleep to the sound of heavy rain. While some people in this part of the world detested the frequent, lingering rains, Summer didn't. She loved rain for itself and for its results: the rich, lush greenery that flourished here. She lay listening for a while, then with a sighing admission that she'd gotten all the sleep she was going to get, she slid out of bed.

After a quick shower, she pulled on a pair of worn, comfortable jeans and a long, soft, pale green sweater that bared one slender shoulder, then padded out to the kitchen to fix herself a cup of hot chocolate. She settled into the cushions of the window seat, looking out at the damp world as somewhere above the clouds heavy with rain, the sun rose.

It hadn't meant anything, she had decided in the dark, sleepless hours. She had remembered, then, when her mind had been spinning so wildly, what the gregarious charter skipper on Key West had told her.

"Yeah," the grizzled old man had said when she'd finally convinced him she wasn't hunting Colter for any nefarious reason, "he's around. Does some work for me and some of the other guys, now and again. Takes over the charters when we need a break, does some other work. Cleans the hulls for us or works on the power plants.''

A smile had creased the weathered, jovial face. "Until he gets enough money to keep him going for a while. Then it's back to that little island of his."

"That one?" She looked toward the one he'd pointed out.

"Yeah." The man looked at her consideringly. "He doesn't take much to visitors. Not even ones that look like you. Don't think he's had a woman over there in all the time he's been there, and I know he hasn't been partying in town, not that the local ladies don't think he's a ... what is it they call it these days? A hunk?"

"That's it," Summer replied with a little laugh. Some things never changed, no matter where you went, she thought, and Colter's sex appeal was obviously one of them.

"Well, it ain't doing any of them any good. He might look, but he don't touch. And some of them ladies have gotten right inventive, too. Why, one of them even pretended to wash up on that beach of his, like off of a shipwreck." He chuckled. "He just sent her back. Just like she came, buck naked and— Er, sorry."

"It's all right," Summer said hastily, hoping her blush wouldn't be noticeable in the bright Key West sun.

"But if'n you're an old friend, like you say, maybe he won't mind. Enrique there—'' he gestured over his shoulder at the boy tinkering with the small outboard motor on his skiff "—can run you over."

So, she thought now as she sipped the chocolate, if the congenial captain had been right, then Colter, as unlikely as it seemed, had been without female ... fraternization for a long time. It was silly to read any more into his reaction; any woman would probably have had the same effect on him.

It certainly couldn't be her. In fact, that was probably why he had left so abruptly, she thought. He must have been embarrassed about it being her, or thought that she would misinterpret a natural response to holding a woman after a long time. Any woman. Not her. Not shy, quiet little Summer. She sipped again, telling herself it was the steam from the mug that was making her cheeks feel so warm.

She wouldn't even mention it, she thought. She'd act as if nothing had happened, at least nothing unusual. If she could save him any awkwardness, she owed him that much. Her mouth twisted wryly. You mean save yourself, don't you? She took another sip of the sweet, warming liquid.

Why had he done it? she wondered. She could understand why he might want to get as far as he could from Seattle, but why had it apparently included cutting himself off from people, too? Especially the women, who obviously found him as intriguing in Key West as they had in Seattle. Had something happened since he'd left? Something in those four years of wandering he'd done before he'd finally stopped, before he'd reached the literal end of the country? Had he fallen for someone on that cross-country trek and been burned?

She lowered her cup as an odd qualm struck her. It was a feeling she'd had only once before, on the night Colter had come to her and told her he was leaving. It was an odd mixture of pain, distress and sadness, and she told herself firmly it was only at the thought that he might have been hurt, not at the idea of him falling for some anonymous, unknown woman somewhere in the vast expanse of country between Washington state and Key West. She had no reason to feel that way. Colter was still what he'd always been—a dear, tried-and-true friend, no more. He'd never felt any more for her and, she told herself firmly, he never would.

She wrapped her hands around the mug for warmth as the rain got heavier, thinking that she would turn up the heat before he got up; this chill air would be a shock for a body thermostat set for south Florida. Just as she thought it, it was too late. At a sound from the hall, she looked up and saw him.

His hair was tousled, as if he'd just run a hand through it, and his jaw was stubbled with the overnight growth of beard. His eyes were bleary, and he rubbed at them as he walked into the small living room on bare feet.

Lord, she'd forgotten. Again. Her eyes seemed riveted on that broad expanse of chest, on the sleek swell of muscled arms. He'd pulled on a pair of jeans; with the top button undone, they rode low on his lean hips and she couldn't seem to help trailing her eyes over him, from the sparse scattering of sun-bleached golden hair in the center of his chest down over the flat, ridged abdomen to where a slightly darker, thicker path of hair began below his navel. His deep golden tan stood out even more now that he was back among the paler skins that populated this part of the world.

His movement as he rubbed at his bare arms jolted her out of her contemplation.

"Good morning," she said hastily.

His eyes flicked from her to the window, wet with a steady stream of raindrops, then back.

"I'd forgotten," he said with a crooked grin.

"I was about to turn the heat on. I thought this might be a shock for you."

"This is not," he agreed, "June in the Keys." He looked out again. "I may have to break down and buy a jacket. Or at least a sweater."

"Yes," she said, too quickly. She blushed when she realized she would have said yes to anything that would cover up that naked chest. He was looking at her rather oddly, and she seized the first thing she thought of to say.

"I . . . maybe I can help with the sweater."

He looked puzzled. "Help?"

She nodded, then slid off the seat and headed for her room. He watched her go, wishing those jeans didn't hug her slim hips quite so lovingly, that her legs weren't quite so long, giving rise to thoughts he couldn't risk.

She was going to play it exactly as he would have wished, he thought. She was going to act as if that brief, fevered moment between them had never happened. As if she hadn't even realized the effect she'd had on him, when he knew she had to have noticed, he'd been so hot and hard. He sat down on the edge of the seat, rubbing once more at eyes that hadn't seen enough sleep since he'd left the Keys.

She was probably so embarrassed, she'd decided just to ignore it. What else could she do? he thought sourly. She had too much class to tell him to go to hell, as she should have. As she probably would tell anyone else, anyone she didn't feel she owed something.

Owed something. Right. For taking to your heels when she needed you most? For—

Anyone else? His mind suddenly reacted to his own thoughts. Had there been anyone else?

A woman like Summer? Of course, there had, you idiot, he told himself acidly. She probably had them lining up at the door. Even in the rain, he thought glumly, quickly ordering himself not to dwell on why the thought was so disturbing.

He looked up when she came back into the room, a white box in her hands. She came to a stop in front of him, gripping the box tightly, as if nervous, and she was looking at him uncertainly. His eyes flicked from the box to her face, his brow furrowing quizzically. She took in a quick breath and handed him the box.

"I saved it," she said in a rush.

Saved it? He lowered his eyes and lifted the lid. The box contained a thick, handmade sweater, with a soft, rough-textured, sea-blue background for an abstract arc of pure black and white in a flat, smooth yarn that had a satin sheen to it. His mind immediately flashed back to that day on the sailboat.

"The whales," he murmured without really realizing he'd said it aloud.

"Yes," she breathed, unable to hide the delight in her voice, delight that he'd seen the intent behind the free-form design that suggested rather than showed.

He touched the heavy sweater with a tentative finger. It felt wonderfully soft and warm, and he couldn't help wondering what it would feel like to wear. But she'd said she'd saved it, so it must have been Terry's. She couldn't mean for him to use it, even if it would have fit. He felt an odd pang of envy for his dead friend as he studied the exquisite work; what had it been like to have someone care enough to do something like this?

"It's beautiful," he said softly. "Terry must have been very proud of it."

She looked puzzled for a moment, then her expression cleared. "Terry thought making a sweater by hand was a complete waste of time."

Colter gaped at her in disbelief. "But this is so... incredible." He lifted it out of the box. "It's... The color, the design... it's like this place..."

He faltered, at a loss for words to explain how it seemed to capture the spirit and feel of the place that had been his home until five years ago. But Summer seemed to understand. And her uncertainty seemed to disappear in the face of his admiration.

"I didn't make it for Terry," she said quietly.

He raised his eyes to her, then looked back at the sweater that had unfolded as he pulled the bottom free of the box. What she'd said was obviously true; the garment would have overwhelmed Terry's slight, wiry frame.

"I started it after we saw the whales that day." She lowered her eyes. "I... You always wore nice sweaters, so I thought you might... appreciate it."

Colter stared at her; she couldn't mean what she seemed to be saying.

"It took me a while to work out the design and get the right material, and I didn't have that much time to work on it, so it took longer than I wanted to finish it."

"It shows. The time, I mean. It's perfect," he said quickly, deciding he'd been reading this whole thing wrong. There was no way—

"Thank you. I wanted you to..." She paused, and a tinge of color rose to her cheeks. "I didn't know I wasn't going to see you again...."

"Summer," he began, speaking slowly, carefully. "Who did you make it for?"

Her eyes widened as she looked at him. "I thought you guessed... I made it for you."

He stared down at the beautiful piece of work in his hands, then back at her. "Why?" His voice was low, almost strained.

Summer sank down onto the edge of the seat. She plucked at a fiber of the soft, blue yarn that had clung to her sleeve. He waited.

"That day," she said at last, "was so special. I thought you felt it, too. Terry... Terry never went in much for that kind of thing. He never understood why I'd want to waste time looking for creatures in the wild. He said they were easier to see in zoos and aquariums. He didn't see any difference in looking at them there or in their natural habitat." She gave a little sigh. "I wanted to . . . thank you for sharing that with me. For understanding."

Colter couldn't speak, his throat was so tight. He couldn't even look at her. She'd made this beautiful thing for him. It had been intended for him from the beginning. The care she'd invested was clear; he could only imagine the hours she'd spent.

His emotions boiled up fiercely inside him and he had to tamp them down. She'd meant it in friendship, he told himself almost desperately, nothing more. It didn't work. For whatever reason, that she had done it at all woke up feelings he had kept buried for five years.

"By the time I got it done, it was almost your birthday, so I decided to wait. But then . . ."

Her voice trailed off, but he knew what she meant. His birthday had come two weeks after Terry had died. He didn't even remember the day. And she had kept it, all this time. . . .

"God, Summer." His voice was tight, husky. "I . . . No one's ever done anything like this for me. . . ."

"I hope it fits. I had to guess."

Good girl, Summer told herself. Nobody would guess that you're lying through your teeth. Ever since that day when she had leaned back against that broad chest, when those strong, muscled arms had come around her, she had carried the memory of his size. With every stitch, she had been aware of it.

It had been that, in fact, that had inspired the idea of the sweater in the first place, in an effort to divert her mind from things she shouldn't be thinking about. Then her world had caved in, and nothing had been strong enough to divert her tortured mind. She stood up abruptly.

"If . . . you like it, why don't you see if it fits?"

"I like it," he said vehemently.

He stood with the sweater in his hands, setting the box aside. He was grateful for the chance at movement, to give himself a moment to pull his rattled thoughts together.

Summer watched as he pulled the sleeves over his hands, then lifted his arms. A sudden rush of heat swept her as she saw the muscles of his chest and belly stretch and flex as he tugged the sweater over his head. Something about that expanse of naked skin lessening as he pulled the edge of the sweater over his shoulders, past the flat, male nipples, over the ridged abdomen and past the navel that seemed infinitely sexy above the trail of hair that arrowed down below the unfastened waistband of his jeans, made that heat spread through her in ever widening ripples.

She couldn't help thinking of the sweater coming off instead of going on, and that rippling heat abruptly changed course and flooded downward to pool in some low, hollow place deep inside her that she hadn't even known existed.

She felt color warm her cheeks and was glad he was busy straightening the edge of the sweater and not looking at her. Then he smoothed one hand down the front of the garment, pressing the thick softness of the sweater against his chest as if he liked the feel of it against his skin. The heat she had beaten down came rocketing back.

She'd never known it would make her feel like this, just seeing him wear the thing she'd made for him. She'd never known it would feel in some odd way as if she were touching him herself, as if—

Lord, what are you doing? She was so startled by the path her thoughts had taken, she nearly gasped aloud. She turned away from him quickly, picking the box up from the seat with more attention than it required.

"Summer?"

She looked back then; she only hoped she had her expression under control. She stared at him and a new, different kind of warmth filled her.

"It looks…just like I always thought it would," she said softly, heedless of what she was revealing by the quiet admission that she had thought of what the sweater would look like on him. Often.

Colter didn't miss it and his emotions took off on another ridiculous flight of fancy. He beat them back again.

"It…fits," he finally managed to say.

"Yes," she said, still in that soft, wondering tone.

"I... Thank you." It didn't seem enough, but it was all he could get out.

"You're welcome."

Fearful of crushing the box with her tense grip, she set it down again. They stood there, looking at each other for one long, awkward moment. Then, slowly, he lifted a hand. He brushed her cheek gently with the backs of his fingers and her breath caught in her throat.

"Summer..."

It was a low, husky whisper, and it made her shiver. Then his hand moved, his fingers threading through the blond silk of her hair. His warmth made her scalp tingle, and she let her head drop back to savor it.

Colter's stomach knotted. She was acting as if she liked his touch, he thought with a trace of wonder. As if she wanted more. The temptation was suddenly too much for him and he lowered his head.

He'd meant only to quickly brush his lips over hers, a soft caress of thanks between old, dear friends for a lovely gift given. But at the first touch of her lips under his, what he'd meant to do vanished in a sudden flare of heat and sensation. His fingers tightened in her hair, his mouth moving, becoming more demanding on hers. His tongue flicked out to trace her soft lips, tasting, seeking.

She had gone utterly still, and a tiny moan of sound from her was the only thing that enabled him to stop, to break away from the sudden, fierce sweetness.

"Colter...?"

She was looking up at him, her eyes a little dazed. No wonder, he thought. What else could she do when a man she thought of as only a friend kissed her like that? Like what he was, a man a hairbreadth away from throwing her over his shoulder and carrying her off to bed. He suppressed a shudder as hot, searing images filled his mind.

Keep it light, Colter, he told himself. You only meant to thank her. And you'd better tell her that, before she slaps you or something.

"I... love the sweater."

It must have sounded as strained to her as it did to him because she looked puzzled. Then color flooded her face.

"Oh," she said as if in sudden understanding. "That's why you . . ." Her color deepened. "Of course. I—I'm glad you like it." She backed up a step. "Would you...like some breakfast?" she said suddenly, a little too urgently. He nodded with a similar celerity.

They ate a quiet meal that was punctuated by Summer's frequent glances across the small table, as if she couldn't quite believe what she was seeing, and by Colter's odd habit of stopping to touch the softness of the sweater. Whenever their eyes met, one of them looked quickly away, as if the memory of that kiss was a physical entity hovering between them. Neither of them spoke.

After the table was cleared, Colter left the room for a moment. He came back with the file he'd gotten from Dave, and Summer felt an odd little chill overtake her.

What's wrong with you? she asked herself. This is what you wanted, isn't it? Not that you expected him to pack up and come back with you, but it's why you went to Florida to find him. So why did the sight of that folder in his hands and that look of purposefulness bother her so?

She stayed quiet, doing small chores around the house as he studied the sizeable stack of papers. It became more of an effort as the minutes passed into hours; with each one, his face became more somber, more taut with painful memories.

She nearly jumped when he slapped down the last page of the last report sharply. Carefully, she set down the can of furniture polish she'd almost dropped at the sudden sound and turned to look at him.

"Fish net," he muttered.

She stared at him. "Excuse me?"

His eyes flicked to her, then back to the pile of papers before him. "That's all this is. A bunch of holes strung together. Not one damned bit of it makes sense."

Slowly, she crossed the room and sat opposite him. "You always said it never did."

"It makes less now. Even if I'd never known Terry, I wouldn't believe it. His record is spotless. There's not one bit of evidence that he ever 'came into' any unexplained money. He was on a legitimate stakeout. There was no indication that he was in financial trouble or needed the money.''

She smiled a little wanly. ''Terry spent what he made, and he didn't believe in saving for a rainy day, but he never went into debt.''

''I know.'' Colter riffled the edges of the stack of reports. ''All they had was that damned envelope.''

''They thought it was enough.''

''Enough.'' He snorted derisively. ''A blank envelope full of money. Any rookie could have seen it was a frame.''

She sighed. This was old, worn ground, and she'd been over it more times than she could ever count. She remembered it too well: the vague allegations, the testimony by the then Sergeant Grissom that Terry had been ''acting oddly'' for some time and his references to supposed clandestine meetings. The fact that no one else, including Terry's closest friends, had noticed anything had been ignored.

Any of it alone wouldn't have been enough to cast a reasonable doubt; together, they had been enough to result in the nebulous, inconclusive verdict. Four years of loyal service had done nothing to exonerate him, a fact that, at the time, had made her first furious, then bitter.

She shouldn't have been surprised, she thought now. How could Terry have had a chance at all, especially when he couldn't defend himself, if almost ten years of brilliant police work, of commendations, awards and a Medal of Valor hadn't saved Colter from the outrage of the questions fired at him in that hearing? True, he'd told her it didn't bother him, that he'd expected it. He'd even, she remembered now, told her that if he'd been on the other side, he would have had to ask the same questions. She supposed he was right, but it didn't make her feel any better.

''And Grissom makes lieutenant by selling Terry out.''

At his harsh tone, Summer's eyes shot to his face. His jaw was rigid, his mouth tight.

''I know,'' she said softly. ''When I heard about it from Dave, all I could think was that I was glad you didn't have to know.''

His expression changed, softened. She'd thought of him then? Colter tried to stop himself, but the words were out before he could.

"What about Terry?"

She shrugged. "They couldn't hurt him anymore." She gave a little sigh, lowering her eyes to the pile of papers. "At least . . . he never had to go through it."

"No. You had to. Alone."

The oddly pained note in his voice made her lift her head. Her eyes went softly warm as she looked at him. "I was never really alone. You were always there for me."

He shook his head. "I should have been able to protect you from those vultures."

"You did all you could. I wouldn't have made it without you." She shrugged again, wondering idly if she'd picked up the habit from him. "It doesn't matter. Not anymore. All that matters now is proving they were wrong."

"Yeah." He toyed with the dog-eared corners of the reports, then leaned back in the chair in disgust. "You know what really never made sense to me?"

"What?"

"Why? Why would Sherwood—assuming it was him—do it? Why would he plant that money on Terry? He had to know it would open up a bigger can of worms, make the investigation even more intense. He's a lot of things, but he's not stupid."

"Maybe it wasn't his idea."

That had occurred to Colter before. He picked through the stack until he found the composite drawing the police artist had done from Albert Webster's description of the man he'd seen crouched over Terry's body, weapon in hand. Colter stared at it for a moment before he spoke.

"You mean the shooter panicked?"

She nodded.

"Could be. But if it wasn't planned that way, then why did he have the money? Even Sherwood doesn't carry around five thousand dollars in a plain, sealed envelope without a reason, let alone one of his flunkies."

"Which brings us back to that same old problem."

"Yes. Who was the money really for. And why."

He said it in weary tones she recognized; it was a question he'd wrestled with fruitlessly, endlessly, five years ago. He tossed the composite drawing down on top of the stack. The narrow, close-set eyes stared back at him from beneath heavy brows, and the unnaturally off-center, wide jaw that was so distinctive, that should have made the man easy to find, seemed to mock Colter.

"That must have been how it happened. Like you said, Terry walked in on a payoff and got killed for it."

He looked at her, one corner of his mouth lifting in a gentle smile. "I didn't think you heard much of what I said then."

"I heard it."

She remembered the long, dark nights when he had held her, when he had soothed her, had told her over and over that she was right, that Terry hadn't done it, that he was incapable of taking dirty money. It had been those nights that had given her the strength to get through the endless, horrible days when she had to sit and watch as Terry's name was dragged through the muck.

"I heard everything. I just couldn't seem to . . . react."

"You'd had about all you could take."

She let out a little breath. "I don't want to think about that anymore. It's over," she repeated.

After a moment, Colter nodded. "But this," he said, flicking the stack of papers, "isn't."

"If anybody can do it, you can."

Her faith both warmed him and frightened him a little. "Don't pin your heart on this, Summer." On me, he meant. "It's back to square one, and the trail's five years cold."

"I know that. I know it may be useless. But you have a lot better chance than I would have."

"Maybe." *God, don't let her depend on me for this. There's too big a chance I'll come up dry, and I couldn't stand to let her down. Again.* "I don't have the resources I had. If I couldn't do it then . . ."

"I understand, Colter. If it's hopeless, it's hopeless. But at least I'll know I tried." She let out a short breath. "Sounds terrible, doesn't it? Like it's all for me, to make me feel better. Maybe it is. Maybe I'm just being selfish."

He reached across the table and laid his hand over hers. Again, he fought off the little jolt that shot through him when he touched her.

"No," he said firmly. "You're not selfish. You wouldn't know how to be. You're just doing what you have to do."

The light green eyes, troubled now, met his. "You mean you're doing it for me."

"No," he said again. "I'm doing it for me. And maybe that is selfish. I'm going to finish what I should have finished a long time ago."

There was a long moment of silence, then Summer looked down at his hand, broad, strong and tan over her fairer, slender one. The moment changed, stretching out between them like something warm and alive. Her lips parted as she suddenly couldn't seem to get enough air.

"Summer..."

She jerked away, unable to deal with how that soft, husky murmur of her name made her feel. In another second, she'd be believing that kiss had meant more than just thanks.

"I—I have to go change. I promised Fiona I'd come and have lunch with her today."

He drew back, his face impassive, showing nothing. She whirled and ran to her room. She knew she must look a fool, running away in her own home, but she didn't, couldn't care; she had to get away from his touch, from the sudden heat in those turquoise eyes. If she didn't, she would say or do something even more foolish, something that would embarrass both of them.

When she came back, having changed into a pair of yellow slacks and a soft yellow sweater that were brightly cheerful on this gloomy day, she felt composed enough to face him again. He was still at the table, going once more through the reports as he sipped at the rest of the hot chocolate she had poured for him earlier.

"I'll be back in a couple of hours."

"Okay." He didn't look up.

"Colter..." she began, her voice strained. He sighed, and set down his cup.

"I'll walk you out to the garage," he said, cutting off whatever she'd been going to say. Whatever it was, he couldn't deal with it right now. His emotions were in turmoil, and he was weary from the constant battle against a suddenly resurgent libido.

As with many of the older houses in the neighborhood, the garage was a separate building, several feet from the side of the house. The ground in between was wet, and they had to walk carefully. If he dared, he thought, he would have lifted her over the small twin rivers that had formed in the two paved tracks that served as a driveway. But he didn't, not when merely touching her hand sent him furiously into overload and sent hot, vivid memories of the feel of her lips beneath his rocketing through him.

He swung open the heavy door for her, then, after seeing the car parked inside, turned to look at her.

"What happened to the Cadillac?"

Terry's father had given Terry and Summer the luxury car on their third anniversary, just before Terry had been killed. Colter wasn't surprised that she no longer had it, only that it had been replaced with an old compact that had obviously seen many better days.

"I sold it," she said sharply, almost challengingly. Then she took a breath and went on more calmly. "I never liked it that much, anyway. It was more Sean's idea of what we should drive, not mine."

She was right, Colter thought, the big sedan hadn't been her kind of car. He could picture her in some elegant European coupe or a sexy little sports car—

Knock it off, Colter, he ordered silently. "Why this?" he asked.

"Why not? It gets me where I'm going."

He eyed the car doubtfully. She could have traded the Caddy for a lot better car than this, he thought. But she said she'd sold it, not traded it. Why? If—

"We're getting wet. Why don't you go back in? I have to get going."

"Are you sure the car's okay?" He stepped into the garage and took a closer look. "It looks like it could break down any second."

"It's fine, Colter. It hasn't broken down in months. I have to go."

"Has it got decent tires? It's really slick out. It wouldn't take much—"

"The tires are fine. Look, I promised Fiona I'd be there by one. She gets upset if things don't go according to her schedule."

"Maybe you should take the rental car."

"There is nothing wrong with my car," Summer said stiffly. "Now may I please leave?"

"If you take the rental car, I'll go get the keys."

"Colter—"

"Please? It'll only take a second."

She let out an exasperated breath. "What difference does it make?"

He glanced at her, then went back to staring at her battered car. "It means I won't sit here and worry all afternoon."

She was taken aback and couldn't think of an answer. He took advantage of her silence and raced for the house. He was back in moments with the keys to the blue coupe parked in front of the house. She began to protest again, but he cut her off.

"Please," he repeated. "Just . . . humor me, will you?"

At last, she gave in and they walked around the house. They stopped next to the car that had at the least the advantage of being several years newer, and she reached for the keys he held out. Even the rain couldn't dampen the little jolt that leapt up his arm as their fingers brushed together. The green eyes came up to his, and she backed away a step.

"It's all right, Summer."

He didn't explain what he meant; he wasn't sure himself. It was all right, just ignore the way he jumped every time they touched? Or it was all right, he knew only he felt that little shock? Or it was all right, he wasn't going to do anything about it? He wasn't too sure about that part. He opened the driver's door for her.

"Be careful." She nodded, and he stepped back.

It's all right. Sure it is, he thought bitterly as he watched her drive away. It's not her problem that every time you touch her, you spontaneously combust. All she knows is you make her feel damned awkward because, to her, you're just Terry's old friend. And all she should be to you is your best friend's wife. The fact that that friend is dead and buried doesn't give you carte blanche to lust after his widow.

He went back inside, closing the door quietly, mainly in defiance of the urge that rose in him to slam it in frustration. It was dry and warm now inside, and he became aware that his new—five years new—sweater was damp. He should take it off and let it dry, he thought. He didn't.

Back at the kitchen table, he turned again to the mass of papers before him with a weary sigh. Again, he relived that hideous night and the nightmare days that followed. He read the transcript of his own testimony at the internal-affairs hearing, then the rest. He managed to smother the churning in his stomach until he got to Summer's long-ago words. Then it took over and he couldn't seem to banish the memory of her as she had been then, a pale, thin child with bruised-looking eyes. God, she'd been so very young!

He stacked the reports neatly when he'd finished, then got up to stretch. It was time for some notes, he thought, and walked into the living room to see if he could find some paper and a pencil in the desk on the wall adjacent to the front windows.

He found a pencil in the center drawer, but the only paper was some stationery that was too nice for his purpose. He closed that drawer and was reaching for one of the side drawers when he stopped at the sound of someone out front.

Summer? No, it couldn't be, she'd only been gone a half hour. And he would have heard the car. The noise stopped, followed only by the sound of the rain. He shrugged and went back to his search until he located a pad of unlined paper.

Back at the kitchen table, he began again, going through everything page by page. Several times he stopped and made notes on the pad, and on a separate sheet, he started to write a list of names and addresses.

He was on his second page of notes when the knock on the door startled him out of his concentration. He dropped the pencil and looked over his shoulder at the front door. The knock came again, and he got to his feet.

He was halfway across the small living room when the knock came again, sharply enough to rattle the old door on its hinges. Only this time, it was accompanied by a voice. A voice making an unmistakable demand.

"I know you're in there! Open up! Don't make me call the police!"

Chapter 6

"Wait a minute, I know you!"

Colter stood in the doorway, staring at the thin, middle-aged woman who was gesturing at him rather wildly.

"That puts you one up on me," he muttered.

"You're the man in the picture," she exclaimed, as if he hadn't spoken.

Colter looked at her blankly. "Picture?"

"In Summer's room." The woman patted at her short, curly, brown hair in a distracted gesture. "That picture of her, her poor husband and you."

"Oh." Summer had a picture of the three of them? In her room?

"I saw a man in here through the window and didn't know what to think." The woman giggled. "My goodness, I nearly called the police, and it was a policeman in here all the time!"

"I'm not—" Colter stopped; explaining seemed beyond him at the moment, at least while he was still wondering about that picture in Summer's bedroom.

"You know, when Summer called to say she was home, she told me she had a friend staying for a while." The woman's curiosity was evident as she looked Colter up and down. "I never would have guessed..."

Colter's eyebrow lifted in sudden understanding. "You're the landlady?"

She nodded. "I'm Gloria Harper." She was looking at him intently, in a way that somehow made him a little nervous. "Well," she said at last, "you must be a special one. Summer's never brought anyone home before. Men, I mean, of course."

"She... hasn't?"

"No." She patted her hair again. "And I'm sure of it. My husband and I live right across the street, you know." She waved toward a neat two-story house on the other side of the narrow lane. "I try to keep an eye out for her, her living here alone, you see."

"I'm glad."

He meant it. He'd never pictured her alone; he'd always thought Terry's parents would be there for her. He'd never imagined that it would end up the other way around.

"Terrible thing," Mrs. Harper said, speculation lighting her gaze as she continued to eye him. "The way her husband was killed. Poor Summer, a widow so young."

"Yes."

The word came out flatly, and Mrs. Harper stared at Colter for a moment. Then a look of chagrin crossed her thin features. "Oh, dear, I'm sorry. I didn't realize. But if you're the man in the picture, you were his partner, weren't you?"

"Yes."

It wasn't much better that time. The thin, beringed hand went to the cap of brown hair again, patting nervously. "I'm sorry," she said, seemingly genuinely upset, although Colter couldn't tell if it was sympathy over Terry or embarrassment. He nodded shortly.

The short brown hair got another pat. "Where is Summer?"

"She went to see her... mother-in-law."

"Fiona?"

He nodded.

"Of course," Mrs. Harper said, "I should have guessed she'd go there right away. She's always so good about that. Such a sweet girl."

"Of course," he echoed. Yes, if Summer O'Neil was anything, it was sweet. He ignored the fact that the first thing he thought of was a sweetness that had nothing to do with her kindness and goodness. Or maybe it had everything to do with it, he thought wearily, tired of having to yank his mind off that particular track.

"I guess I can go get the things I was going to bring over for her now," Gloria Harper said, studying him once more. "Are you staying for a while?"

"Yes," he answered. Then he saw the speculative glow that had returned to the woman's eyes. "Summer's loaning me her guest room for a while," he amended quickly.

"I see."

I doubt it, he thought wryly as she left to go and get whatever it was she had intended to drop off. He could just guess what she saw, or thought she did. He hadn't really thought about that aspect when he'd come here. He'd only known that, despite the hell it would be, he wanted to be close to Summer. He was beginning to realize he might have made the biggest mistake of his life.

He watched the woman as she reached the narrow road. Then he closed the door and turned around. He didn't even try to resist the urge; he knew it would be useless. Still, he felt odd as he went into Summer's bedroom, as if he were trespassing on her privacy.

It was there. He hadn't seen it in the darkness before, but it was there. It had been taken that golden day, he remembered; Dave had snapped it just before they'd dropped anchor in that cove. She'd had it enlarged and framed, and it sat on the polished oak of the dresser.

Why that picture? he wondered. They had taken dozens that day, including several of Terry and Summer alone. He knew, because he'd taken a couple of them himself. But this was the three of them, with Summer in the middle. It made him oddly uncomfortable, both to look at it now, knowing Terry was dead, and to wonder why she had chosen this particular picture.

And, he acknowledged ruefully, to see himself captured forever in frozen color as he looked down at his partner's wife. You're damned lucky she's as innocent as a day-old puppy, he told himself, or she couldn't have helped but see everything written all over your face.

He turned on his heel, a sharp, jerky motion indicative of the effect this room was having on him. He had to get out of there, get away from the faint scent of sweet honeysuckle that lingered, floating on the air to tickle his senses and rouse memories better left hidden. Yet he couldn't seem to move until a noise at the door signaled Mrs. Harper's return.

When he opened the door again, the woman came inside, arms full. She hung two dry cleaner's plastic bags full of clothing on the back of the door to the small entry closet and set a stack of mail on the small table next to it.

"There. Now she's all set for work when she has to go back." She looked at him as if she was about to say more, but then changed her mind. "You tell her to call me when she gets home."

"I will."

He tried to go back to work when Mrs. Harper had gone, but the interruption had destroyed his concentration. And it wasn't, he insisted silently, because of the look in Gloria Harper's eyes that had made it all too clear what she was thinking. He paced the living room, restlessly awaiting Summer's return without acknowledging that that was what he was doing.

He reached the closet door, the end of his path, and began to turn back. Then something caught his attention and he froze. He hadn't looked at the contents of those plastic bags, had only noted that the clothes were dark in color. But now he looked, something nagging at the edges of his memory. And after a moment, he reached for one of the hangers, removed it from the door and tugged off the plastic bag.

Summer was in a fairly good mood when she turned onto the narrow lane that led to her house. Although still in her fantasy world, Fiona had been cheerfully happy, and her mood had been catching despite the pain of her withdrawal from reality.

The damper on Summer's afternoon was that, unfortunately, Mr. Webster had not improved. A call to the shelter from Fiona's room had netted the information from Tim that Mr. Webster was as bad as he'd been the day before. She sighed as she pulled into the drive. This was the longest he'd ever been this way, and she tried not to think bitterly about poor timing.

There was a light on in the living room, so she decided to go in the front instead of the back as she usually did. She was a little startled to find Colter sitting in one of the two armchairs, staring at the door as if he'd been there for hours, waiting.

"Hi," she said. He didn't answer.

She hung up her damp coat on the hall tree, walked to the chair next to his, set down her purse and the keys to the rental car, kicked her shoes off her chilled feet, and he still hadn't answered. She sat down.

"Are you all right?"

"Fine." It was a flat, toneless word.

"Colter, what is it?"

His eyes flicked from her to the entry closet, then back. She lifted her head to see what he'd looked at, then froze.

"Would you like to explain that to me?"

There was a barely perceptible pause before she said carefully, "My laundry?"

"Don't play games, Summer. You know what I mean."

She sighed. "I gather Mrs. Harper was here."

"Yes."

"She told you?"

"No."

"Then how—"

"I was a cop, remember? A trained observer."

She stared at him.

"The airport," he said flatly.

Her eyes widened. "Jenny."

"Funny how your laundry looks an awful lot like her uniform."

Summer looked down, picking at an imaginary thread on the arm of the chair.

"You work with her, don't you? That's why she knew you were gone. And your flight wasn't just a standby, it was an employee standby, wasn't it? That's why you knew all about the flights back to Miami. And you moved here to be closer to the airport, didn't you?"

Slowly, her head came up. She just looked at him.

"And I suppose you're the one who found Webster hanging around the airport? While you were working?"

She answered then, short, flat and without emotion. "Yes."

He closed his eyes for a moment, as if he'd hoped up until the last moment that he'd been wrong. Then he opened them, zeroing in on her face.

"Why?"

"I needed the job." She said it simply, without explanation.

"You had a job. At the aquarium."

"It . . . didn't pay enough."

"Money." His face contorted oddly. "You always said it didn't matter, as long as you could get by. You said as long as it was in marine biology, if you could use your degree—"

"I . . . don't have a degree."

He sat up, staring.

"What?"

"You heard me."

"But . . . you only had one year left."

She stood up abruptly. "I quit, all right? I gave up. I couldn't do it. It was too tough. So I work at the airport, for decent money."

Her words were coming in short, choppy bursts and sounded so twisted with pain that he almost reached out for her. As if she sensed his near movement, she backed away.

"It was . . ." She swallowed, and he could almost feel the tightness of her throat. "It was just a silly dream, anyway."

She whirled and ran, and this time when she closed the door of her room, he heard the lock snap.

What the hell? He stared after her, his mind whirling. Getting that degree and using it in her life's work had been so important to her.... He'd never forgotten the fire that lit those lovely green eyes that Saint Patrick's Day night when she told him of her plans. She'd been almost through her second year at the University of Washington then, she was shyly proud of her excellent grades, and he, for some reason he hadn't yet understood, had been very proud of her.

But she had quit. Too tough? He doubted that; she had sailed through classes that had nearly strangled him in school. Not that she hadn't worked hard, he knew she had, but she just wasn't going to let anything stop her.

But something had. Had Terry's death done that to her, too? Put out that wonderful fire? Why hadn't she gone back?

He'd always had this picture of her in his head. No matter where he went, whether he was on that ranch in Colorado, the farm in Oklahoma or that riverfront bar in Louisiana where they'd somewhat doubtfully hired the big Yankee as a bouncer, he'd always had this safe, secure image of her.

And when he'd at last landed in Key West, he'd perfected it. He didn't do it often, but now and then, the urge became too strong as it battered at the doors of his mind. It was then that he would surrender. He would sit down, close his eyes and let her in.

She was fine, he'd reassure himself. She would get up each day and take the walk she always took around the acre that surrounded the house, the land that she loved so much. Then she would drive—in the Caddy, in his mind—to the Aquarium, to spend her day working with the creatures she loved, enjoying the opportunity all her hard work had given her.

He always tried to end it there, tried not to let his mind slip into the useless self-torture, but often, he couldn't help it. Had she found someone to fill the hole Terry had left in her life? Had some unknown man slipped into that place beside her? Was he enjoying the pleasure of looking at her across a restaurant table or cozying up with her before a fire on a wet, Seattle night? Was he kissing her, touching her—

Damn! Colter got up in one violent movement, resuming the pacing he'd stopped so abruptly when he'd realized just what Mrs. Harper had hung on that door.

He'd had that pretty little dream of her, and now he was confronted with the brutal reality. Guilt gnawed at him and he bitterly refused to try and fight it off. He deserved it, he thought. Every damned bit of it. He'd left her thinking the worst was over, only to find now that Terry's death had only been the beginning. The destruction of her life had been complete, and he'd left her to face it alone.

God, if he'd only been here, he—

You weren't, he snapped silently. You turned and ran like a coward. She faced Sean's death, Fiona's deterioration and the death of her dream, all alone.

He paced faster, as if trying to keep up with the roiling emotions inside. Self-contempt warred with sorrow for what she'd gone through. Fury at the fates that had struck so harshly at someone who deserved it so little warred with anger at the fates that made her the one, the only woman who had ever tied him up in knots like this. And all of it was overlaid by an odd, strangely powerful pride in her; she had handled it. He didn't understand what had happened, but he knew she had done what she had to do with the class, the grace, that in her ran clear down to the bone.

Of course, she did, he told himself bitterly. What else did you expect? You're the one with the staying-power problem.

It erupted then, the anger, the self-contempt. He had to do something, no matter that it was much too little and much too late.

He strode into the kitchen and grabbed the notes and the list of names he'd made. It wasn't complete, but it was a start. He grabbed up the keys from beside her purse and headed out the door.

The front room light was still on, casting a rectangle of golden warmth into a chilly darkness. The rain had stopped, but the night was punctuated by the reminder of it as occasional lingering drops fell from the branches of the trees and bushes and from the eaves of the old house.

The lamp was next to the sofa, its circle of light only reaching to the windows that faced the road. The window seat, which faced the yard, was in shadow, and he nearly missed the shape huddled beneath a thick, handmade afghan on the soft cushions.

Quietly he set down the keys and shrugged off the jacket he'd bought this afternoon. He slipped off his soggy running shoes, wishing, now that it was too late and his feet were frozen, that he had gone ahead and gotten a pair of boots, as well.

After shedding his equally wet socks, he walked barefoot across the room and sat carefully on the edge of the seat that was just long enough for her if she curled up. She didn't stir, and he wondered how long she'd been there.

She looked so sweetly innocent, he thought, with her hair tousled and the thick fringe of her lashes resting on her cheeks. Her head was resting on one slender hand, the other hand held the heavy, warm wool of the afghan. The intricate pattern, the rich combination of color, told him who had made it, not that he'd doubted.

He thought of just letting her sleep; it was nearly two. But this close to the window, it was cold; he knew this old house didn't have the double thermal glass that was now common in the northwest, making the windows themselves, and the air trapped between them, a form of insulation. And it was going to get colder. He lifted a hand to touch her shoulder and wake her, then stopped.

Don't, he ordered himself firmly. Don't start something you can't finish. Don't. His body ignored the command. He bent over and pressed his lips lightly against her cheek.

What happened then stunned him. She stirred, murmured something. Something that, incredibly, sounded like his name. He stared at her sleeping face, his heart pounding.

Don't be an idiot, Colter. At least not more of one than you've already been. With a tremendous effort, he quieted his racing imagination. He reached for her shoulder and shook it gently.

"Summer."

She murmured, unintelligibly this time.

"Come on, baby, wake up. It's cold out here. You need to be in bed."

She moved then, and her eyes fluttered open. When she saw him, a soft, warm smile curved her mouth, a smile that set up an answering warmth inside him unlike anything he'd ever felt with anyone else.

How did she do it? he wondered. How could she make him feel so warm, so thankful for her friendship, and yet with a certain glance or just a movement, make him so hot, he could hardly stand up? It was a combination he'd never encountered before, and it scared him a little.

It always had, even before. Even if she'd been free, he wasn't sure he'd have known what to do. If he pursued the friendship, he'd wondered, would he always be hungering for the heat, the passion? And if he pursued that, would the friendship, surprisingly precious to him, be lost?

She reached up to rub at sleepy eyes with an almost childlike gesture, then came abruptly, totally awake and sat up with a start.

"Colter!"

He stared at her, all thought of innocence, of her being childlike, singed away by that one, sudden movement. It had sent the afghan tumbling to her waist, baring to his eyes the delicate white satin of the nightshirt she wore. It shimmered in the dim glow, flowing over her like the light itself. In her sleep, the top two buttons had come unfastened, and he could see the ripe inner curve of her breasts. The quickness of her movement had made them sway slightly, and the motion of that soft, tempting flesh beneath the sleek, glistening fabric sent a white-hot rocket of flame through him.

He tore his eyes from her, but the way that fine fabric had peaked over her nipples was seared into his mind, and the sudden, fierce tightness of his body told him he wasn't going to forget it soon.

"I was worried."

Her voice was still husky with sleep, and he nearly groaned in answer. He wanted to reach out, to touch, to cup that tempting feminine curve of flesh in his palm, to let his thumb flick over that little nub, teasing it to hardness, he wanted—

Desperately he reined in his soaring senses.

"You didn't need to be." His voice was thick, but, still a little groggy, she didn't seem to notice.

"I was. I didn't know where you were." She flushed. "Not that you have to tell me, but—"

"Hush. I know. I should have left you a note, at least."

She lowered her eyes to the afghan, as if she had never seen the complicated pattern before and was fascinated by it.

"I . . . thought you were angry at me."

"At you?" Don't, he told himself. He reached for her hands anyway. The little shock rippled through him. "No. Never. Only at me."

She looked startled. "Why?"

He sighed heavily. "I should have been here for you. I know," he said quickly when he saw that proud little chin come up. "But I can't help the way I feel."

She stared at their hands for a moment. Her fingers moved, but not, as he'd expected, to pull away. She seemed to be measuring the difference between them, comparing the slender delicacy of hers to the broad, calloused strength of his. She stroked soft fingertips along muscle and bone; he clenched his jaw against the fiery little darts of sensation that shot through him from every nerve there. When she traced the strong curve between his thumb and forefinger, he was unable to suppress the shiver that rippled through him.

She stopped and looked up at him. He lowered his eyes, afraid of what he knew she would see there—sheer, hot pulsing need.

"Where did you go?" she asked at last, and he realized she'd been considering whether or not she had the right to ask. Someday, he thought, maybe he'd have the nerve to tell her she had the right to ask anything. He made himself look up.

"I decided it was time to get started."

Her eyes shot up to his. "Get started?"

"Talk to some people, walk some streets, see what the word is. The usual."

She nodded slowly. Dave had once told her that Colter had the most incredible network of contacts, sources and snitches that he'd ever seen. "They trust him," Dave had said, "because they know if he makes them a promise, he'll go to the mat to keep it. They respect him because he's tough, and trust him because he's fair."

"Did you find out anything?"

"Yeah," Colter said dryly. "An awful lot of people are either dead or gone." He shrugged. "I'll hit the day people tomorrow. Maybe something will turn up."

"I'll go with you."

"Summer—"

"I can't just let you do it all. It's bad enough I turned your life upside down. I can't just sit back doing nothing while you do all the work."

Lady, you turned my life upside down years ago. "I'm not doing much, yet. Just walking, talking, feeling out the street. You can't help with that."

She frowned. "I could talk to some people. Those small-business owners you talked about, the ones Sherwood was trying to shake down for protection money, maybe they've seen the shooter around again—"

"Maybe. We'll talk about it tomorrow. Right now, you need to get to bed."

And I need to climb right in after you. He shuddered at the thought of lying beside her in that big four-poster, of at last turning his hands free to roam over her slender body, to caress that silken skin; of skimming that shimmering white satin off her; of cupping her breasts in his hands....

"You too," she said, and his heart slammed to a stop. "You must be freezing—you're shivering."

His heart began again. "Yeah," he muttered.

She got up, and he smothered a groan at the sight of long, statuesque legs beneath the edge of the thigh-length night-shirt.

"Go ahead," he said hoarsely, "I'll get the light."

Her delicate brow furrowed at the odd note in his voice, but she went. *Thank God,* he thought. *She takes one look* at me now and it's going to be obvious what I was thinking. If I just stay behind her, it'll be all right. If, he thought sourly, I can walk at all.

He did manage to walk, but a couple of hours later, he had to admit that sleep seemed beyond him. It had been a day of too many ups and downs, and of too many memories. Driving the streets he had known so well had begun the process, getting out and walking them after dark, as he had done so often before, had finished it. It was as if he'd never been gone, he'd thought at first, the darkness, the damp, the sometimes-furtive, sometimes-bold figures that populated this nighttime world.

But then something out of synch would strike, a building no longer there, a doorway that had once been littered with sleeping drunks gone, and the truth came home to him: the city was different, just as he was different.

He'd found people he'd known, some that greeted him with pleased surprise, and some that had greeted him with loud catcalls. He took it in stride, never really thinking about the fact that those calls were in themselves a form of respect; not many cops would have been remembered at all after five years. He found none of Sherwood's people, at least none he knew, but the man could have a whole new army signed up by now.

Colter knew it didn't matter; everything on the street got back to Sherwood eventually. So Colter had begun slowly, never mentioning his real reason, figuring it was enough for now to get the word out that he was back. He had no illusions that this was going to go quickly, and he was prepared for it to take as long as it took. For now, he would relearn the streets he'd once known so well.

Yes, the streets were different, the people were different, he was different. The only thing that never seemed to change was that Summer O'Neil drove him out of his mind.

Summer nearly cringed when she looked at his eyes as he stumbled into the kitchen; Colter looked as if he hadn't slept in days. Once she'd known he was safe at home, she'd slept fairly soundly herself, and she knew she'd dozed on the window seat—

Home? Her coffee cup paused halfway to her lips. Is that really what she'd meant? Quickly, she composed her features as he brought the mug he'd filled to the table and sat down.

"You look like you need about twelve more hours of sleep."

He chuckled ruefully. "More? You have to get some before you can get more, don't you?"

"Poor Colter," she said sympathetically. "Jet lag, still?"

"Mmmph."

His mutter was unintelligible through the mouthful of hot coffee. Summer stirred hers idly, waiting until he had swallowed the bracing liquid.

"Have a cookie, if you like. They go good with coffee."

He eyed the plate of obviously homemade cookies, rich and thick with nuts and chocolate. "When did you do that?"

"Last night. I . . . needed to do something."

His jaw tightened a little. Needed to keep busy, he thought, because she was worried. Nice move, Colter. He looked at her, blond head bent over her steaming mug of coffee. Then she lifted her gaze to his face.

"I called the shelter this morning."

He set down the cup and looked at her.

"They said Mr. Webster is doing much better today. He's been talking up a storm with Tim, they said. Seems completely back to normal."

She was talking neutrally, as if it meant nothing, carefully avoiding any hint of suggestion in her voice.

"Then I guess we'd better go see him," Colter said. He would have done a lot more than spend some time talking to a confused old man for the smile that had earned him.

He downed the coffee, then a couple of the chewy, delicious cookies, and was awake by the time they got into the car. He drove this time, and they'd been on the road a few minutes before she quietly spoke.

"Was it different, last night?"

"Last night?" he asked, shaken out of his reverie. No, it wasn't any different last night. She'd torn him up into little pieces just as she always did. But she didn't know that. Did she?

"Being out there. Has it changed?"

He could breathe again. Her words had done what he'd been unable to so far this morning; they beat back the image of her in that clinging sweep of white satin.

"Yeah," he said after a minute, "it's changed. But it hasn't." He shrugged.

"Are you sorry?"

"That it's changed?"

She looked up then. "That it's not . . . yours anymore."

He stared at her. He hadn't expected her to understand that. Terry had always said he never talked to her about work because she didn't like it, didn't understand. Yet Colter knew she understood without explanation how he'd felt about this city.

"It just felt strange," he said after a moment. "I saw a couple of kids doing a coke deal on a corner. It was weird to just keep going."

He shook his head and laughed. "You know what's really crazy? I saw all this stuff, and deals ten times that size, all over the place in the Keys. Real calm, real quiet, but there. And I never felt like I should do anything. I never felt . . . I don't know, responsible. But here . . ."

"Because it *was* yours, once? Because it's still home?"

"Yeah. I guess so." He glanced at her. "Nuts, huh?"

"No. You cared. It's why you were so good."

Why did he go all soft inside when she said things like that? He'd heard other people say similar things and had felt only a mild gratification. When she said it, he felt as though he'd been given a prize he'd never expected and wasn't sure he deserved. The feeling humbled him into silence.

"Is it all right if we stop so I can see Fiona?" Summer asked when they neared the quiet neighborhood where the rest home was.

He glanced at her, then shrugged. "Sure."

When they arrived, she looked at him uncertainly. "You . . . don't have to go in if it bothers you. I'll only be a minute." She picked up a plastic container that she'd placed beside her on the seat. "I just want to drop off the rest of these cookies. She likes them."

"I'll go with you," he said. If she could stand it, he could, he thought. She'd done too damned much alone already.

Many of the residents of the rest home were outside, enjoying the rain-washed freshness. They found Fiona sunning herself in the front yard.

"Hello, dear," the older woman said. "How nice to see you! It's been such a long time."

"We had lunch yesterday, Fee. You remember, we had that salmon mousse you like so much."

"Oh, of course! I declare, I don't know where my memory is these days."

She looked up at Colter. "Oh, good, you brought your young man again." A smile creased her worn face, lighting it up radiantly. "At least I can still remember a good-looking man."

Colter shifted his feet uncomfortably, and Summer could have sworn he was blushing. Then he looked at Fiona and said with a sincerity that warmed Summer to the core, "And I'll bet you've had a few to remember."

Fee giggled delightedly, like a girl, and for a moment, she was the lively, vital woman Colter had remembered. She chattered on for a moment, pointing out, with a sly glance at Colter, Summer's baking prowess.

Blushing, Summer broke in. "We have...an appointment, Fee. I just wanted you to have these. I'll be back later, when I can stay awhile."

"That's fine, dear," the older woman said, her eyes twinkling as she teased Summer, "you and your young man go and have a good time."

Embarrassment kept Summer silent until they got to the shelter. Then hope began to course through her and she hurried inside, noting wryly that while she was almost at a trot, Colter had merely lengthened his stride to stay even with her. She glanced at him, feeling yet again that sense of controlled, restrained strength she'd always felt around him.

They found Mr. Webster out in back, on the porch that had been constructed there when the building had been converted. He was sitting in a chair placed to take advantage of the sun, a book open across his lap. He appeared engrossed in it and didn't look up until Summer knelt beside him.

"Well, hello there, young lady."

"Hello, Mr. Webster."

He waved a hand at her. "I told you to stop that mister stuff. Makes me feel as old as I am."

"Okay," she said easily. "Albert, then."

"That's better."

"I brought someone to see you."

"To see me? Nobody comes to see me. Except for you, of course, sweetie."

Colter had held back; he hadn't wanted to see Summer's face if the old man didn't recognize her again. But now he stepped forward, coming into the man's range of vision. A pair of dark, quick eyes fastened on him, eyes that bore no resemblance at all to the vague, clouded eyes he'd seen before.

They seemed to size him up, to search him out, to peer into the depths of his mind. Colter held the man's gaze, searching the wizened face for any sign of recognition. He found himself hoping, for Summer's sake, that Albert Webster wasn't just a befuddled old man.

Summer had straightened up, and Colter knew he wasn't imagining her sudden tension. Her eyes flicked to Colter, then back to Webster. She took in a deep breath and started to speak.

"Albert, this is—"

"Never mind, girl."

Webster looked him up and down again, and suddenly Colter knew she'd been right. This man knew him. And, at least right now, was no more senile than he was. Sensing it was somehow important to the old man, he spoke first.

"Don't bother, Summer. He knows who I am. Don't you?"

A smile creased the old man's face and lit up his eyes.

"Been a long time, Detective. Colter, isn't it?"

Chapter 7

He understood now. Colter knew why she had refused to give up, why she had confronted the department's disinterest, why she had crossed the country to find him.

After nearly two hours of listening to Albert Webster, of questioning him about every little detail he could think of about what he'd seen, Colter had no doubts that the old man had a crystal-clear memory of that night five years ago.

The man had never faltered. With the transcript of the testimony fresh in his mind, Colter knew that the version he'd heard today matched almost perfectly. Webster had been out for a drink at a local bar run by an old friend, as he had done every Friday night. He had walked, as usual, from the small apartment he had lived in then; it was only a few blocks. He had talked with friends in the bar. Then he had started home. And stumbled onto murder.

And as clear as that memory was, Colter found it hard not to believe that Albert Webster was as certain—and as right—about who he had seen in the limousine.

"I'd go find the son of a bitch myself if I could get out of this place," the old man was saying. Then his eyes narrowed as he looked at Colter. "Still might, if you don't."

"I'll find him."

Colter said it evenly, without heat, but Webster seemed to find what he wanted in the quiet words and the casual posture as Colter lounged in the chair he'd pulled up. The gray head nodded.

"Hmph. Gettin' away with what he did to that little girl." He glanced toward the end of the porch where Summer was waiting. "Oughta string him up."

"I know." Colter liked this old man, he thought, smothering a grin.

Albert's eyes narrowed again as he studied the younger man. "She's a pretty special lady."

"Very."

"I'd be out on the street if it wasn't for her. She got me in here." Albert grimaced as he looked at the building. "It ain't much, but it's a roof and dry at night."

Colter glanced over at Summer, who had tilted her head back to savor the rays of the sun. She seemed to shimmer in the light, as if it had come down to earth simply to caress her. He shivered as if a feather had been run up his spine.

"Some folks give more than's good for them," Albert said casually, but when Colter looked back at the old man, the bright, dark eyes were fastened on him intently.

"I know." The words came out a little huskily. That was Summer, all right, Colter thought. She gave and gave and gave. Except to herself. Only then, it seemed, did she give up. Her home, her school, her dreams...

Why? It doesn't make sense, he thought as they drove in silence back to the little rental house. Then he smiled at himself humorlessly. You're just upset because all your pat, easy answers, all your pretty little visions of what happened after you left her don't fit anymore.

Deserted her, you mean, he corrected himself sternly. Left her to deal with the crumbling destruction of her life alone. That he hadn't known was no excuse. He sighed inwardly. Even if she would have come to him, which he doubted, she couldn't have found him. He'd cut his links here too thoroughly, too completely. God, Summer, I'm sorry.

She didn't ask what Albert had said. She responded to his silence with her own. She didn't speak, didn't even look at him as he drove. But when he pulled up in front of the house and turned to face her, leaving the engine running, her brow furrowed.

"Where are you going?"

"To work."

"Work?"

"So to speak."

"Then you . . ." She faltered, as if she didn't dare ask.

"Yes," he said softly. "I believe him. The shooter's here."

She let out an odd, shaken sound, and he saw her shudder. The shiver took her again, and she quickly turned her head away, staring out the window of the car.

"Summer?"

She didn't answer. He reached for her shoulder and turned her to face him. And caught his breath at the sight of the tears glistening on her cheeks.

"Summer!" He groaned her name aloud, pulling her across the seat and into his arms. "Sshh," he soothed as she shook against him. "It's okay."

"I—" She gulped and tried again. The words came out between choking sobs. "I was so scared . . . you wouldn't believe . . . came all this way . . . because of me . . . you were happy, at peace and I dragged you back—"

"Hey," he interrupted gently, squeezing her shoulders, "you didn't drag me anywhere. I don't," he added wryly, "drag easily."

"But—"

"Hush," he said softly.

She did, but he could still feel the little quivers that shook her. He pulled her closer, lifting one hand to stroke the tousled silk of her hair. She was incredible, he thought. After all she'd been through, she still felt guilty about him coming back to do what he should have done long ago.

She was clinging to him, and he could feel the dampness of her tears through the cotton of his shirt. This is the way it should have been then, he thought. He should have been here for her. She shouldn't have had to face it all alone.

Well, he was here now. And even if it was too late, he would do what little he could to make it up to her. Instinctively, he lowered his head and before he even realized what he was doing, he was pressing his lips to the golden softness of her hair.

God, she smelled good. Rain and honeysuckle, he thought again. Fresh and sweet together. He'd never forgotten that scent. There had been times in the sultry heat of the Keys when he had awoken with it filling his nostrils, when it had seemed so real, he had sat up looking for her before the fog of dreams had cleared.

And then she lifted her head, looking up at him, green eyes wide and glistening with abating tears. Her lips were parted, her breathing quickened; he told himself it was from the strain of crying. But then she lifted one slender hand to touch his face, her fingers blazing a trail of tingling heat along the line of his jaw.

He groaned, low and harsh and deep, his hands tightening around her slim shoulders with a grip that was almost painful. The tip of her tongue crept out to wet her lips, and somewhere deep inside him, a glowing ember that had been radiating a steady heat since the first time he'd seen her again burst into flame.

"Colter," she said breathlessly, the sound of her voice fanning that fire until the last bit of his resolution was turned to ashes and his body leapt to life.

Just once more, he thought. Surely he could taste that sweetness just once more? Just a touch, to appease this gnawing hunger? He lowered his head, his lips tingling as if he could already feel the soft warmth of hers beneath them. He could feel her breath, hot and sweet as it came through those soft, tempting lips, and it made him shudder.

"Summer!"

They jumped apart, startled by the shrill sound of Mrs. Harper's voice, then her tap on the car window. Confusion flooded Summer's light green eyes and color flooded her face. She turned and rolled down the window for the older woman as Colter smothered an oath.

"My goodness, dear, I've been trying to catch you for days, it seems like. A package came for you. They didn't know you were back, so they brought it to me—"

The woman chattered on, oblivious, Colter thought, to what she had interrupted. No, he amended as he caught a glimpse of her eyes, not oblivious; she was looking at them both with an avid curiosity. Probably came over to see what was steaming up the windows, he thought dryly. Well, it was me. It was definitely me.

Just as well, he thought grimly. He doubted if he would have been able to stop with just a kiss, not when his mind was sizzling with memories of that first taste of sweet fire that was no less searing for its quickness. And mauling her in the front seat of a car is not what he had in mind. What he had in mind was her naked in front of a crackling fire or sprawled in limp, sated exhaustion in a tangle of sheets on the big four-poster bed. What he had in mind made him feel so damned guilty, he was tied up in tight, bitter little knots. What he had in mind had him so hot, it was about to kill him. A low, stifled sound escaped him. As if it were a signal, Summer cut off the seemingly endless stream of the woman's monologue.

"Thank you for taking it for me. I'll pick it up soon."

"Oh, that's all right, dear." The inquisitive eyes flicked to Colter. "You've had . . . other things on your mind, I'm sure."

Summer blushed, staring at the dash of the car as if caught between Mrs. Harper's curious gaze and Colter's steady, unreadable one. At last, Summer chose his and raised her eyes to him.

"Thank you," she said softly.

He shrugged, then cleared his throat; anybody with ears could have told by his voice exactly what he'd been thinking. When he was fairly certain he could do it steadily, he answered her.

"My pleasure," he said, his voice slightly husky with the lingering effects of what had almost happened. Her color deepened.

"You—" She broke off, and Colter guessed that she had barely managed not to glance at her hovering landlady. Summer's color was still high when she spoke. "You're going into Seattle again?"

He nodded. She settled back into the seat and reached for the seat belt she'd unfastened.

"No." He said it gently but firmly. "Not this time."

"But—"

"I know. And I promise, we'll start on those other people soon. Right now, where I'm going is no place for you."

Her chin came up defiantly and he felt that little burst of pride once more; God, she had learned to fight!

"I'm not some fragile little flower, Colter, who's going to wilt at the first sign of trouble."

"I never thought you were. Never," he repeated in emphasis. The chin came down a little. "We'll start on them Monday. They'll be at work then."

The "we" seemed to placate her and after a moment, she surrendered with a little nod. "Will you be late?"

"Maybe. Don't wait up."

The memory of her curled on the window seat, of the light and shadows of her body beneath soft, lustrous white satin, of the equally soft satin of her breasts leapt to life from the corner of his mind where he'd tried so hard, so futilely to keep it. God help him if she asked him anything else; any control he'd gained over his voice was shot to pieces by that glowing image.

"Be careful," she said softly. He sighed in relief and gave her a nod. Under Mrs. Harper's watchful eye, Summer opened the door and slid out of the car.

He hadn't, Summer found to her relief, just been appeasing her. When, on Monday morning as promised, they began to make the rounds of several small businesses that had been listed in his file on Sam Sherwood, she had found herself doing considerably more than just tagging along.

They had worked out a system after the first couple of small stores they'd gone into. One of them, whichever one the person they were talking to seemed to respond to best, would take the lead while the other one faded into the background.

Sometimes the reasons were obvious, such as the women who looked Colter up and down with open appreciation, leaving Summer wondering why it bothered her so. At the same time, she didn't even realize what was happening when some of the men took one look at her delicate beauty and couldn't seem to talk fast enough. And sometimes, it was the opposite, the women who seemed to find Colter too intimidating but responded to Summer's quiet manner, or the men who were more impressed by Colter's size and aura of power.

Some people were wary; whether it was because they believed their unofficial status or didn't, Summer wasn't sure. But sometimes it had been easy. Like the moment they had gone into one small, surprisingly bright and cheerful bar, and the owner had looked up from behind the long counter. After a moment of shocked silence, a smile had creased his thin face.

"I'll be damned!" He dropped the bar rag and strode out from behind the bar to shake Colter's hand enthusiastically. "When did you get back? Are you staying? Going back on the force?"

Colter laughed. "A couple of days ago, for a while, and no."

The young bartender who had been replenishing the stock on the shelves behind the bar had stopped his work and was watching them curiously, his eyes flicking over Summer with interest.

"Come here, Chad, let me introduce you to the guy who saved this place so you could laze around and get paid for it!"

Comprehension dawned in the young man's eyes as he walked toward them. "You're Colter?" At Colter's nod, Chad held out his hand. "Man, I've heard a lot about you. Jim's always talking about how you saved this whole neighborhood when that crook tried to take it over."

Colter let out an embarrassed chuckle. "I had a lot of help."

"Yeah," Jim said, "but who backed that slimy jerk down in his own house? Who lived in that little room upstairs here for weeks, just so he'd be around when we needed him to fight off that scum? Who scared him out of the protection business altogether?"

Colter shrugged off the praise. "Ancient history."

"Not for some of us. We remember, Colter. We always will." The man's eyes flicked over Summer, who had been standing quietly aside, taking in everything with an odd sense of pride she didn't quite understand. He'd been, she thought again, one hell of a cop.

"Now," Jim was saying, "who's this?"

Colter introduced her to the two appreciative men, and Summer tried not to blush as they offered her a seat at the bar and some rather extravagant compliments. She was thankful Colter gave only her name and made no further explanation that might give rise to awkward questions.

She accepted the soda Chad drew for her with a flourish after she had politely refused something stronger. Colter sat on the stool beside her, and when he took another of the copies they'd made of the drawing of the shooter out of his pocket, she'd known he was about to get down to business. Business that was almost as much ancient history as the extortion racket he'd beaten and dismissed so casually.

Unfortunately, it seemed doomed to stay that way. Neither Jim nor any of the others they talked to had seen the man in the drawing or anyone who might belong to Sherwood's forces. They'd spent two long days talking to any and everyone, Summer's spirits alternately rising and falling, and the results were always the same. No one had seen him.

And tonight, Summer thought as she lifted her tired legs up and stretched them out on the window seat, just as last night, Colter had gone out again. Out into the night where the relatively peaceful streets they'd walked in daylight became a different world. She wondered wearily where he found the energy.

They had stopped at a small seafood restaurant on the waterfront for dinner, and the normalcy of the surroundings, of the act of ordering, chatting idly about nothing in particular as they waited, then eating the savory meal, seemed odd to her after the hours of ups and downs.

"I think I'm beginning to see," she said slowly as they sipped at a final cup of coffee, "why it's so hard for cops to come down, sometimes."

His head came up, his eyes intent as he looked at her.

"It must be hard to find the Off switch." Her voice was tentative; she was afraid he might think her foolish.

"Sometimes," he said huskily, "it's impossible. Sometimes, it goes on for days, even weeks, when you can't stop, can't let up. When you know you're too close to the edge but you can't step back. When you can feel your mind stretching so tight, it's about to snap but you can't slow it down."

Impulsively, she had reached for his hand, closing hers over his finely muscled fingers where they were wrapped around the cup of coffee. She didn't know why she'd done it, only that, at that moment, she needed to touch him so badly, she couldn't resist.

He stared at her for a long moment, his eyes bright and intense. Then something happened to cloud them and he lowered his gaze to his empty plate.

"But I'm sure you know that. From Terry."

She drew her hand back as if stung. Why did he always bring up Terry? Was that really all she was, just the widow of a long-dead friend? With no existence for him beyond that? Not Summer, but only Terry's wife?

"I know," she said coolly, "absolutely nothing from Terry. He never talked to me about his work. No matter how often I asked, he wouldn't tell me. He said I didn't need to hear about it, that I was better off." A trace of bitterness crept into her voice. "He wanted me naive and innocent, and if shutting me out of the most important part of his life was what it took to keep me that way, he was more than happy to do it."

Colter had stared at her then, shock mixing with a touch of anger in the turquoise depths.

"Oh, yes, I know," she said sharply, "I shouldn't talk that way now that he's dead. But I got so damned tired of being locked out all the time...."

She crumpled up her napkin and tossed it onto the table. She got to her feet and started away, blinking rapidly against the sting of tears.

Colter caught up with her just outside the restaurant, a few yards down the walkway that edged the water. He took her arm gently but insistently and turned her back to face him.

"That's not what I meant," he said softly. The tight line of her mouth softened a little, but returned as her eyes narrowed.

"You were angry," she stated flatly.

"Yes. But not at you." She eyed him doubtfully. He let out a long breath. "Terry shouldn't have done that. It's hard enough holding a law-enforcement marriage together when both people understand what the job is. If one doesn't, it's damned near impossible." His mouth quirked. "Believe me, I know."

She looked at him, the anger fading from the green eyes. "Is that . . . what happened to you?"

For one long, silent moment, she thought he wasn't going to answer at all. Then he turned and leaned his elbows on the boardwalk railing, staring out at the water.

"Not quite," he said at last. "At least you *wanted* to know."

He let out a sigh, and she saw his jaw tighten, then release. And finally he went on.

"Cheryl and I got married right after I graduated from the academy," he said slowly. "She thought it was exciting then. Watched too many TV cop shows, I guess. When the reality set in, the long days and the longer nights, she began to hate it. I tried to talk to her about it, tried to explain so she would understand."

Colter seemed to be watching a freighter making its way out to the shipping lanes, but Summer had a feeling he wasn't seeing it at all.

"I asked her to go to some of the support meetings. . . ." His voice trailed off, shrugging.

"Support meetings?"

"Yeah. You know, the program the department had for spouses. Some of the guys give talks and arrange for people to ride along on a shift so they can get an idea what it's really like—" He broke off at her odd expression. "You didn't know about it?"

She shook her head, that tightness back around her mouth again, this time joined by a look in the green eyes that seemed almost like pain. "I wish I had."

Irritation flooded him. What the hell had Terry been thinking of? She was too smart, too vital to be kept in the dark, wondering. Hadn't he seen that he was only hurting her, hurting their marriage, by keeping her so isolated from the reality of his work? Hadn't he thought of what it would do to her to have to face it all at once, as, in the end, she had had to?

"Cheryl wouldn't go?"

Colter shook off his annoyance to answer her. "No. She wasn't interested." He let out a breath. "She was... very social. Always wanted to go out, go to parties. She got tired of me canceling out so often or being late because something came up. I was still in Patrol then and got my share of late calls. She got angry about my days off not even being my own because there was always a court subpoena, a case to testify on. It got so she never wanted to hear anything about my work, never even wanted it mentioned."

Summer watched him as he talked, aware by the odd strain in his voice that this was a subject he was not used to talking about. His eyes were lowered toward the water, and she found herself staring at the sweep of long, thick, sun-tipped lashes that shadowed the vivid eyes. She saw his hands, fingers laced together as he leaned on the rail, tighten.

"One night, I got in a pursuit of a stolen car. Couple of runaway kids ripped off a hopped-up Camaro from the sub base over at Bangor. Two hours later, I found them cruising down Alaskan Way, cool as can be, and the chase was on. It was a mess, to put it mildly. It went on for miles. Nearly lost them a couple of times. Then..." He stopped and took a deep breath. "Then they lost it. Went into a bridge abutment. Killed both of them." His voice was tight, harsh. "They were sixteen years old."

"Colter," Summer began, wishing she hadn't started this, it was causing him such pain. She reached for him, her vision blurred by the moisture gathering in her eyes. He had begun to turn toward her, and her outstretched hand missed his arm and touched his chest. Inadvertently, two slender fingers slid between the buttons of his shirt and across the bare skin of his chest.

He stiffened, and Summer quickly started to pull her hand away, embarrassed. And froze when his hand shot up to cover hers, to hold it there, her fingers pressed against his skin. She could feel his heart accelerate, although the reason why it would escaped her. Maybe it was her own pulse, she thought, hammering even to her fingertips; the way her heart had begun to pound, it seemed all too possible.

As if of their own volition, her fingers moved, and the feel of his hot, sleek skin beneath them made it impossible for her to stop the small, stroking movement. She could feel the hard, masculine curve as muscle swelled out from his breastbone, and that imaginary picture she'd had of the sweater she'd made him coming slowly off, baring his broad chest in slow stages, flashed through her mind and set her heart on a wild race. Shocked by her own boldness in touching him like this, she tried to pull away again. And again he held her there.

And again he began to talk, to finish the grim story he'd begun, in a voice oddly thick and husky. But he did it staring down at their hands, as if meeting her eyes while she was touching him like this was too intense for him to bear.

"We stood out there in the rain for hours while they pried the bodies out of what was left of the car. When I finally got home that night... that morning, really, Cheryl was gone. She left a note saying she'd send for the rest of her things. And goodbye."

"Oh, God, Colter," Summer breathed. "After all that..."

"It wasn't her fault. Not really. She had a right to be angry." He lifted his head then, staring across the water to the tree-covered shore on the other side. "That night was our fourth anniversary. I'd promised her a big night out, and I couldn't even get to a phone to call her. I had the dispatcher call, so she wouldn't think something had happened to me, but..."

"I'm sorry. God, Colter, to have to watch those kids die, and then have that happen."

"That's what I couldn't make her understand. That I felt . . . responsible. Yeah, they'd stolen the car and they deserved to be punished for it . . . but did they deserve to die for it? They were just kids. . . ."

"No," Summer said softly, "but it was their decision, not yours. Once they made it, they set their course. And you did the only thing you could. What you had to do."

His head came around then, his gaze meeting hers at last. God, he thought, why on earth had Terry ever thought she wouldn't understand? Why had he cut himself off from this comfort, this incredible solace? He stared at her, his throat tight. And with a sudden, convulsive movement, his grip on her hand tightened fiercely, flattening her palm against him. His other hand came up to reach for her, but he made himself drop it, knowing he was teetering too close already to a very dangerous edge.

"Cheryl . . . she never understood. Not like this. All she could see was that I'd let her down. Again."

Summer remembered his expression now as she stared out at the lengthening shadows in the yard. It had been weary, regretful, but not pained, and for that she was glad. She told herself she was glad because it didn't hurt him anymore, that it had nothing to do with relief that he obviously no longer loved the woman he'd lost.

It was crazy, she told herself firmly, just the way it was crazy for her to want him to react to her as more than just Terry's widow. He'd been there for her when she'd needed a friend. That's all he was, all he wanted to be, and she had to stop these ridiculous flights of imagination. That night he had held her so close, his body telling her exactly how true the charter captain's words had been, had been a fluke, that's all. And the day she'd given him the sweater . . . that kiss had been meant for thanks, that was all. It wasn't his fault that her senses had gone haywire. And he hadn't been going to kiss her again, out there in the car. And tonight, it had been only that he needed a human touch as he walked through the horrible memories. . . .

Imagination, she told herself firmly. She would stop it, and now. She would accept it all for what it was, not decorate it with her silly dreams, trying to make it into something she knew was impossible. But, oh, it had felt so good to touch him, to feel that sleek, smooth skin...

"No!"

The lonely sound of her exclamation echoed around the empty room. Flushing at her own silliness, she shook her head as if that could rid it of all these foolish ideas. She just wouldn't think about it anymore. And she wouldn't, she ordered herself, lie awake tonight until she knew he was home. Colter could take care of himself and didn't need her worrying about him.

With an abrupt little movement, she got up, heading for the little kitchen to make a cup of hot chocolate, hoping that the activity would help her smother the thought that she had believed Terry able to take care of himself, too.

Colter shoved his hands deeper into his jacket pockets as he walked down the darkly shadowed street. He should be aching to get back to the warm, tropical clime of the Keys, he thought, but for some reason, he found himself oddly invigorated. He'd forgotten how crystal clear, how pure, a summer day was here, and how breathing the cool night air was almost like a drink of the sparkling water he only now realized he'd missed so much.

He tried to concentrate on that alone, tried to stop the conversation that was replaying in his head, over and over, like a record with a skip.

He'd gone by the station again after calling Dave to be sure he was there. It hadn't taken much persuasion to get him to run the check Colter wanted, finding that Sherwood did, indeed, own a limousine. Two, in fact. And one just happened to be white.

"He still on Queen Anne Hill?"

Dave had grinned sourly. "Nope. Not fancy enough, anymore. He's moved up in the world since you left." He flipped on the computer terminal, typed in a query and waited. When the response hit the screen, he turned the monitor around so Colter could read it.

"Mercer Island?" His eyebrows rose.

"Yep. Nothing but the best for Sam Sherwood these days."

"A little far out, isn't it?"

"From his, er, business interests? Yeah, but they say he's working real hard on a new image. Upstanding business-man, pillar of the community, all that."

"Right. A model citizen," Colter said acidly as he grabbed a piece of paper from Dave's desk and wrote down the address.

"Uh, not that I'm trying to tell you what to do, old buddy," Dave said as he watched Colter pocket the note, "but you're not planning on paying your old friend a visit, are you?"

Colter grinned. "Not today."

Dave sighed. "Why don't I find that comforting?"

"'Cause you're an uptight cop, old buddy."

"Don't rub it in. Everything around here's uptight lately. And you aren't helping matters."

"Me?"

"Yeah, you, buddy. Grissom's been pacing like a caged goat ever since he heard you were back."

Colter's brow creased. "How'd he hear that?"

"Come on, you remember the grapevine around here! You can't expect a legend to show up and not have word spread like wildfire." Dave chuckled at Colter's sour face. "I'm serious, man. About Grissom, anyway."

"About him pacing or being a goat?"

"Both," Dave said with a laugh.

"Well, he'll just have to live with it. No law says an old retired cop can't drop back in to see his buddies, is there?"

"You'll be in a lot of trouble," Dave warned him. "But then, you always did like taunting tigers, didn't you?"

"Me?" Colter asked innocently.

"You." Dave grinned wryly. Then, seriously, he eyed his old friend. "You sure about this, Colter? I mean, I know how you feel. Terry was my friend too, and Sum-mer...well, you know. But I talked to that old man.... It's a dead end—"

"Is that your opinion or the party line?"

Dave flushed. "Maybe both," he admitted. "But I can guarantee you one thing. You keep digging, Grissom'll do his damnedest to make your life miserable."

"As I recall," Colter said dryly, "his damnedest was never very good."

Dave laughed. "Still isn't. But you might want to think about going back to fishing and lying in the sun just to avoid having to deal with the blockhead."

"I don't have to deal with him anymore. You do."

"Don't remind me." Dave glanced at his watch. "Is Summer with you?"

"No. I've got some places to go that—" Colter broke off, but his one-shouldered shrug said it all. "Not that she's convinced of that, of course," he added wryly.

Dave grinned. "Yeah. She's become pretty independent, hasn't she? A long way from that quiet little girl we used to know." His grin faded. "Of course, she had to, didn't she?"

"Yes." Colter tried to stifle the stab of pain that hit him every time he thought of what she'd had to do. "I just wish she hadn't quit school. I don't understand it. It was so important to her."

"I know. I...Joyce and I offered to try and help out, but you know Summer. She wouldn't take anything, even after that rotten mess with the insurance."

"Insurance?"

"Yeah. You know, after Terry was killed."

Colter was sitting up straight now with the instinctive knowledge of yet another blow to fall. "What mess?"

"You didn't know?" Dave's brow furrowed. "No, I guess you were already gone when all that happened." He picked up the pen Colter had used and toyed with it.

"All what?" Colter enunciated carefully.

Dave dropped the pen, then spoke in a rush. "The insurance company wouldn't pay up on the line-of-duty clause. Said that since there was a chance Terry was involved in criminal activity when he was killed, that negated the extra payoff."

"But they didn't prove it!"

"No. But the inconclusive verdict was enough, the company said. So they got away with the absolute minimum.

Bastards,'' Dave spat out suddenly. ''There was barely enough to pay the bills she already had after the funeral. Terry didn't leave her any kind of a cushion. So she had to quit school, her job at the Aquarium, sell the car and the house and get a full-time job somewhere else.''

Colter sagged in the chair. Would it never stop? How much had she had to take? And how much was he going to have to live with knowing he'd left her to face it?

''And then Terry's dad died and she had all that to do, too,'' Dave was saying. ''Some of the guys got together and tried to help then, but she was so determined to do it all herself. She said she'd taken what you'd raised for Terry's funeral, but that was because it was for him. She wouldn't take anything for herself.''

No, she wouldn't, Colter thought grimly now as he rounded another corner. Yes, she'd come a long way from that quiet, innocent little girl they'd all known. And she'd made the journey in the hardest, most painful way possible. But the woman she'd become was, if anything, more dangerous for him than the girl had been. The girl had stirred his blood and his senses; the woman stirred his very soul.

He saw the man a split-second too late. The dark shape lunged out of the alley he'd just passed, and Colter only had time to spring sideways, all but his left arm eluding the clawing grasp of the black shape. He used his own momentum and the man's fierce grip on his arm to hurtle them both into the alleyway. They crashed against the closest wall.

Colter did nothing to ease the impact. The man's head snapped back, a hollow thud sounding as it hit the wall. He sagged. Footsteps, running; Colter whirled and crouched. He came up low and hard into the belly of the second man. He heard the whoosh as his shoulder drove the air out of a pair of shocked lungs. And then the third was there, almost on top of him. Colter dropped to his knees. The bulky body faltered at the sudden change. Colter came up fast and solid, catching the man midthigh and virtually tossing him over his shoulder.

More footsteps. Colter whirled again, ready, but the deadly, unmistakable click of metal on metal stopped him.

He'd heard that sound too often. A .45, he guessed. And the safety had just been flipped off and a round chambered.

"Smart move, Colter."

He peered through the darkness, but all he could see was a shadow with just the barest darker outline of a bulky coat and a hat. A formal felt hat, out of place in this grim back alley. The memory clicked.

"Hello, Billy."

He heard a chuckle. "Say that for you, Colter, you were always cool under fire."

"Am I?"

"What?" The raspy voice sounded puzzled, and as if its owner didn't like it.

"Under fire."

The chuckle again, less amused this time. "Only if you keep poking your nose where it don't belong."

"Me? I'm just taking a walk."

No chuckle this time, only ominous threat. "Don't play games with me, man. You're not a cop anymore. You ain't got that tin badge to hide behind now."

"Sam send you?"

"Nobody *sent* me."

Anger this time, unexpectedly. Colter filed away the fact for future reference. If, he thought, as the three men he'd put out of commission began to stir, he had a future.

"Then what do you care what I do?"

"Maybe I just don't like you stirrin' up the streets. Maybe I just don't like you on my turf. Maybe I just don't like cops."

"Make up your mind," Colter returned mildly, "you just said I'm not a cop anymore."

He felt the anger coming off the shadowy figure in waves. He'd arrested Billy Marx many times for everything from petty theft to assault. He served as a messenger for some of the big dealers, but he was small time and doomed to stay small because of his hot temper and a weakness for some of the stuff those big movers sold.

"Yeah, Colter. You're not. And everybody on the street knows why."

Colter stayed quiet. He knew Billy wouldn't be able to resist taunting him, and it would only goad him more if Colter didn't ask. The silence lasted only seconds.

"Everybody knows you split because you didn't want them lookin' at you real close. Like your partner, man. That money he was gettin' went somewheres."

"You're blowing smoke, Billy." He'd heard worse, and it would take a lot more than a cheap taunt from a punk like Billy Marx to get to him. "Make your point and do it now. I've got things to do."

"No, you don't. Not anymore. Not if you know what's good for you."

Colter cocked an eyebrow in exaggerated surprise. "A warning? You come up in the world? The big boys usually only trust you with delivering their laundry."

Billy took a step toward him, and the three men hovering close behind followed suit. At the last second, Billy stopped, regaining his judgment, if not his temper.

"You just keep going and you'll find out, Colter," he spat out. "Keep on listening to that crazy woman and that drunk old man, and you'll wind up right next to your partner."

Billy's words hit a sour note. How had Albert and Summer's part in his return filtered down so fast? But he didn't have time to think about it now.

"You through yet, messenger boy?"

The words and Colter's cool tone infuriated Billy even more. "You think this is some kinda joke, man?"

"No. I think you are."

He knew instantly he'd pushed too far. Billy had changed too, he thought. His fuse used to be a little longer.

"I'll show you who the joke is, Colter!" Billy's eyes flicked to the other men and Colter sensed them begin to move in again.

"Still letting somebody else do your dirty work, Billy?"

"Oh, they're not gonna do it, Colter. I am. They're just gonna make sure you don't leave the party early. And I'm gonna like this party."

Colter saw the movement as Billy set the automatic on a nearby crate, then began to flex his hands. He could feel the others approaching warily. He knew just how much room he had; he'd been gauging it ever since the moment when he'd known he'd pushed Billy too far.

He'd faced worse odds, he thought, but it had been a long time ago. He was rusty, he knew; they never would have gotten this close if he hadn't been. But he'd make it as hard for them as he could. He knew Billy didn't mean to kill him, but he wondered what his chances were of walking out of here under his own power. Right now, it didn't look very promising.

Circling like a school of sharks on the scent of blood, they closed in.

Chapter 8

Summer wasn't certain what had brought her suddenly, sharply upright. She only knew that by the time she was fully awake she was already sitting up in bed, her ears straining. Had she heard a car? Or the front door? She shook her head, trying to clear away the last foggy wisps of sleep.

Then she heard a familiar sound; the creak of the warped floorboard in the hall outside the bathroom door. She looked toward her own closed door and saw the narrow band of light that suddenly leapt along the carpet from beneath it.

He was home. She didn't even blink at the word she silently used; she'd quit fighting the habit of thinking of it that way. She glanced at the clock on her nightstand. Her eyes widened when she saw it was nearly four; she didn't feel as if she had slept that long. She'd kept to her promise not to wait up and had gone to bed early, but sleep had eluded her until after midnight.

He was awfully late, she thought. He hadn't been gone this long before. Had he found something? The possibility banished the last remnants of sleep and she tossed back the covers and swung her legs over the edge of the bed. Then she stopped. If he hadn't, if he was just late, would he feel pressured by her sudden appearance? She hovered uncertainly, one hand still clutching the edge of the comforter.

A sudden, heavy thud decided her. She jumped to the floor and headed for the doorway. Whatever had fallen, it had hit the wall with enough force to rattle the bathroom window. She pulled open the door and went quickly down the hall.

He was hunched over the sink with his back to her, the tail of his unbuttoned shirt half out and hanging lopsidedly. The water was running steadily. She paused in the doorway.

"Colter?"

He stiffened, and she heard an odd sound that sounded almost like a gasp. He moved as if to straighten up, then, as he stopped abruptly, she thought she heard him suck in a short, harsh breath.

"Sorry if I woke you."

His words had a strange edge and an oddly muffled sound. He didn't turn around.

"It's all right. I . . . went to bed early. Did you drop something?"

He was hunching over again, even more, his head down below the level of the mirror over the sink.

"Bumped the wall. Sorry," he said again with that same peculiar tension, that same muffled sound. "Go back to bed."

She stared at his bent body for a moment longer, her eyebrows drawn together.

"Good night, Summer."

The words were a little too insistent, his posture a little too tense. She stepped into the small room and he went rigid.

"Summer, don't."

Now his words were ripe with warning, but drawn by a compulsion she didn't completely understand, she ignored it. She took another step. His shirt was torn, she thought with a little shock. That's why it was dangling so crookedly. And then a startled exclamation broke from her. Her eyes were fastened on his right hand where it was braced against the sink. It was spattered with blood, and three of his knuckles were split and bleeding, the others scraped and raw.

"Colter, what— Oh, God."

His body had gone slack in resignation at her first cry, then he had moved with painful slowness until she caught a glimpse of his face in the mirror.

"What happened?" It was a hoarse, shocked whisper.

"I ran into an old friend."

The statement came out slowly, word by careful word, and he grimaced with the effort. She realized why he had sounded so odd, now. She stared, stunned.

"Oh, God, Colter." Her voice shook.

The left side of his mouth was red and swollen, his lower lip split and bleeding. His left cheek was coated in blood from a cut beneath an eye that was reddened and swollen nearly shut. His left hand nearly matched the right, his fingers raw and swollen, with two knuckles trickling blood over the back of his hand.

Without realizing it, she reached out, but stopped when she realized that touching him would probably be the worst thing she could do. Pull yourself together, she ordered. Worry about what happened later. Right now, he needs help. You finally have a chance to do something. Don't fall apart now. She suppressed one last shudder as she watched him swipe with a swollen hand at the blood trailing down his face.

"Sit down."

He looked startled at her sudden firmness, then winced as the expression tugged at bruised, torn flesh.

"Sit down," she repeated, gesturing at the stool to the small vanity that was tucked in the corner of the room behind the door. He sat.

She pulled open the medicine cabinet and took out a couple of bottles, a tin of adhesive bandages and some cotton balls. She took a clean washcloth off a shelf and put everything down on the small table. Then she stopped to look at him.

"I presume you won't go to a doctor or the hospital?" Her tone was matter-of-fact, and his eyebrows began to rise in surprise again before he remembered and stopped in time.

"Can't," he mumbled, his voice worse now that he wasn't trying to hide what had happened. "They'd have to call the cops. Don't want that."

She looked puzzled, but only said, "Hold still, then."

With gentle hands, she began to clean him up, managing with an effort to keep her expression even when he winced despite her care. She swabbed the cut beneath his eye and closed it with a row of small butterfly bandages. Then she tended the other cuts and bruises, moving methodically, carefully. He bore it all silently, but she could tell by the rigidity of his muscles and the way he held his breath when she hit a particularly sore spot that she was hurting him. It made her want to hurry, to get it over, but she knew she couldn't. At last, she'd done the best she could with his battered face.

"Now for your hands," she said.

"They're fine." He drew back as if to keep her from touching them.

"Sure. That's why they're still bleeding and your fingers are the size of bananas." She went to rinse out the blood-stained washcloth, then came back. "You'd better take off your shirt," she said, eyeing the cuffs of his sleeves, "it's already getting stained."

"It doesn't matter."

"It will only get worse—"

"I said it doesn't matter!" He took a breath and tried again. "Sorry. But it's already shot, anyway."

"You have a point." Her eyes flicked to that ragged tear in the pale blue fabric. She'd liked that shirt, she thought, especially the way it lit up his eyes. "Well, you'll have to take it off anyway, unless you want to sleep in it."

"Just leave it," he ground out.

"Colter..." she began, exasperated.

"I can't!"

He jerked his eyes away from her, letting out a short, compressed breath. She stared at him for a moment, then painful realization struck her. He couldn't because his swollen, battered fingers couldn't manage the small buttons at the cuffs.

"Oh, for heaven's sake. Why didn't you just ask?"

He made a low growling sound of disgust. Because, he thought. Because when I think of asking you to take my shirt off, this isn't at all what I have in mind. Because my shirt isn't the only thing I want you to take off. Because if you touch me, I'll probably jump out of my skin. And if you don't touch me, it won't matter because I'm going to curl up and die anyway.

And then her slender fingers were at his wrists, gently tugging the buttons loose. He sucked in a sharp breath and she stopped.

"Am I hurting you?"

Yes. God, yes. A relentlessly building pressure low and deep in his body told him that the pain wasn't enough to combat the fierce, driving need that had begun in him the moment he'd caught a glimpse of her reflection in the mirror. She was wearing a pale green version of the same satin nightshirt, this one almost the exact color of her eyes. Her hair was tousled, the thick, blond bangs falling over her forehead, making her eyes look even more enormous and delightfully, sexily sleepy.

"Colter?"

"Go ahead," he grated out, closing his eyes tightly. He hoped she would think it was against pain and not from the fact that he didn't dare look at her when she was so close and wearing only that shimmering sweep of pale green, her breasts swaying slightly with her every move, her long legs bare beneath the edge that stopped above midthigh.

She moved around behind him and slipped the ragged shirt over his shoulders. Her fingers brushed the back of his neck and she heard a small, low groan. She stopped, startled; he'd never made a sound while she'd cleaned up his battered and bloody face. Slowly, she pulled the shirt the rest of the way.

Colter's eyes snapped open again as he heard her smothered gasp. She was staring at his back, and he could guess at what. When Billy had gotten tired of using his fists, he had begun with his boots, and his cohorts had gotten in a few licks of their own, maliciously enjoying the chance to get even. Lying curled up in that darkened alley as their feet battered him was the last thing Colter had remembered before waking up, shivering, having no idea how long he'd been out. He could imagine what his back must look like.

He could almost feel her draw up straight, sense her steadying herself. She tossed the ripped shirt aside, then stepped back around to reach for the washcloth. She began to wash away the blood, cradling his hands gently in hers.

"What do the other guys look like?"

His eyes snapped up to hers. "What makes you think there was more than one?"

She smiled crookedly. "Fishing for compliments, Colter?" He flushed and dropped his gaze to his hands, watching the careful way she was cleansing his battered knuckles. "How many were there?" she asked again.

He shrugged, then regretted the movement as his bruised muscles protested.

"Half a dozen?"

He chuckled wryly. "Try four."

Something flickered across her delicate features, and he realized he had been neatly maneuvered into answering her question. He was a little startled that she had done it so easily. He was finding facets in her he'd never known existed. Or perhaps they never had before. The girl he'd left here had truly become a woman.

"Three to hold you down and one to do the damage?"

His right eye narrowed; the left had already swollen shut. How had she known that?

Summer read the answer in his lopsided expression. "People you arrested before?"

"One. Billy Marx, a small-time errand boy. With three playmates." His mouth twisted wryly, and he winced again at the tug on his split lip. "They were all very glad I wasn't a cop anymore."

Finished, she rinsed out the cloth and hung it up. She turned back to look at him and leaned against the sink, trying not to look at the marks that marred the sleek skin of his torso. He saw her look away, saw in her face the determination not to betray her distress.

"Terry was wrong," he said quietly, unexpectedly.

Her head snapped around and the peridot eyes fastened on him.

"You could have handled it. All of it."

He saw the sudden gleam of moisture in her eyes, the rapid blinking as she held it back.

"Thank you." Her voice was soft, and a tremor of emotion shook it slightly.

There was a long, silent moment as they looked at each other, feeling a closeness, a warmth that threatened at any second to turn into something more. They both knew it, they both looked away at the same instant. The sudden tension was almost tangible, and he was grateful when she abruptly moved.

"I'll get some ice for your hands and your eye. They'll be better in the morning if you ice them now."

She returned with a bowl of water with several ice cubes floating in it, more ice in a small plastic bag, a glass and a bottle of aspirin. She handed him the bowl.

"I thought it would feel better than straight ice." He nodded as he balanced it on his knees. "Here, take these first."

She handed him two aspirin and the glass she'd filled at the sink. He managed to take the pills and hold the glass, but his fumbling efforts told him he wasn't up to anything more dextrous than that. Swallowing was painful, and he could taste blood from where his teeth had cut the inside of his mouth with the impact of Billy's first punch.

She took the glass from him, and he dunked his hands into the bowl. He tried to suppress the hissing breath that escaped at the shock of the cold on his swollen fingers. His head came up and he closed his eyes against the sudden wave of pain.

"I know," Summer said sympathetically. "But try and hold your head still."

She held the small bag of ice against his eye. Distract him, she thought when she saw the lines of pain deepen in his tanned face.

"You're not going to report it at all?"

"No."

"Why?"

"No point."

"But you knew one of them, you could identify him—"

"Don't want to drag in the police."

Her eyebrows rose. "That, from you?"

He realized then just how much he had come to rely on a shrug when he didn't want to answer. He moved his hands instead, sloshing the ice water. "Don't want them involved. Not yet."

"Involved?"

"Too early. Don't have anything yet."

Her brow furrowed. Then her expression cleared, replaced by one of dismay.

"Then it wasn't just a payback."

He let out a compressed breath between sore lips. He hadn't meant to let that slip, but he was aching all over, and that brief, silent moment of rapport had him shaken. Still, he should have realized she would pick up on it; she was too quick not to.

"It was over this, wasn't it?" Her voice was tight, distressed.

"Summer—"

"It was a warning, wasn't it? To back off?"

"Look, these guys are funny about anybody poking around their territory. For any reason."

She looked at him steadily. "You said Terry was wrong. That I could handle it. Was that just to pacify me?"

Something in the troubled eyes told Colter just how much Terry's shutting her out had hurt her. Not for anything would he add to that look, not for anything would he treat her as a child, as Terry apparently had.

"No." He flexed his fingers tentatively, the floating cubes rattling against the sides of the ceramic bowl.

"Then I was right?"

With a sigh, he nodded. Distress filled her eyes, her voice. "God, Colter, I'm sorry."

"It's not your fault." He was pleased that he sounded a little more normal; he knew his short, clipped sentences were worrying her.

"Yes it is. I brought you here—"

"Stop it, Ms. Martyr." She blinked, startled in turn. "I came on my own. You didn't force me. I knew it wasn't going to be easy."

She shifted the ice bag with trembling fingers. "But this . . . for just asking some questions?"

Damn, he thought, how many muscles did it take to shrug, anyway? "They wanted to be sure I got the message." He flexed his fingers again. "I'm just not sure who sent it."

"I thought. . . . It wasn't Sherwood?"

"Billy said no, not that he wouldn't lie through his teeth if it suited him. But I think I'll pay a visit to some of Mr. Sherwood's people tomorrow, anyway."

Summer's breath caught in her throat at the thought of him venturing into that evil man's domain. Even Terry hadn't been able to keep her from hearing about Sam Sherwood. If there was organized illegal activity in Seattle, Sherwood's fingers were in it somewhere. Yet the man remained aloof, apart from the grim dealings that had made him one of the wealthiest, most powerful men in the state. Never had any of the unsavory residue of his business clung to him. Never had any charges been made to stick; the man had never even had to appear in court.

She wanted to tell Colter no, he couldn't risk it, but she knew it wouldn't stop him. She tried another tack. "You won't be going anywhere tomorrow," she said sternly.

He looked startled. "What?"

"You'll be lucky if you can move tomorrow."

"I'll move."

"You can wait a couple of days—"

"It's got to be tomorrow."

"Why?"

"Because that's the way the game's played. If he was behind this, I can't let him think they put me out."

Summer eyed his bruised face and the discolorations that were beginning to surface on his chest and ribs.

"Men," she sniffed with all the disdain of civilized woman. Colter grinned. He couldn't help it and didn't mind that it hurt.

Something about that lopsided, swollen grin tugged at something deep inside her, releasing a flooding, rushing warmth. She wanted to soothe away all the hurt, to smooth back the tousled sun-streaked hair, to ease the pain from his aching muscles with her hands. She wanted to touch, to caress—

God, what was she thinking? Summer backed up a step hastily, staring at him, the bag of melting ice dangling forgotten from her slender fingers.

Colter's breath had caught in his throat the moment he'd seen that soft, caressing look fill her eyes, the moment he'd seen her lips curve into that gentle, tender smile. Never in his life had he ever thought to see her look at him like that, and it shook him to his soul. When she stepped back, he felt such a wrenching disappointment that it overpowered all the signals of pain and weariness his body was sending his tired brain.

"You'd better get some rest," she said hastily.

It took him a moment to shake off the effects of that look and he could only nod. Slowly, he got up, fumbling with the bowl. The ice was melted now, but his fingers were so numb, he nearly dropped the container. She took it from him and dumped the water into the sink, leaving the bowl out in case it was needed again. She emptied the plastic bag and set it aside.

"Do you need any help?" she asked as they stood at the door of the guest room he'd been using.

He tried to bend his chilled fingers again. "I don't..." His voice trailed off as he looked at her helplessly.

Without a word, she followed him inside. She hadn't been in the room since he'd arrived, and she found herself taking an odd pleasure in the sight of masculine clutter here and there—a comb tossed on the dresser, tennis shoes kicked off beneath the small chair that held his knapsack, a towel draped over the doorknob.

When she saw the sweater she'd made folded carefully and placed on the second chair, unlike the haphazard tossing of the rest of his possessions, she felt an odd tug at her heart. He'd never worn it when he went out at night, when he would most need its warmth, she realized now with a little shock. Even if he'd had it on during the day, he always took it off before he plunged back into that dark world that had sent him back as he was tonight. Had he guessed, or even known, that something like this might happen?

Feeling she would never know the full truth about what life was like on those darkened streets he had once roamed as a keeper of the peace, she knelt at his feet as he stopped beside the single bed that was covered with a handmade quilt in rich shades of green.

"You need something without laces," she said dryly as she undid his boots.

He'd bought a pair of army boots because he'd always found them comfortable when he was on uniform patrol; he hadn't thought about the intricacies of lacing them. Should have gotten some of the new ones with zippers, he thought.

"I hadn't planned on this," he said, trying once more to flex his uncooperative fingers, then wished he hadn't said anything, because Summer went suddenly still. Then she tugged the boots off and straightened up. Hurt and guilt warred in her eyes; he wanted to pull her into his arms and erase those emotions. Instead, he made himself reach for the top button of his jeans, wondering if he could undo it.

He couldn't. His fingers just weren't working right, and he couldn't make them grip the brass button. He clenched them into aching, useless fists. He'd sleep in the damn jeans, he thought, closing his eyes against his frustration.

The feel of her hands at his waist brought them open again abruptly. She was tugging at the button, sliding it through the heavy denim.

"Summer," he choked out.

"You need help," she said evenly, two spots of color in her cheeks the only sign that this was any different than unbuttoning his shirt.

He couldn't help the visions that sprang to his mind as she undid the button and reached for the tab of his zipper. His body forgot the aches and discomfort, responding to the vivid images instantly, fiercely. As her hand moved, sliding the tab down slowly, he thought for one crazy moment that she was doing it intentionally, moving so slowly just to make it even more arousing.

Then he saw her expression and knew it was only embarrassment and awkwardness at an unfamiliar task. The realization didn't help; his body rose to that hesitant touch as surely and as quickly as if she'd meant it to be the sensual caress it had seemed. And, he thought, if she opened that zipper another inch, she was going to find that out. He grabbed her wrists with his aching hands.

"I can manage now. Thanks."

She stopped, curling her fingers back away from him. Her eyes were fastened on his hands, then slowly rose. He saw the barely perceptible tightening around her eyes when they reached the particularly sore spot on the right side of his rib cage; he imagined the bruise was beginning to show. When the light green eyes reached his, they were wide and troubled and full of an emotion he couldn't pin down.

"It's not worth it," she whispered.

His body went taut as he stared down at her.

"I didn't want revenge, I just wanted to clear Terry. I didn't want anyone to get hurt."

Colter sucked in a short, harsh breath and held it as she freed one hand from his grasp and reached out tentatively to touch that heavily bruised spot. The feel of her fingers gently brushing his skin, even in that aching place, sent a little burst of heat rippling through him.

Her voice dropped, went low and husky. "Especially you."

"Summer."

It was all he could say; he was too busy trying to beat down the surging response of his emotions to her words and the sound of her voice. She didn't mean it that way, he told himself, ordering his leaping heart to calm down.

"No more," she said softly, her fingers still touching that discolored expanse of skin. "They can't hurt Terry anymore, but they can hurt you. It's not worth that. Nothing is."

With a strangled little groan, he lifted his battered hands to her head, cupping it gently. His eyes searched her face, her eyes, looking for some sign that he wasn't out in left field, that the soft, tender note in her voice was truly for him.

She tilted her head back to meet his penetrating gaze, and her lips parted as she tried to take in the air that seemed suddenly in short supply. She heard that odd, strangled groan again, sounding as if it had been ripped from deep in his chest. Then his head lowered, slowly, as if he were fighting it every inch of the way.

When his lips brushed hers, Summer was stunned by the electric surge that shot through her. After the slightest of caresses, she felt him start to pull back and was startled by the instant protest of her senses. Involuntarily, her arms went around him, in an impulsive attempt to keep him from pulling away from her. She felt him go rigid, felt his muscles tense under her hands.

Embarrassment flooded her. He didn't want this, she thought, and began to pull away. Then his mouth was on hers again, harder this time, more urgent, heedless of the pain she knew it must be causing him. She couldn't seem to breathe, but it didn't matter. She didn't need to breathe, didn't need air; all she needed was the growing warmth that was spreading through her. Her hands flexed on his back, her fingers sliding over his skin, tinglingly aware of the hardness of the muscles beneath that sleek surface.

Colter couldn't believe how she had gone soft and warm in his arms. She was clinging to him. Her lips were pliant and yielding to his, her fingers were stroking his bruised back, not hurting, but sending rockets of heat through him, heat that careened around inside him before it settled low and deep, hardening his body until he wondered why the zipper of his jeans didn't give the rest of the way under the pressure.

He barely felt the pain of his lip as he crushed her mouth with his, all he could feel was the surging, blazing waves of sensation. She was all heat and light held in his arms, and he was rapidly losing control. With the last singed remnants of his will, he slid his hands to her shoulders and straightened his arms, holding her away from him.

She was staring at him, her eyes wide with wonder, her lips parted. A chill swept him when he saw the bright red of blood glistening on her lower lip, but when she raised an unsteady hand to touch his mouth, he realized it was his own.

She opened her mouth to speak, then shut it again, lowering her eyes. He let out a long, compressed breath. He understood, he thought. She was upset, she hadn't wanted this but didn't know how to tell him. With a muttered, inward curse at himself for his lack of control, he released her and backed up a step.

"Good night, Summer."

His voice was unsteady, and it echoed oddly in his ears. He saw her draw herself up straight and slowly lift her head. When her eyes paused just below his waist, he felt the touch of her gaze on his swollen flesh as if it were a physical caress.

When her eyes seemed to rivet on the narrow triangle of flesh above the half-open zipper and the trail of sandy brown hair that disappeared below the brass fastener, he was torn between wanting to wait, to see what her reaction was to his obvious state of arousal, and wanting to run like hell before he did something he'd regret. He compromised by abruptly turning his back on her and repeating his goodnight.

Summer didn't remember leaving his room or walking to her own. She only knew she was there, curled up on her bed, shivering. She couldn't seem to move, even to pull the covers over her and shut out the chill that had taken her over.

She'd made a fool out of herself. Colter had only meant to thank her for tending his injuries, and she'd reacted like the proverbial love-starved widow. She'd embarrassed him, until the only way for him to avoid further awkwardness was to turn his back on her.

In her humiliation, she was certain that although he might have responded, as any man long without a woman would, he hadn't wanted to, hadn't wanted her, and had taken the only way out he could think of without telling her directly to leave him alone.

Quit kidding yourself, she thought grimly. He told you as directly as if he'd shouted it. How many times do you have to tell yourself he only sees you as Terry's wife? And what did you expect? He finally walks away, finds his peace, and you drag him back so he can get beat up.

She reached for her pillow with hands that were shaking, buried her face in the softness of it and wished she could shut out the world as easily as she could shut out the light.

*   *   *

She'd been right, Colter thought ruefully as he gingerly pulled himself upright. Every muscle in his body screamed in protest against any movement at all, and his head ached with a fierceness that he knew aspirin wasn't going to handle. He set his feet carefully on the floor, trying to ignore the way the room seemed to spin around him. After a moment, using the chair beside the bed for support, he pulled himself upright.

It shouldn't be so hard, he thought vaguely. Down was where the floor was, up was the other way. Easy. Then why was he clinging to this chair as if it were the only solid thing in a dissolving world?

It was a good thing he'd wound up sleeping in his jeans, after all, he thought. He never would have been able to pull them on now, just as it had been too much for him to take them off last night. His mind shrank away from the other memories of last night like a horse shying away from the spot where a rabbit had once burst from the brush and spooked it.

It seemed as though he stood there forever before the whirling finally stopped. He lifted his head tentatively, testing his shaky equilibrium. He could barely see out of his left eye, and his mouth, although less swollen, was sore as hell. Still, he thought he could chance it and made it to the dresser to get a fresh shirt. It took long, painful minutes to pull it on. He felt a hundred years old as he began to move toward the door, knowing he was shuffling rather than walking, and he hunched over to ease the strain on his bruised, tender stomach muscles.

He stopped in the bathroom to take more aspirin and to look at the remains of his face. It wasn't as bad as he had expected, except for the now near-black contusion beneath his eye. There were a few other, less-intense bruises. His lip was still obviously split, but the swelling had gone down, as it had in his hands. He could move them now, and although his fingers were sore, they were operative.

It was his ribs that were the problem now, and his back where Billy and company had vented their rage. It hurt just to breathe, and he looked like the muddy palette of some grim, dark-souled artist.

Summer was at the kitchen table, a cup of coffee before her, staring at the steam rising from it as if it were the most fascinating thing she'd ever seen. She looked up as she heard him in the doorway, and in the split second before an unreadable mask descended over her face, he saw embarrassment and pain and something else he couldn't name.

Disappointment? Was that what had been there in that brief tightness of her mouth and eyes, that hollowness in the green eyes? At what? That he'd stopped last night?

His heart leapt once more. It was getting harder and harder to beat it down, but he did it resolutely. If it was disappointment, he told himself firmly, it was more likely in you because you kissed her at all. Because she expected better of you than to treat her as every other man probably did.

His recoil from the thought of those other men was almost violent. He knew they had to exist, never mind that there had been no sign of them since he'd been here, never mind that Mrs. Harper said Summer never brought them home. No woman who looked like Summer, let alone one with her quick intelligence and warm heart, would be alone for long.

So why not you?

Stop it, he snapped at himself. You're only thinking that way because you're hurting too much to stop it. You know why. Because Terry was your best friend. Because you feel guilty enough already for having fallen for her while he was still alive. Because she deserves better than somebody who was supposed to be a friend but deserted her when she needed help the most. And she doesn't want you, not like that.

But she had kissed him back. Before, it had been too quick, too brief to be sure, but last night, she had kissed him back.

And there it was, the pesky thought he'd wrestled with until, at nearly dawn, his aching body's need for sleep had at last won out.

She was startled, that's all, he told himself. And worried because you were hurt. And feeling guilty, thinking it was her fault.

He knew it was true, just as he had last night, but he couldn't quite seem to bury that last little glow of longing that his heart clung to stubbornly.

"I made some soup. You should be able to eat it. Sit down and I'll get it."

Her voice was inflectionless, even, as if she were talking to a stranger. He cringed inwardly, reading her intent clearly; a stranger was exactly what she wanted him to be. You've been warned off, Colter, and this is a warning you'd better listen to.

He managed to sip the hot, savory broth she'd made and was surprised at how much it settled him. He took a second cup when she offered it, thanking her with formal politeness. At least, he thought glumly, he could let her know her message had been received and understood.

Summer wanted to put his coolness down to his being in pain, but she was certain he was as mortified about her actions last night as she was. She had awakened early and had spent the dawn hour calling herself every kind of a fool she could think of. He could have any woman he wanted with one look from those turquoise eyes, what on earth would he want with the shy little mouse who had been his best friend's quietly proper wife? She didn't feel like that woman anymore, but it was clear he still saw her that way, and probably always would. And maybe he was right. Just a mouse.

When he was done, he thanked her gruffly for the soup and got slowly to his feet. She took the cup and carried it to the sink, dumping her own unwanted coffee down the drain and putting both mugs aside to be washed later. When she turned back, she caught him tentatively probing his side as he tried to stand up straighter.

"You should go back to bed." She hadn't meant to say anything, but he looked so sore....

"Can't. Things to do."

She eyed him warily. "Don't tell me you're going down to his turf again."

"Okay."

She relaxed until she realized all he'd agreed to was to not tell her he was going. "Colter—"

"Don't argue." He suppressed the need to drop back in the chair and cradle his aching head in his hands. "I'm not up to it."

"But you're up to tromping through the devil's domain?" Her tone was biting.

"It doesn't matter if I am or not. All that matters is that he thinks I am."

It was all some kind of crazy game, she thought incredulously. The good guys and the bad guys, cops and robbers, with a set of rules, a code, not written down anywhere but understood by all those who played by them. A game in which Colter had been an all-star.

And a game in which her husband had been murdered.

"I wish I'd never come to you."

I'll bet, he thought, a different kind of pain knifing through him. *I wasn't here when you needed me, and now that I am, I fall all over you like a teenager in heat.* His heart was aching relentlessly, twisting with a pain that was somehow worse than all his other hurts put together.

She sighed, a weary little sound of resignation. "I'll drive you."

"No."

"You're in no shape to go at all, let alone drive."

"I'll manage."

"I brought you here—"

"Summer, I told you, it's not your fault."

"I know you did. But you wouldn't be here if not for me, so it's my party, too. I'm not backing out now. Besides, there's safety in numbers."

Sherwood, Colter thought sourly, would have as little trouble disposing of two of them as he would one. But he didn't tell her that. He ground his teeth in frustration, an action that made his already aching jaw throb. He couldn't tell her it was too dangerous and then tell her he was going alone. He couldn't tell her it wasn't dangerous because, then, there was no real reason for her not to come along.

"Summer—"

"Look, I'd be doing this myself, alone, if you hadn't come back."

"No," he repeated.

"I won't get in the way. I'll just wait in the car, if you want," she said equably.

"It's not that—" He broke off. "No."

"You're not up to arguing, remember? So accept it, Colter. You've got a chauffeur." She smiled, better this time. "But I refuse to wear a hat."

"What you should wear," he said grimly, "is a warning sign. All that stubborn in such a pretty package."

She blushed suddenly, so furiously that it startled him.

"Okay," he said hastily, "maybe not stubborn, but—"

Her color deepened, and she spoke hastily. "I'll get the keys while you put your shoes on."

She raced to the living room, leaving him staring after her in puzzlement. He hadn't meant to insult her, in fact, in a slightly backhanded way, he'd meant it as a compliment. He was laboriously putting on his second shoe before it dawned on him that what had made her blush was not his comment on her obstinacy, but that he had called her pretty.

He stopped, staring at the battered running shoe—he'd forgone the lace-up boots in the interest of finishing sometime today—as if the worn leather held the answer. It couldn't be that compliments were so rare for her, not the way she turned heads in a room. So it must have been because it came from him.

Maybe she'd thought he was making a pass at her, he thought glumly. And after last night, it was certain that that was the last thing she wanted. He finished with the shoe and straightened up, wincing as the muscles of his torso cried out another protest.

Good, he thought grimly. Think about that, Colter. That way, you won't be able to think about that stupid idea you somehow got into your head that she kissed you back because she wanted to.

Chapter 9

She hated it. She had known this side of the city existed, the dark, seamy side. She had realized that no city of five hundred thousand people, even beautiful Seattle, could exist without that underlying layer of corruption, of barred windows and street crime, but she hadn't had to come face-to-face with it before.

This, she thought, was what Terry hadn't wanted her to know about. This was what he and Colter had dealt with every day, and she began to understand them both a little better. Terry had wanted her insulated from this, protected. Colter hadn't wanted her here, but once she'd made her decision, he'd accepted it with enough faith in her to think she could handle it. His trust made her feel a warmth unlike anything she'd ever felt before.

She was fascinated by the way he seemed to change. The battered, bent man she'd seen disappeared so completely, he seemed never to have existed; he seemed totally at ease. His hands were casually in his pockets, and if she hadn't known, she never would have guessed it was to hide his battered hands. He walked with that coiled grace she remembered so well, without a visible trace of the pain and soreness that she knew must be making him want to double over in response. Even his bruised face seemed to fade into insignificance.

They were deep in Sherwood's territory, Colter was talking to people who reported directly to the man or to his small army of employees, and he never showed a sign of strain. Only when Colter got back into the car did the pain show, in the way he sagged into the seat and the tight lines that grooved his face.

She herself was decidedly nervous; every time he left her, she locked the car with the haste and apprehension of one who wasn't altogether sure it would help. She was painfully aware of the looks she got, a lone female parked in a part of town where men walked with care. Colter was always back before anything could happen, but by afternoon, she was ready to admit this hadn't been her brightest idea. And she began to realize what a fool she'd been to think she could have ever done this herself.

"I've had it," he said at last at the end of a long afternoon.

Summer looked at him suspiciously, thinking he was calling a halt early for her sake, but the pain and weariness in his eyes told her differently. Before she could speak, he read her look.

"I've planted enough seeds for one day. If Sherwood was behind this, he knows I know it now. If he wasn't..." He shrugged, then winced.

It wasn't until they were back at her house that she asked the question that had been gnawing at her since he'd said those words. She sat watching him eat the stew she'd made, chewing with slow care for his sore mouth.

"If he was behind those men coming after you," she said, knowing she didn't have to explain who, "then he knows you didn't listen to his warning."

Colter shrugged; it was a little easier this time. "He knows I wouldn't, anyway. I never did before."

"Then why did he bother?"

Colter's brow furrowed, then cleared as he was reminded just how sore his face was.

"I've been wondering about that myself."

"Maybe he thinks you've changed," she said tentatively, answering her own question.

Colter let out a wry chuckle. "Yeah. Maybe he believes what Billy said."

"What did he say?"

"That I took the money Terry was getting and ran with it."

Summer wrinkled her nose and made a delicate sound of disgust. "Then he's a fool."

There hadn't been a second of hesitation, and her faith filled him with a sudden warmth.

"You said maybe he thought I'd changed."

"I meant because you weren't a cop any longer."

He looked at her curiously. "Is that what you think?"

"What?"

"That the only change is that I'm not a cop anymore?"

"No. I think you're not a cop anymore because you've changed." She studied him for a moment. "I understand why you had to leave, Colter. More now than I did then. All I knew then was that you were leaving and I . . ."

Her voice trailed off, and she lowered her eyes.

"You what?" he asked softly.

She stared at her own empty bowl. "I didn't know what I was going to do without you."

He went tense, his eyes fastened on her lowered lashes. "Without me?"

She sighed and lifted her head. "You were the only thing that kept me going. I would have fallen apart completely after Terry died and during those awful hearings if it hadn't been for you."

Terry. Of course. It was always Terry. Colter sagged back in the chair and relaxed his death grip on the spoon he'd been holding. He wondered if she would ever leave it behind, then ruefully knew the answer to his own question. How could she when she still loved Terry? She'd loved him most of her life, since they were children together. That wasn't something you turned off at will. Firmly, Colter shoved his recently overactive libido back into its cage and slammed the door.

They spent a quiet evening, Summer curled up in a chair, knitting needles clicking rhythmically as she worked on the intricately patterned sweater she was making for Fiona, Colter stretching his aching body out on the couch as he watched a local news broadcast with his one open eye. He felt oddly, unexpectedly comfortable, a kind of comfort he'd never known.

He would glance at her now and then, watching the needles flash dexterously in her slender hands, seeing the intensity of her concentration on the complex design. He imagined her like that, working intently on a different garment, a sea of blues broken by a smooth black and white arc. Had she thought of the person she'd been making it for then? Or just the design forming beneath her nimble fingers?

Occasionally, she would catch her lip lightly between white, even teeth as she studied her work. It was then that he had to look away before that heat he had only managed to bank erupted again. It was then that he was thankful for the throbbing pain, thinking that it was the only thing that kept him from going to her.

He didn't remember falling asleep, but on some semiconscious level of his mind, he knew he must have because he could smell that sweet honeysuckle scent that always seemed to accompany his dreams of Summer. It was an exceptionally vivid dream; he could even feel her fingers threading through his hair, brushing it back from his forehead and sending shivering little currents of sensation through him.

He tried to talk, to tell her how good it felt to have her touch him, but as it always was in those dreams, he couldn't form the words. Then he felt the soft, warm touch of her lips on his forehead and the dream gained a new, more tangible aspect; it seemed so real, he could feel the sudden quickening of his pulse, the sudden surging of his body.

Then the sweet, warm feeling was gone. He felt a tugging at his feet, and then a different kind of warmth enveloped him as something soft and thick was pulled over him, tucked around him. The honeyed scent faded, and so did the dream.

He awoke just after dawn when a chill roused him enough to reach for the afghan he'd kicked off in his restless sleep on the couch. He tugged it back over him, burrowing into the warmth, glad Summer had covered him with it. She must have taken off his shoes, too, he could feel—

Summer. He sat up with a jerk. She *had* put the afghan over him. And his shoes were off. If that part had been real, had the rest? Had she touched him? God, had she kissed him? Of her own volition?

All chance of going back to sleep had been seared away by his thoughts. He was up, pacing, noticing only vaguely that he felt much better than he had yesterday, as if the worst was over.

Had she? Of her own will, had she touched him with those gentle fingers, had she pressed her soft mouth to his forehead?

He glanced at her closed door, barely able to stop himself from going to her. He wanted to know, had to know. But if he went to her now, he didn't trust himself to leave. She'd be wearing that damned nightshirt, her hair would be tousled, her face flushed with sleep, and he knew damned well he wouldn't be able to keep his hands off her.

The house was suddenly much too small and he quickly crossed to his room. He changed clothes hurriedly, went for the car keys and pulled open the door. Then he stopped, glancing once more at that closed door. She might worry, he thought. Maybe he should leave her a note. He'd promised, almost, after the last time.

He stared at a blank piece of paper for a moment, wondering what to write. It had been a long time since he'd accounted for his time to anyone and it felt strange. In truth, it felt right, and he didn't quite know how to react to that. At last, he wrote a few brief words telling her he wanted to check something out and he'd be back by noon. He had no idea what he was really going to do, he only knew he had to get out of there. Now. He closed the door quietly behind him.

A few hours later, he sat in front of a glowing computer screen in the office that had once been his. After two hours of fruitlessly driving in circles he had called Dave Stanley from a pay phone, knowing that he usually got to the station early. Reluctantly, Dave had agreed to let Colter have an hour or so at the computerized files while the weekly staff meeting was going on.

"Find something else to do," Colter had told Dave when he arrived. "If I get caught, I'll say I snuck in. Besides, what can they do? Fire me?"

He knew there was a lot more they could do, like pressing criminal charges, and he knew that Dave knew it, but his old friend had accepted his decision to take the risk. Colter wasn't sure what he was looking for, only that it made him feel better to at least be doing something. The computerized files were five years more up-to-date than his own; he might find something.

He pulled up the file on Terry's case, his jaw tightening despite the time that had passed as he read that faintly damning "inconclusive" decision. Idly, he looked it over, page after gruesome, familiar page.

A .38-caliber bullet to the chest. The kind of gun a thousand street hoods carried. Owned by thousands of law-abiding citizens. And cops. Casing not located. Weapon never found. He called up another page.

Nothing new. Everything was just as it was in his own pilfered copy of the file. On a sudden spark of curiosity, he called up his own file. His own part in the detailed inquiry glowed in soft amber letters on the black screen. Again, nothing new. He reached for the key to return to the query mode.

His finger stopped in midair. He stared at the last line of the last page that stared immutably back at him. "Officer resigned, investigation terminated prior to resolution."

What the hell? Prior to resolution? He'd been exonerated long before the prolonged, extensive investigation had ended. If he hadn't been, he never would have quit, even though he had wanted to the moment he realized they were treating the ridiculous charges against Terry seriously. He had stuck it out, refusing to leave under a cloud.

Billy's words came back to him as he stared at the screen. He had dismissed them as a typical punk's taunts, not taking them seriously enough to even think about them beyond wondering where the man had gotten the crazy idea. Colter knew his own reputation on the street, and it wasn't ego that made him believe that no one who knew him would swallow that crap. Yet here, veiled in department double-talk, was that same insinuation. And he knew damned well it hadn't been there before.

He was tempted to go find Dave now, but realized he'd better get this done while he had the chance; he could ask about this particular bad joke later. He hit the keys to call up the criminal inquiry and typed in Sherwood's name.

The screen went blank, then spit out a string of numbers and a rather rude "Unauthorized Request." He blinked and tried again. On the third try, he stopped, studying the machine for a moment, thinking.

He tried another name, a flunkey of Sherwood's he'd arrested a few times. The data popped up nicely, including Sherwood's name under "Associates." He hit more keys, trying this back door to get the file he wanted.

A short beep, then the same results as before. He was locked out. Yet Dave hadn't said anything and had been able to pull up the file the other day without a problem. And if the system password had been changed, he wouldn't have been able to pull up anything else, either.

Quickly, he tried several other names, digging back into memories he'd put in mothballs. They all showed up, nice and complete, leaving only one answer. It was only Sherwood's file that had been locked out. And it had to have been done after he'd been here the first time.

Damn, he thought, he should have paid more attention at that computer class they'd given when they installed this system. There had to be a way to get to that file. Or at least to find out who had locked it up. He tried to call it up again, then stared at the string of numbers on the screen. Was that a date? The date the file was sealed, maybe? No, that was the terminal number, he realized with a self-deprecating laugh. A computer whiz, you're not, Colter.

Then he stared at another set of numbers, just before the abrupt denial of access. If that were a date, it would be the day after he had arrived here. Coincidence? He shook his head sharply. Hell, you don't even know if that's what it is, he told himself wryly.

He stared at the unhelpful screen for a few minutes, then idly tapped a few more keys. The booking records appeared, and he began scanning them, not certain what he was looking for. He went back, then further back, memories tugging at him as he began to hit some familiar names. It gave him a funny feeling the first time he hit his own name as the arresting officer, and he stared at it for a moment. Then with a rueful chuckle, he started to run forward again.

He had to admit Grissom had, as Dave had said, made a lot of arrests. Small amounts, true, the biggest being a couple of kilos and a bust of a small lab on the south side, but they had been fairly regular. Some of the names he knew, some were only vaguely familiar, and there were a few Colter didn't know at all.

And probably not a year of jail time done amongst them, he noticed glumly. Great system. The dispositions on those cases all looked alike, credit for time served or charges pleaded down to a lesser charge. Crazy. His brow furrowed. More than just crazy, he thought. And something else—

"You done yet, man?" Dave's voice came anxiously from the doorway. "The brass is out of that meeting."

Colter sighed but reached over and shut down the machine. Dave breathed a sigh of relief.

"Did you find anything?"

"Nope. Except that Sherwood's file's been deleted."

"What?"

"No access."

"That's weird. We just looked at it."

"I know. When did you see it last before that?"

"Not too long ago. When Summer first came to me."

"So it's been locked out since I got here. Who has authority to do that? Or," Colter added, remembering his own file, "change an existing file?"

Dave shrugged. "Same as when you were here. Brass only."

Colter considered that for a moment.

"You know," Dave said, "there wasn't much in there the last time I looked at it that wasn't already in your stuff. Hasn't been much on him since you left." He grinned crookedly. "Been keeping his nose clean, Mr. Sherwood has."

"I doubt that," Colter said wryly.

"Yeah." Dave contemplated him for a minute. "You're not dropping this, are you?"

"You think I should?"

Dave's eyes flicked to Colter's blackened eye. It was better now, not swollen shut any more, although it still looked terrible. Dave had winced at his first sight of his friend; he grimaced now.

"Somebody thinks you should."

"Maybe. Maybe somebody just doesn't like me."

Dave laughed. "Hard to believe. You made so many friends."

They heard a loud, disdainful voice chastising some poor soul in the outer office; both of them recognized it immediately.

"I'm outta here," Colter said hastily, knowing the last thing his friend needed was to explain what he was doing here. "Thanks, Dave."

Dave nodded and kept a wary eye out as Colter slipped through the back door. Then he reached for the stack of reports on the desk and tried to look as if he'd been buried in them for hours.

Summer looked over at Colter as he drove. He was moving much more easily. Although he still winced now and then when a too-quick move tugged on still-sore muscles or skin, the lines grooved into his tanned face by pain were easing.

Those lines had been nearly gone last night while he slept. When she had realized he had dozed off, she had dropped her knitting in her lap to watch him. With his hair tumbled over his forehead and his mouth softened in sleep, he had looked for all the world like a mischievous little boy who'd gotten into a fight and gotten a black eye.

When he had shifted, murmuring something in his sleep, she had been unable to resist the powerful urge to go to him. She had sat on the edge of the sofa, at last giving in to the need to brush that thick, errant lock of hair back off his forehead. And then a stronger urge overtook her, one she didn't even try to fight, and she bent to press a soft kiss on his brow.

It had been a restless night for her, with long periods of wakefulness in which she tossed and turned while trying to understand what was happening to her. She'd never felt anything like this constant awareness, the feeling she had of always being strung taut, of always being on the edge of something, although she didn't know what.

She'd been surprised when she'd gotten up to find him gone, but even more surprised when she saw his note. She'd recognized the bold scrawl immediately and was touched that he'd bothered; he'd told her once that having to report his comings and goings to the department had used up his supply of dutiful accounting for his whereabouts.

Colter had arrived home just when he'd said; the small brass clock on the mantle was chiming the noon hour when she heard the car. He'd helped her fix a quick lunch, said nothing about what he'd done all morning, then told her what he wanted to do this afternoon.

Colter hadn't been able to explain why he wanted to go see Mr. Webster again. He hadn't really tried; he was afraid it would come out as simply not knowing what else to do. He knew he'd struck some kind of nerve somewhere—he had the now-purple eye to tell him that—but he didn't know where. Or whose nerve it was. And he didn't quite know how to find out, except to keep going. And wait. And that, as it always had been, was the hardest part.

At least going to the shelter would keep his mind occupied, he thought, although keeping his mind off Summer when she was right there beside him in the car was an impossibility. Don't kid yourself, Colter, he thought wryly. It doesn't matter if you're here with her or clear across the country, you can't stop thinking about her.

At the shelter, they found Albert on the porch again.

"You want to go through it all again?" Albert asked, a little testily.

"I know," Colter said patiently. "And I can't explain why. Something just feels wrong."

"Some of that police instinct stuff that the sergeant talked about at the hearing?"

"Sort of."

"Hmph." It was an eloquent snort of disdain.

"I know it's hard to believe—"

"What's hard to believe," Albert Webster cut in dryly, "is that that pompous windbag has any of it."

Colter stared at him and Summer stifled a giggle.

"Albert," she said with a broad wink, "I always knew you never missed a trick."

"Hmph," the old man said again, but his lively eyes glowed with pleasure. "I've seen a lot of men full of their own importance in my life, girl, but never one with as little reason as that man."

"He's not my favorite person, either," Colter said with a grin.

"And you're not someone else's, are you now?" Albert eyed Colter's face speculatively. "You hit a nerve somewhere, son?"

Colter's grin widened as the old man gave his own words back to him. "Guess so," he agreed. "Now, if I could just figure out whose...."

"Well, 'fraid I can't help you with that."

"You can help, though."

"All right," Albert said, "if you think it will do any good."

Summer had thought she would dread hearing it all again, but somehow, it wasn't as painful this time. Perhaps it was knowing Colter believed the old man, or that he had already made progress, although painful. Or maybe it was just Colter's presence that had soothed her, made her look at things differently.

She sensed rather than heard Colter smother a sigh when Albert had finished; nothing different had come out of this account of what he had seen that night. He leaned back in the deck chair, lifting one leg to rest his ankle on his other knee. She saw his hand come up, the knuckles still red and raw, to run over his hair. She felt a little rush of warmth as she remembered what the heavy silk of his hair had felt like slipping between her fingers.

"So," Colter said wearily, "he came out of nowhere that night, dropped back into oblivion, and now he's back again."

"Well, I wouldn't say that."

Colter's hand stopped. "Wouldn't say what?"

"That he came out of nowhere."

Colter stared at the older man. "He didn't?"

"Heck no. Saw him around a lot before that night."

Colter's feet hit the deck with a sharp thud as he leaned forward. "You did? Before the shooting? You never said so."

"Nobody ever asked."

It was so simple an answer, Colter had to smile. "Okay. I'm asking now."

"Not much more to say. Saw him around all the time, that's all. Daytime, nighttime. Wasn't drivin' a limousine then, though. Always on the street. Saw him from my window, coming and going at all hours. Didn't look then like he did that night, either."

Colter's brow creased. "He didn't?" he asked carefully.

"Nope. Had a beard then. And a moustache, one of those long ones, handlebars they called 'em in my day."

"You're sure?"

"'Course I am. Take more than shavin' some extra hair to fool me."

And once again, as he and Summer drove back to the house in the rain that had suddenly begun, Colter found himself believing the old man. He didn't know what it meant, but it gave him something else to work with.

Summer could feel the new tension in Colter; she could practically see it crackling around him. She doubted if he even tasted the dinner they'd had, and he'd attacked the clean up with a lot more energy than it needed.

In the living room, he was restless, sitting down only to rise a few minutes later and cross to the window to stare out at the rain. Then he would sit again, then up and over to the fireplace where he had built a roaring blaze to jab at it with the poker. Then back to the chair, where he would sit for a few minutes before starting the cycle over again.

He was acting, Summer realized with a growing dread, as Terry had while wrapped up on a big case. It had enveloped him; he had eaten, slept and breathed the case until it was over, until there was no room for anything else. Only where Terry had been a bundle of barely suppressed excitement, Colter reminded her of a caged tiger, restrained only until the door opened and that coiled, suppressed power would erupt.

Without warning, an image of him lounging in total relaxation under a palm tree, on a white beach beside crystal water formed in her mind with relentless clarity. Distress flooded her; what had she done to him? Her throat tightened until she couldn't swallow, couldn't even breathe.

She couldn't bear it. All he'd wanted was the peace he'd earned, and she had destroyed it. He'd always been so good to her, and now she'd done this to him. Her anguish got all mixed up with the crazy feelings she'd been having lately, bubbling up inside her until she ached with the pressure.

Colter turned away from the window and started back. There were too damn many pieces, he thought. Why had the man risked coming back? Who had that money really been meant for? What had really been behind Billy's—

He stopped dead. "Summer?"

She made a furtive swipe at her cheeks, but it was too late; he'd already seen the sheen of tears. He knelt beside her chair.

"Summer?" he said again, softly.

She made a small, choked sound and shook her head. He reached out and grabbed her hands, nudging aside the knitting needles and yarn that lay in her lap.

"What is it?"

She shook her head again, but in the flickering firelight, he saw the glistening track of a fresh tear and tightened his hands around hers.

"Summer, please, talk to me."

Her hands drew into hard little fists beneath his, and he felt a tremor go through her. "I . . ." She swallowed, then tried again. "I wish I'd never gone to you."

He stiffened. It stung as much now as it had the first time she'd said it. He released her hands and sat back on his heels. He looked away from those clenched hands, a long, weary breath escaping as he felt his only chance slipping through his fingers. Hell, he told himself coldly, you never really had a chance.

"I'm sorry," he said stiffly. "I never meant to bother you. I tried. I really did, but I—" He paused, shaking his head. "I never should have stayed here. I should have known."

She stared at him, puzzlement having stopped her tears. "What—what do you mean?"

Her confusion was unmistakable. His brow furrowed. "What did *you* mean?"

"I . . . That I hate what this has done to you. It's bad enough that you got hurt, but . . . it's changed you, wound you up until it's like you never left." Her eyes brimmed again, the tears threatening to spill over. She blinked rapidly. "I never meant for that to happen. Not to you."

He reached for her hands again, feeling somehow that this was very important, that he had to ask the right question and that the answer could change his life.

"Why, Summer? Why does it matter so much?"

She choked back a sob but held his gaze. "Because you matter so much," she whispered.

"Oh, God," he groaned, standing up and pulling her with him in one smooth, urgent motion.

Summer went into his arms unhesitatingly, eagerly, seeking the haven she had only found in their strong warmth. That long ago Saint Patrick's Day, that day of the whales and the long, hard days before he'd gone. . . . It was here that she'd felt safe, felt understood, felt as though there was something still to hope for in the world.

His head bent over her, and she felt his lips press against her hair. It sent a quivering little bolt of feeling through her, but it wasn't enough. She wanted those full, warm lips on her skin, on her mouth, on her body. . . .

With an electric snap of shock, she realized that that was exactly what she wanted. She wanted him to touch her, she wanted to touch him, she wanted to know every inch of that golden body she'd seen, and then she wanted to explore every inch she hadn't seen.

Heat flooded her like a dam bursting and she reeled under the force of it. She hadn't felt the slightest flickering of desire for any man for so long, it was as if she had been saving it, all this time, for this moment, for this man.

Then his mouth was on hers and she knew the burst of heat she'd felt had only been the beginning, a pale precursor of what he was capable of causing in her.

His lips rocked over hers, coaxing, urging, while his arms held her tightly against him. As great as the heat rising in her was, it was dwarfed by the answering fire of his big, hard body. Being pulled against his muscled chest was like touching a wall that held back an inferno; it was hot and hard and solid, but never without the knowledge that that inferno could blaze free at any second. A tiny, throaty sound escaped her and his arms tightened around her.

His tongue crept out to flicker gently, suggestively over her lips. She recognized the silent question and responded to it instantly, uncontrollably. Her lips parted, giving him access, and she was pressed so close, she felt the groan that rumbled up from his chest before she heard it. Then his tongue was stroking, caressing, tasting, and all she could hear was the pounding of her blood in her ears.

He tasted her lips, then pushed past them, sending steady, pulsing beats of rippling heat and sensation through her in time with the rapid thump of her heart. He ran the probing tip of his tongue over the even curve of her teeth, then past that slight barrier, and she moaned low and deep in her throat.

Unconsciously, she arched against him, knowing only that the solid heat of his chest was the only thing that eased the aching of her breasts. The movement rubbed her already-tingling nipples against him and a gasp of surprised pleasure broke from her.

She was whirling out of control, and she didn't understand. How could she be feeling like this, feeling this much, when all they'd done was kiss? Her bones were melting, her muscles liquefying into some golden, flowing mass, and he'd barely touched her.

She'd long passed the pleasant, floating sensations that had been the height of her past experience; *pleasant* was much too tame a word for this. This was fire, this was soaring, this was…this was killing her, and she didn't, couldn't care. She lifted her arms to lock them around his neck, knowing that if she didn't, she was going to slide to the floor in a puddle of boneless, quivering jelly.

She twisted sinuously in his arms, wanting, needing more of his fire, more of that solid, masculine feel of him. Her fingers tangled sensuously in the thick, shaggy silk of the hair at his nape. A harsh, throttled groan ripped from him, and his tongue suddenly plunged deep and hot into the depths of her mouth. Sweet, shimmering fire swept through her and without thought, she lifted her tongue to meet his, never expecting the blast of wildfire that took her at the first mating of their mutual wet heat.

She made a tiny sound of protest when at last he tore his mouth from hers, but it ended in a moan as he trailed hot little kisses over the curve of her jaw and down one side of her throat. His hands had slid up her slender rib cage to hold her steady, stopping with a convulsive little jerk when they reached the outer curves of her breasts.

He shuddered, his lips pressed to the hollow of her neck where her pulse leapt beneath his touch, his fingers quivering against her tender flesh. She didn't know if it was because he was trying to make them move or to stop them, and she no longer cared. Feeling his hands on her had become the single most important thing in her life, and when she moved again, it was to twist her body so that the full curve of her breast molded itself into his hand through her thin T-shirt.

She heard his choked cry, but it was the last thing she heard. His strong, gentle fingers had found her nipple, stroking and teasing it until she was gasping at the stunning pleasure of it, and all her other senses seemed to fade away. When his other hand moved and found the other taut, begging peak, paying it equal attention, she sagged against him, letting her head loll back, both in sudden weakness and because the movement offered her breasts to him more completely.

She trembled, shocked at how her entire being could be reduced to the twin points of fire beneath his hands and the growing, throbbing ache between her thighs. How could she feel so hot, so swollen, and yet so empty?

The answer came to her suddenly when, as she went even limper beneath his tugging caress of her nipples, her lower body pressed harder against his and she felt the full, rigid heat of him against her.

Yes, she thought blindly, caught up in the swirling firestorm of heat and sensation, that was the answer to the hollowness inside her. He could end it, could fill her with his strength, his heat, his essence. He could make her whole as she'd never been before. She lifted herself, arching into that ready male flesh, wanting, needing. She felt him shudder violently and an echoing thrill rippled through her.

"Summer," he said hoarsely, "stop me. Now."

She murmured in protest and the negative little sound sent a tremor through him again. He buried his face in the curve of her shoulder.

"Got to," he gasped against silken skin.

She withdrew her hands from the tousled hair and gripped his shoulders for the support her wobbly legs could no longer provide. "Why?"

Her voice was low and husky and sent a shiver of sensation racing down his spine so strong that every muscle in his body tensed in response, as if it were a physical touch. He tried to remember her question and the answer that he'd had so ready a moment ago.

"Because..." he choked out. "Because..." Why? What reason on earth could be important enough to forego this soaring, searing pleasure? He knew there was one, but...

"Terry," he said suddenly, desperately. She still loved Terry.

It was as if he'd dropped her into the Sound in January. The shock of her sudden chill, of the sudden removal of all her light and heat, left him shivering. And convinced he was right. She didn't want him, not really. All it had taken was the reminder of Terry to make her pull away from him.

He could see her shaking as she raised her eyes to his. There was a flat, dead look in them, unlike anything he'd ever seen there before, even in the grimmest days they'd been through. It made him even colder, this time from a frost that came from within, as if seeing her look like that had frozen his soul.

"Terry is dead." Her voice matched that look in her eyes, icy, flat. "Perhaps I should have climbed into that grave after him. That's where you seem to think I should be."

Without another word, she turned and walked straight out the front door into the rainy night.

Chapter 10

Colter stared after her. What the hell had that meant? He sucked in a deep breath, trying to beat down his surging senses, none of which understood what had happened. Hell, *he* didn't understand what had happened. Those last cryptic words had thrown him a curve.

He'd thought he understood. He'd thought it was the memory of Terry that had brought things to a painful halt. He'd tried to do the right thing, which meant not doing what his body, his mind, his entire being was screaming to do— make hot, sweet love to her. But somehow, he'd wound up hurting her. And badly; even in the worst days after Terry's death, those normally vivid green eyes had never looked like that.

And she was out there in the rain, hurting for reasons he didn't understand, while he stood here like an idiot. Suddenly galvanized, he raced to the door.

A blast of cool rain hit him in the face as he stepped outside, and he was surprised it didn't sizzle on his overheated skin. She had lit a fire in him that surpassed anything he'd ever dreamed of even in his most vivid imaginings, and they'd been pretty vivid over the past five years.

He looked around, searching the wet darkness for any sign of her. Where would she go? God, she'd be soaked in minutes out here, and even though it was summer, it wasn't warm enough to be running around on a rainy night in only jeans and a T-shirt.

He headed toward the road, thinking she might have gone across to Mrs. Harper's. But the house across the narrow lane was dark, not even a porch light on, and he stopped before crossing the wet strip of pavement.

He turned away from the road, looking back at the house. The light spilling from the windows made it seem like the warmest of havens in this dark, wet world. But he knew it was empty without her presence, that whatever warmth this place held for him was in her. That whatever warmth the world held for him was in her.

He realized it suddenly, standing there in the rain. He had kept a careful distance between them when he'd been here before; distance and Terry hadn't been enough. He had put a continent between them, and it wasn't enough. And now, after all this time, Terry's memory wasn't enough.

He had told himself he'd come back for Terry, to finish what he should have done long ago, to prove his friend's innocence. And he'd meant to do it. He still meant to do it. But he could no longer kid himself about the real reason. He had come back for her. To find out if she still had that same, incredible power over him. What Colter had found was that the pull she had exerted on him before had been a mere tug compared to the magnetic force she had now.

And in that moment, with the Washington rain pouring down his neck, he knew he couldn't fight that pull any longer. If she told him to go to hell, he would live with it, but he couldn't live in this limbo anymore.

He turned up the collar of his shirt, although it was so wet already, he didn't think it would do much good. The cotton cloth clung to him, as did strands of his hair, forming paths for little streams of water. He thought of Summer's fingers running through his hair, of the tiny sounds she'd made when he was kissing her, and a blast of inner heat beat off some of the chill.

On a sudden impulse, he headed for the small grove of trees that the window seat faced, recalling that she had once talked of sitting out there when she wanted to think or just wanted to savor the clean scent of the cedar and pine.

He found her huddled under the largest of the trees, her knees drawn up in front of her, encircled by her arms. Her head was down, resting on her knees, her face hidden. She seemed oblivious to the rain that was pouring over her even in the shelter of the trees, darkening her hair, wetting it until it clung to the delicate line of her head like drenched silk. He dropped to his knees beside her.

"Summer, come in. You're soaked."

She didn't react. He put a hand on her shoulder and felt her shiver. She pulled away from him.

"Please," he urged, "you're freezing."

She made an odd sound, a choking kind of laugh. "Isn't that what I'm supposed to be? Frozen? In cold storage?"

She wasn't making any sense, but he couldn't worry about that now. He had to get her inside where it was warm. He reached for her again and she recoiled.

"Summer, please. I didn't mean to—" He broke off as another shiver, more violent this time, rippled through her. "Look, whatever it is, whatever I did, can we talk about it inside? You'll get sick if you keep sitting out here."

She looked at him then, her eyes going over him as he knelt beside her, rain streaming over him. It seemed as if she could see, even in the dark, the golden sleekness of his skin where his soaked shirt clung to him. The bruise around his left eye looked like merely another shadow, but she didn't notice. All she could see was the concern that marked his face, carving lines in the tanned skin almost as deep as those his pain had. And suddenly, her anger died away.

It wasn't his fault, she thought tiredly. He couldn't know what he'd done to her, that he'd made her feel things she hadn't known she was capable of, long for things she'd never had. He'd made her feel alive again. He'd made her forget everything, including the ghost that stood between them. But he'd remembered. He'd remembered and he'd stopped.

Whatever he'd felt, it hadn't been enough to make him forget. If she wanted out of this deep freeze she seemed to be in, if she wanted to break free of the shadows of Terry's memory, she was going to have to do it without Colter. But no one except Colter made her want to come out, she thought with a smothered little sob.

Colter saw her shoulders sag and it tore at him. He still wasn't sure what had set her off, but he couldn't bear to see her like this. He reached for her, expecting her to push him away again, but unable to stop himself. She didn't move, didn't speak, and he gathered her into his arms and lifted her.

He carried her inside, expecting at any moment to be told to put her down and leave her alone. The words didn't come. He kicked the door shut behind them with his foot, not daring to release her while she was so quiescent. Trying not to think about how she felt in his arms, he went all the way into the small bathroom before he gently set her down and reached for a towel.

He dried her face, then ran the towel over her sopping hair. She just stood there, numbly, her eyes fixed straight ahead, as if she wasn't even aware of what was happening. He forced himself not to look at how the thin cotton T-shirt she wore, drenched now, clung to every lush curve, outlining the lace edge of her bra. He tore his eyes away from the taut thrust of her nipples, ordering his mind not to think of how they had felt against his hands, his chest.

"You'd better get out of those wet clothes," he said, his voice gruff as he tried to keep it steady. He draped the towel around her shoulders and backed up hastily. He left the room before he surrendered to the overwhelming urge to get her out of those wet clothes himself.

Summer sank down on the edge of the tub, unable to control her trembling now that he'd gone. She sat there for a long time, her arms wrapped around herself until at last, the tremors eased. Then she got up, tugging off her wet clothes and tossing them over the shower rod. She reached for the terry cloth robe that hung on the back of the door and wrapped it around her.

She wanted to creep unnoticed into her room and shut the door. But she owed him something and she couldn't leave things like this. She glanced toward his door; the room was open and dark. Steeling herself, she made her feet turn toward the living room.

He was sitting cross-legged before the hearth, his elbows resting on his knees as he stared into the flames. He had changed out of his soaked clothes, putting on a pair of dry sweatpants that rode low on his hips. He had run a comb through his wet hair, and she could see the golden gleam where the heat from the fire had dried the surface layer to its streaky blond.

He hadn't put on a shirt, and the firelight flickered over him in rippling sheets, making the bruises on his body seem only part of the shadows. He looked like some kind of beautifully formed sculpture, steel dipped in gold, each powerful curve of muscle gilded with dancing light.

He was beautiful, she thought, her steps faltering. He was beautiful, and she was a fool. She was quiet, shy, with nothing to recommend her to someone like him. She was the meek little mouse Terry had always called her and no match for the potent likes of Shane Colter. She never had been.

She made herself cross the room. She was glad that he was on the floor; her legs were about to give way anyway. She dropped down a safe distance away. Not that any distance was safe, not when she had to contend with that broad expanse of naked chest.

He lifted his head, his eyes meeting hers. There was something odd in his gaze, something she'd never seen before, something she couldn't put a name to. It made her feel suddenly warm, warmer than the heat from the fire. And confused. She took a deep breath, trying to pull together the fraying threads of her composure.

"I'm sorry," she said stiffly.

His eyebrows went up. "For what?"

"For putting you in such an awkward position." She grimaced, but held his look. "I'm sorry I came on like . . . the proverbial lonely widow. I had no right to—"

"Summer."

He said it sharply, his body suddenly rigid, his turquoise eyes glowing with a new intentness as he looked at her. He had meant that decision he'd made out in the rain. He was through living in this limbo, through denying the truth of what he felt for her.

"Please. This isn't easy. Just let me finish." She took another quick breath. "I never meant to... I know you don't want..." She made a frustrated little sound. "I know you don't think of me like that...."

He was staring at her. That new, unknown look in his eyes had become a fierce glow and it made her falter.

"And just how do you think I think of you?"

It took her a moment to answer; that vibrant undertone in his voice disconcerted her as much as that look in his eyes. When she did, she couldn't seem to help the barest hint of bitterness that crept into her voice.

"I... Like everyone. I'm just... Terry's widow. I'm supposed to have buried my heart with him. I was Terry's wife, and now I'm his widow. Just an appendage, even now. You wouldn't even be here except for him."

The pain in her voice tore at Colter. He wanted to tell her, to explain why he had tried so hard to keep it that way, but his throat had closed up. As he had before, he saw her draw herself up, squaring her slender shoulders. His heart twisted at her quiet courage, the courage that had carried her through hell.

"I'm sorry," she said again. "I had no right to get angry at you. You can... have anyone you want. There's no reason you should want a... mouse."

A mouse. A memory of Terry referring to Summer as his "little mouse" came to Colter, and he winced, only now realizing how it must have sounded to her. He remembered the girl she'd been, the quiet girl who had held the promise of the woman she'd become. She'd fulfilled that promise beyond any expectation, and he ached inside because she didn't know it.

She was shifting uncomfortably, color staining her cheeks at his continued silence. Her distress helped him find his voice, although he had to swallow heavily past the lump in his throat before he could speak. He had just, finally, realized the implications of what she'd said. He'd realized she thought he didn't want her, but only now did he see that that wouldn't matter to her...unless she wanted him. The thought sent a heat that far outstripped that of the fire spiraling through him.

"You're wrong, Summer."

Her nervous movement stopped. "I...am?"

He wanted to tell her she was wrong about everything, about being a mouse, about how he thought of her and above all, about him wanting her. But he couldn't seem to find the words, not when she was sitting there glowing in the light of the fire, water from her hair beading on her silken skin. And especially when every nerve in his body was screaming with the knowledge that she was probably naked beneath the thick, fluffy robe.

"You are," he said thickly.

And then he reached for her, hauling her up hard against him, his mouth taking hers in a sudden, fierce rush. She made a small, startled sound, and he felt her stiffen. His mouth gentled, became coaxing, and his hands slid up to cup the sides of her face, his fingers tangling in the wet silk of her hair.

He felt the heat of battle begin to grow in him, the knowledge that he needed to go slow with her warring with the urgent need that had erupted in the first second his mouth had touched hers. His body's need for haste strained against his mind's awareness of the need for control, and his muscles ached with the conflict.

His tongue slid gently, teasingly over her lips, and he felt them part for him in the same instant her rigidness faded and she sagged against him. Slowly, he invaded that sweet warmth with his tongue, savoring the honey he'd only begun to taste before. When her tongue hesitantly rose to his, he shivered at the sensation. He felt her hands slide up his arms, felt her slender fingers digging into his bare shoulders, and the pressure released a current of heat that cascaded through him until it settled into a hot, pulsing river that jammed against the rigid barrier of his flesh, demanding release.

He ached with the pressure of it, the pressure of a body too many times aroused and too many times denied. He'd never known it could happen so fast, never known so fierce a need. He needed her more than he'd ever needed anyone or anything, more than he needed his next breath. All the years, all the long lonely nights haunted by her image boiled up inside him, making need a pitiful, tame word for the urgency he felt.

He couldn't control this, he thought wildly, he couldn't stop the wildfire she lit in him. But he had to. This wasn't some casual encounter, this was Summer. He had to slow down.

Summer felt the moment when he changed, felt the taut urgency replaced by a sweet tenderness she'd never known before. His hands slipped to her shoulders, his mouth left hers and trailed soft kisses down her neck to the hollow of her throat. A tiny sigh escaped her, carrying with it the last of her doubts. She couldn't think of them, not now, not when his mouth was on her, blazing those fiery paths.

The last sane remnant of her mind warned her, told her this was only for the moment, that her need and his had just happened to mesh at this point in time. It warned her that when it was over, nothing would have changed, she would still be Terry's widow, an extension of a man long dead, and he...he would still be Colter, strong and golden and utterly unattainable for someone like her. But none of it mattered next to the aching heat that was growing in her.

She felt his lips on the soft, tender skin below her collarbone, his hands sliding down her back to her waist, and she made a soft little sound as her fingers flexed convulsively. His skin was so sleek, so smooth, like hot satin. It would have seemed too smooth for a man had it not been stretched over rock-hard muscle spun in taut cords beneath that golden surface.

His head was bent to her, and she surrendered to the irresistible urge to thread her fingers once more through the damp, heavy strands of his hair. At least that's what she meant to do; instead, she found herself pressing the back of his head gently to hold his mouth against her body.

She heard a low groan rise from him, as if torn from him by this indication that she wanted more. His hands slid up from her waist, tracing her rib cage with tender strokes, pausing for half a heartbeat when he reached the outer curve of her breasts.

Summer knew that the small begging sound had come from her, but she hadn't been conscious of making it. All she knew was that she needed him to touch her, she needed to know if the feel of his hands on that soft flesh could truly turn her into such an aching mass of need. Then he moved, and she knew it was true.

Her back arched involuntarily. She wanted more of that sweet pressure, more of that loving touch. He groaned again, his mouth returning to crush hers once more, his tongue plunging deeply. She gasped, opening for him eagerly, welcoming that hot, probing touch as she welcomed the searching caress of his fingers as they found nipples that were already taut in anticipation.

Never had the thick cover of her robe been so unwelcome. Her cheeks heated when she realized that she was thinking of it only as a nuisance, a layer that was stopping her from feeling his hands on her naked flesh. She was seized with a sudden, wanton desire to bare her breasts to him, to beg him to continue that stroking caress without the heavy cloth between her tender flesh and the gentle touch of his strong, masculine hands.

She couldn't do it. She wanted it so badly, but the shy little mouse couldn't do it. But perhaps she could show him, she thought dimly through the golden haze of pleasure. She slid her hands down from his shoulders, her fingers stroking, sliding over his sleek skin with slow delight, amazed at how much pleasure she got from the feel of him.

She was careful to avoid the livid bruises, and she tried to ignore the stab of pain they gave her. She paused over the scattering of hair in the center of his chest, fingers tingling at the feel of that slightly rough patch after the slickness of his skin. Then her hands moved outward until she found the flat nubs of flesh she'd been seeking.

She heard his sharp exclamation as his mouth left hers for a gasping breath at the same moment she felt that small disk of flesh tighten under her touch. Her fingers stroked, caressed and finally tugged, her body heating violently at his response and at the thought of him returning that intimate caress.

"Oh, Summer!"

He moved urgently now, and her blood sang in triumph that he'd understood her unstated need. His hands slid beneath her robe, moving to cup the fullness of her breasts. She pressed herself into his hands, urging him on, and when his fingers found and caught her nipples, she cried out.

She was melting, turning into some hot, flowing liquid contained only by the boundaries of skin that had never been so tinglingly alive. And then his mouth came down on her, claiming the breasts he had teased into throbbing awareness, first one, then the other, his hot tongue flicking, circling the rigid peaks, and all boundaries, all limits, were forgotten. She had become that mass of pulsing need, a quivering bundle of heat and flame surrounding that hollow ache she'd never known before.

She arched in his arms, not even aware that she was lying on the thick rug in front of the fireplace now, knowing only that he was driving her mad. Her hands went to the back of his head, pressing him to her breast as she moaned low in her throat.

He growled against her breast, a low, harsh sound, and she felt his hands at the tie that belted her robe. Somewhere in the heat of his touch, the shy little mouse had been seared to ashes, and Summer wriggled to help him, conscious of nothing now but a driving need to feel his touch everywhere, on every inch of her naked, trembling body.

The robe fell away, was pushed aside and forgotten as quickly as the rest of his own clothing. Colter stared down at her, his chest rising and falling rapidly with the quick, harsh pants of his breath, his expression that of a man who had woken from a precious, treasured dream to find it real and within his grasp.

"Summer. Oh, Summer."

The moan came from deep within him, and it plucked at some answering chord deep within her. The flush that had spread over her at being naked before his heated gaze receded. When he moved again to skim his hands lightly over her slender body, she had the oddest feeling of security, of warmth and familiarity, a feeling she didn't understand. Then he came down beside her and pulled her into his arms, and nothing mattered except the fact that he was holding her.

And that was all he did for a moment. He held her, cradled her against his body, and for one shocked moment, she thought he was trembling. He was holding her as if she were fragile, some delicate, breakable thing that he'd never thought to hold. It made her feel so warm, so safe that she never wanted to leave his embrace. She'd never felt so cherished before, and no matter how sternly she told herself she was reading too much into his tender touch, she couldn't deny the feeling.

She twisted in his arms, trying to get closer. She heard a tight little gasp from him when her hips shifted, and she became suddenly aware of the hot, hard length of him pressing against her. She smothered a gasp of her own, a muffled little sound of pleasure. Her breasts felt heavy and swollen against his chest, the crests that were still wet from his mouth rising tautly to his heat. Then she moved her head and pressed her lips softly against his chest.

That slight touch galvanized him and he began to move again. He rained hot, sweet kisses down on her, moved his hands over her in smooth, caressing strokes. He was relentless, never stopping until she was writhing in his arms, little cries of pleasure rising from her at every touch.

Her hands grasped at his back as she strained upward to him. She was beyond worrying that she'd never felt anything like this, she was beyond caring that she was responding so fiercely; all she knew was she had to have more. Her hands slipped down the muscled contours of his back and narrow waist. Then with a boldness that would have stunned the little mouse she thought she was, she slid her hands down to the taut swell of his buttocks.

Her fingers flexed convulsively against the muscled curve, and an explosive burst of heat shot through her when he groaned in response. She had long ago left behind what experience she had; nothing in her life had prepared her for this, for how merely touching him made her feel.

She wanted to know every inch of him, every muscled curve, every flat, hard plane. Her fingers moved eagerly, over his back, down his sides, until she had returned to that tempting curve of muscle that seemed made for her hands to cup and hold.

He cupped her breasts, lifting them for his mouth once more, and she sucked in her breath as she awaited that fiery burst of sensation. It came in a fierce, rippling wave, sweeping through her, filling every part of her except that aching, empty hollow place that yearned for him.

Then his hands began to move again, stroking, sliding over her skin, leaving sizzling trails. His mouth slid over her, one breast to the other. One hand slid down her body and she felt the muscles deep in her abdomen ripple in an involuntary response to his touch. She couldn't help the moan that escaped her.

"Please," she gasped out, not even certain what she was asking for. Then his hand moved farther down, cupping her heat, and she knew it had been this. She was barely aware of parting her legs for him, of tilting her hips to give him access. When his probing fingers parted the golden curls to stroke her, she gasped at the new and exquisite sensations that blazed through her.

Had there been any sane part of her mind left functioning, it might have astonished her, this wanton response, but now, all she could do was feel. Only the incredible fact that it was Colter doing this to her, that it was Colter's hands, his mouth that was driving her to the brink of insanity, had the power to penetrate the thickening fog of pleasure.

She heard him groan as his fingers slid over her hot, slick flesh, and she felt a shudder ripple through him, as if the realization of how ready she was for him had overwhelmed him. He stroked her, caressing that exquisitely tender bit of flesh until she was writhing, arching her hips against his hand, then her breasts against his mouth. She was caught between an inferno and a conflagration, and when the two met, she was certain she'd be consumed. She didn't care, she couldn't care, not when she was soaring, flying higher than she'd ever gone, her body reaching for a peak she'd never thought possible.

He began a rhythmic, circular motion with his fingers, and her body responded with a fierceness so swift, she cried out at the power of it. With a sudden, convulsive movement, he raised himself over her, his mouth darting to hers almost desperately, and she felt the searing heat of his hardened, swollen flesh pressing urgently against her. Hot, demanding need boiled up inside her and her hands went around his waist, pulling him tighter against her.

When her hands slipped down to once more cup his buttocks, Colter let out a throttled groan and went rigid beneath her touch. With agonizing slowness, he lifted his head, bracing himself on his elbows, every muscle taut with the strain of holding himself still.

"Summer," he gasped, "I want to go slow, to wait, but I—"

"Don't wait." Her voice, low and husky, held a beseechingly eager note that ripped at what was left of his fragile control. "Not anymore. I've been waiting all my life to feel like this."

He groaned, a low, vibrant repetition of her name. And then he was moving, his hips shifting between her thighs, blunt, male flesh probing. At the first caressing touch of her slick heat, he shuddered. He knew he should be gentle, knew how long it had been for her, but how could he, when all he wanted to do was drive into her with all the force of years of longing? And then she whispered, throaty and feather light against his ear.

"Now," she pleaded, "please, I can't wait any—"

Her words broke off with a sharp, gasping cry of pleasure as his hips jerked forward, joining them with one long, hard stroke. A harsh, guttural cry broke from his lips as he buried himself in her, and his arms slipped beneath her, his hands curling back over her shoulders to brace her for the driving thrust.

He'd known in the long, dark nights when he'd dreamed of her, that making love with Summer would be unlike anything he'd ever done, ever felt before. What he hadn't known was that he would lose control so swiftly, so completely. He had never been so recklessly aroused, never been so helpless to stop himself.

He pulled back, hating the chill that touched the heated flesh he withdrew from her body, but needing more than anything to plunge into those satin depths once more. She made a small sound of protest, as if she felt the same regret, and as he slammed forward again, she rose to meet him, adding her own impetus to his force, and the driving collision sent the breath spinning out of both of them in a mutual gasp of pleasure.

He was careening recklessly, all restraints shattered, thrusting with a ferocious rhythm that echoed the pulsing, pounding currents of pleasure that were catapulting through him. He was barely aware of the sounds he made, deep, short cries of pleasure at the depth of every stroke. He didn't know how they roused Summer to an even fiercer need, he only knew that she was with him, her hips bucking beneath him, her own little cries urging him on, removing his fear that he was hurting her.

His grip on her slender shoulders tightened, holding her in place, bracing her to take the full length of his ever more powerful strokes. The sound of their bodies coming together echoed in his ears over the pounding of his blood and the snap of the fire.

Summer looked up at him, watched the firelight dance over his straining body, over the planes of his face taut with both need and pleasure. Whatever happened, she had this moment, and it was more than she'd ever had in her life. He was golden, he was beautiful and, for now, he was hers. Then he drove into her fiercely once again and she shuddered at the beautiful pressure, the wonderful fullness that had replaced that hollow ache. She marveled that he filled her so completely, stretching her eager body until she knew she could take no more, and yet, she could still feel herself clasping at that swollen male flesh.

"Summer!" The cry burst from him raggedly as he sheathed himself savagely in her once more. "No," he protested in an agonized voice, "not yet..."

She didn't understand, but then he slammed his hips forward, grinding flesh against flesh, arching into her, his head thrown back as her name again ripped from his throat, his face contorted with a pleasure so great, it was almost pain. Just the sight of him like that was enough to send her tumbling over the precipice, and she cried out his name as the convulsions took her.

She felt him freeze for one split second in surprise, whether from the sudden contraction of her body around his or the fact that she had called him Shane for the first time since he'd known her, she didn't know. Then, as a hoarse cry broke from him, he exploded within her, shudders racking his powerful body as he gave himself to her in boiling, throbbing pulses that seemed to go on and on.

The hot, seething pleasure seemed to build on itself, returning to her from him in waves until her body was convulsing in rhythm with his, her muscles rippling in fierce, helpless response. In the final seconds, she locked her legs around him, moaning his name over and over, her voice echoing with wonder and pleasure.

Feeling drained, weakened by the sweet fury of the most shattering climax of his life, Colter nuzzled the curve of her neck. His breath came in hot, quick pants against her skin; he couldn't tell if the hammering heart he was feeling was hers or his own. He knew he should move, that he was crushing her with his full weight, but he was clinging to the sweetness of their intimate contact.

When his pulse gradually slowed and he could breathe more slowly, he began to press a soft trail of kisses up to the delicate line of her jaw, then up to her temple. A sudden spurt of alarm seized him as he tasted a salty moisture and realized what it was. He jerked up to stare down at her.

"Summer?"

She sniffed, blinking rapidly to clear her eyes, biting her lip as if it would help hold back the rest of the brimming tears.

"Damn," he swore softly, "I hurt you, didn't I? I knew I was being too rough, I—"

He stopped when she lifted one slender finger to his lips.

"No," she whispered. "Oh, no, you didn't hurt me. I— it was just so beautiful...."

A sighing breath of relief escaped him. A soft smile curved his lips as he realized that the gleam in her eyes was of joy, not pain.

"You're beautiful," he murmured, bending to kiss away the last dampness from her tears.

"I feel...whole." She sniffed again and lowered her eyes. "For the first time in so long..."

He let out a choked little breath as he slid to his side, taking her with him and pulling her close against him. He shivered as he remembered the first moments of that rippling convulsion of her body, the last moments before his own world had gone spinning away. She had been so openly responsive, so sweetly hot in his arms, he didn't think he could ever again deny himself the pleasure of feeling her unravel at his touch.

She snuggled closer, the ebbing glow of the fire painting her with golden light as she laid her head on his shoulder. That trusting little movement stuck a chord deep inside him.

He wanted to tell her so many things; how he felt, how he'd always felt; how wrong Terry had been to call her a meek little mouse; how proud he was of the woman she'd become; and how sorry he was that he hadn't been here to see it. It didn't strike him as odd that he who had always kept himself apart, even from the women who had occasionally shared his bed, wanted to bare his soul to her; this was Summer, and all holds were off.

And he realized in the moment when he had admitted that much, that the reason he had held himself apart for so long was because of her, because even though she'd always been out of his reach, he wasn't willing to settle for less.

He wanted to tell her all of this, but before he could gather in the remnants of a sanity that had been scattered by the unbelievable, explosive sweetness of making love to her, before he could find the words to express what her generous giving had meant to him, he realized she had drifted into sleep.

He stared down at the semicircles of her lowered lashes. The quiet faith of surrendering to the vulnerability of sleep in his arms tugged at him in a way he'd never known before. He felt the protectiveness that had begun to grow in him ever since he'd begun to realize what her life had been like since—and now before—he'd left. It was combined with the sense of pride in her that he'd always had, even before he realized why. Pride at who and what she was and, now, at what she had become. Pride that she didn't need that protection, yet a warm satisfaction that she was accepting even this tiny bit of it.

He would tell her, he thought, in the morning. She needed rest now. He considered carrying her to her bed, but she was so tenderly nestled against him he couldn't bear to risk waking her. Being careful not to jostle her, he reached out with one arm and tugged at the afghan that lay on the couch. The one she had covered him with the other night.

He froze with his fingers clutching the soft thickness of the wool. It hadn't been a dream. She had kissed him. He knew it now as surely as he knew anything. She had wanted him even then. He'd been reading her wrong all along.

He pulled the cover over both of them, tucking it around her with gentle care. Then he settled down beside her, lifting one hand to smooth back from her forehead the hair that had been dried by the fire into a tousled mass of golden silk. He pressed his lips to the gleaming strands in a soft kiss, then shifted to pull her gently closer, tucking her into the curve of his body. She made a small murmuring sound of satisfaction and nuzzled his shoulder.

The smile that curved his mouth at that innocent action was only the outward sign of the warmth that spread through him. It matched the languorous contentment that had filled him, and the combination lulled him into a sleep that was, for the first time in longer than he could remember, not haunted by the image of the woman he held in his arms.

Later, when his sleep was disturbed, it was by a shyly gentle touch that made his heart soar. He couldn't quite believe that she had truly reached for him, that she was silently asking what she seemed to be asking. But when her fingers slid over his chest to tease the flat disks of his nipples, his body surged in answer to the question he was afraid to ask.

"Summer?" he whispered into the darkness.

She froze as if she hadn't known he was awake. He felt her begin to pull her hand back, but he moved his own to cover hers and hold it there.

"Do you want me again?" he asked softly. She made a tiny, embarrassed sound. "Because I want you, love," he said, moving his other hand to return the caress she'd given him. "Always."

He groaned as her nipple rose eagerly to his touch. His fingers toyed with the sensitive flesh, his body surging to painful fullness as it became a tight, hard bud beneath his fingers. And later, as they both trembled on the brink, she cried out his name again, the name he'd never heard from her before tonight. He grasped it like a physical thing and held it tight as he went hurtling into space.

The feel of Summer going suddenly rigid in his arms awoke him from a deep sleep. He shook his head groggily, aware from her stiff posture that something was radically wrong. He pried open eyes that were sticky with sleep, startled to be met with the full light of late morning. It wasn't until he sat up that he noticed that Summer, her eyes wide with shock, was staring past him at the chair she'd been sitting in last night. He twisted around to peer over his shoulder.

And looked straight into the cool, assessing eyes of Sam Sherwood.

Chapter 11

In that first stunned moment, all Colter could do was fight down the shock that he had slept through it. Talk about rusty, he thought bitterly. Sherwood and two of his trained gorillas had come in and made themselves at home, and Colter had never heard a thing, never been roused from his sated, Summer-drugged sleep.

Summer. His head whipped around, his eyes fastening on her pale face. She was clutching the afghan to her naked breasts, and he could see her trying to suppress small shudders of distaste as she stared at the two bodyguards, who were standing by the door, watching her with hot, avid eyes. A red, murderous rage erupted inside Colter, and it took every bit of his considerable will not to launch himself at the two leering men.

Then Summer's eyes shifted to him. Embarrassment and fear were both there, but beyond that, down in the light green depths, he saw a spark of anger. She was amazing, he thought. And a million miles from the shy mouse she thought she was.

That tiny flash of fire had the odd effect of cooling his own rage, enabling him to regain control. She would be all right, he thought, a new rush of pride filling him. He gave her a nod of reassurance before he turned back to the man in the chair. When Colter spoke, his voice was icy and his eyes were just as cold.

"Get them out of here."

One of the groomed black eyebrows rose.

"And why should I do that?"

"Because if you don't, you'll be dead before they get to me."

Colter's cool, implacable tone seemed to take the man aback. His dark eyes skimmed over Colter's naked, powerful body, only half-covered by the afghan, consideringly.

Don't doubt it, Summer told the man silently, Colter could do it. Apparently Sherwood reached the same conclusion.

"Which leaves the lady alone with them."

"Only if you decide their company is worth dying for."

There was a moment's pause, then Sherwood's stern expression broke as he laughed in delighted amusement.

"Oh, I've missed you, Colter! There's not a man on the force who's a challenge anymore!"

He glanced at his two bodyguards and jerked his head toward the door. Their eyes gleamed with resentment, but they went without question, only pausing for a last lascivious glance at Summer. Her head was high now, the spark of anger having caught and kindled, and she glared at them so furiously, their eyes widened in surprise.

God, I love her, Colter thought as she stared them down. She'd become everything he'd known she could be, and he was going to make damn sure before long that she knew it, too.

When the men had gone, her eyes flicked back to Colter's. He put every bit of reassurance and warmth and pride he could manage into his gaze, and he saw by the widening of her eyes that she understood. He glanced toward the robe they'd tossed aside last night, then back to her. She read his message, and with a dignity that belied her state of undress, she turned her back on Sherwood and picked up the discarded garment.

Slipping it on, she turned back in time to catch Sherwood's eyes on her. While his gaze was more appreciative than the luridly suggestive looks of his men, it fueled the already roaring fire of indignation in her.

"Can't get a girl of your own to look at, Mr. Sherwood?"

Sherwood's carefully groomed eyebrows shot upward in surprise, then down, as if a suitably tamed house pet had just turned on him. His startled gaze went to Colter, who hid his amusement at the man's discomfiture.

"That peek will cost you someday," Colter promised coolly.

Then he rose, kicking aside the tangled afghan, heedless of his nudity before the man who was, in his twisted way, one of the most powerful men in the metropolis of Seattle. Summer watched the muscles rippling under sleek skin, saw the barely leashed power, savored the tightly coiled grace of his movements as he went, without any evidence of haste, to pick up and pull on his sweatpants. The bruises that marked him were no longer signs of pain, but badges of honor. She was so proud of him in that moment that it made her eyes brim and nearly took her breath away.

"Perhaps, Mrs. O'Neil, you might make us some coffee?"

She turned on Sherwood, eyes flashing. "Off to the kitchen? Do you really think that's wise, Mr. Sherwood? Who knows what I might slip into your cup."

That startled look flashed across his face again; it was clear that had never occurred to him.

"Don't worry," Summer said in cool satisfaction at his reaction, "I have something much more painful in mind for you."

The surprise changed to delighted amusement once more, followed, as before, by the laugh. "Colter, I do believe you've found your match! Who could have known that beneath that exquisite-but-quiet exterior beats the heart of a wildcat?"

"I knew," Colter said quietly, his eyes fastened on Summer, willing her to understand everything he hadn't been able to tell her. Her look of puzzlement told him she didn't see it yet. But she would, he promised himself. And soon. No more writing yourself off as a shy little mouse, love, he told her retreating form as she went into the kitchen.

"I must say, Colter, this is one particular piece of information that my sources managed to miss. I had no idea you and the lovely widow were, er, involved."

"It seems your sources aren't infallible."

"Oh, but they are. That's why this is such a surprise." He looked at Colter speculatively. "Unless, of course, this is a recent development?"

Colter didn't think he reacted, but Sherwood had not gotten where he was without being perceptive.

"Ah, I see! Oh, dear, have I interrupted the new-found lovers? I'm so sorry. But how interesting! The ex-cop with his dead partner's widow? Fascinating. But it does, of course, lead to speculation on exactly how long this had been going on, doesn't it?"

Colter resisted the urge to bury his fist to the wrist in the man's silk-suited belly, knowing that it was exactly what the man wanted. He hadn't forgotten Sherwood's favorite technique of engaging his opponent's defenses elsewhere while he prepared his real strike. Reining in his anger, he managed a faintly bored tone.

"Cut to the chase, Sherwood. Why the hell are you here?"

The thin mouth smiled. "You never were much for the niceties, were you?"

"It seemed a pity to waste them," Colter said dryly.

Sherwood lifted a hand to smooth dark hair already slicked back as he chuckled. "I think that's what I always liked about you, Colter. You were never afraid of me. You always— Ah, that was quick, my dear."

Summer set down the steaming mug. "Instant," she said shortly. "Because that's how soon I want you out of here."

"My, my, she has grown teeth, hasn't she?" Sherwood reached for the cup.

"She always had them," Colter said. "She just didn't know it."

Summer stared at him, knowing from his tone and the way he looked at her that his words were meant more for her than for their uninvited, unwelcome guest.

"If you're here to find out if I got your message," Colter said, "I did."

He had taken a seat on the sofa, and somehow managed to look casually relaxed and poised to strike at the same time. Sherwood studied him for a moment, his eyes resting on the large, fading bruise that still colored his rib cage, then moving to the darkly shadowed flesh around his eye.

"I presume that is what you mean? I heard about your . . . little encounter."

Colter eyed him coolly. "I'm sure you did."

"I also heard you put two of your opponents in the hospital and sent another home in a cast."

Colter shrugged, hiding the fact that he didn't remember much after Billy had first begun pounding on him. Summer registered Sherwood's words with quiet satisfaction.

The man was polished, she thought, from head to toe. His head was covered with polished dark hair, his mustache shone as if polished, his immaculate fingernails looked buffed if not polished, even his skin looked polished. She'd seen only pictures of him before, but she'd known him in the first second she'd awakened to find his narrow little eyes on her.

"You hurting for manpower, Sherwood?" Colter asked sardonically. "A gutter rat is a little low, even for you."

"From you, I'll take that as a compliment." Sherwood leaned forward in the chair. "You may find this hard to believe, but I had nothing to do with that little contretemps."

"Oh?" Colter's voice was only mildly inquisitive, giving no indication that he had already heard that from Billy.

"Yes. And if Marx told you otherwise, he was lying."

So Sherwood knew it had been Billy Marx. The man's sources were, Colter thought, incredible. He wondered how much the man shelled out a month just to informers. Probably more than a cop makes in a year, he speculated sourly. "I see," he said, mildly enough. "And I suppose you have an excellent reason why I should believe you."

"Because I'm not a fool, Colter. And I know that that—" he indicated Colter's bruised side "—would never work. You're many things, Colter, but a coward is not among them."

Colter's expression never changed at the implied compliment, he just kept that cool, turquoise gaze on the man in the chair until he went on.

"If there's anything I learned about you during our, er, association, it was that threats only made you more... determined."

Colter knew what the other man was thinking. It had been Sherwood's attempts at intimidation that had driven him so hard to destroy the man's attempts to control the business owners in the whole neighborhood. His neighborhood, his beat. His people.

"I'm not a cop anymore," Colter said tentatively, thinking of Summer's words, studying the man's eyes for a reaction. "Maybe I've changed."

"If I believed that for a minute, Colter," Sherwood returned, his thin mustache twisting in a dark line as his mouth quirked wryly, "I'd offer you a job right now."

Surprise flicked across Colter's face. "You'd what?"

"I always said you were the kind of man I needed. Tough, strong, smart.... Unfortunately, you were also utterly incorruptible." He sighed regretfully. "I tried, remember?"

"Yes."

"Unfortunate," Sherwood repeated. "That core of unyielding, upstanding morality. Laudable, I'm sure, but useless for my purposes. No, however much I admire you, Colter, you're not the kind of man who would work for me. Too bad. We could have been an excellent team."

Colter's posture, his expression didn't change, but his voice was intent when he said, "My partner was the same kind of man."

"And look where it got him," Sherwood said, not denying the assertion. Colter sensed Summer go tense beside him, but his eyes never left Sherwood.

"You should know."

Sherwood drew himself up in the chair. All sign of the urbane, witty man disappeared, and into the dark eyes came a chilly hardness. This was the man who ran a huge criminal operation, whose evil tentacles spread into nearly every corner of one of the loveliest cities in America.

"All right," he said sharply. "Let's get down to it. I'm here because you've been shaking up the streets with a lot of questions, Colter. You're making my people nervous. They remember you."

There was no flattery in his tone, merely factuality. What an odd relationship, Summer thought, vaguely surprised that her mind was functioning at all. She should be terrified, she thought, with someone like Sherwood sitting in her living room, but somehow, she wasn't. She glanced at Colter, who hadn't said a word. He merely watched Sherwood, waiting.

"I don't need the aggravation, Colter. I run a very finely tuned organization, and you're messing up the balance. You've got my people on edge, jumping at shadows."

"And you want me to stop?"

Sherwood grimaced. "I know better. I know you won't, cop or not. But I also know that, unlike some of your former colleagues who just want a big arrest, you want the truth. You always did. So I'm going to do you a favor."

"Your favors are too expensive."

"This one's on the house. Because I don't like being used." His mouth twisted into a crooked smile. "Call it a token of my esteem."

"I'm flattered."

"Don't be." Something akin to admiration flickered in the narrow, dark eyes. "No one's ever faced me down and lived to tell about it, Colter. No one but you. I was almost sorry when I heard you'd quit." He looked suddenly thoughtful. "But I was more surprised that you left some things unfinished. I should have known you'd be back eventually."

"Oh?"

"To find the man who killed your partner."

Colter's eyebrows lifted at the placid tone. "That doesn't bother you?"

"No."

Colter sat back, watching Sherwood silently.

"I see that you understand the implications of that, so I won't waste your time. But I'm forgetting the favor I promised you."

Colter waited, still silent. A genuine grin creased Sherwood's face. "If you could bottle that cool and sell it, you'd be rich."

"You said something about not wasting my time."

After a short, appreciative chuckle, Sherwood's face became serious. "Yes. So I'll make this quick. You're hunting in the wrong field, my friend. You should be checking your own backyard."

Colter's eyes narrowed. "That's it?"

"You're the smart one. You'll figure it out."

Sherwood got up then, turning to bow to a startled Summer. "My apologies, Mrs. O'Neil, for any embarrassment or distress I may have inadvertently caused you. And may I say now how highly I have always thought of you, as well. You conducted yourself with great dignity during very trying times."

He walked around the chair and started toward the door. When he reached it, he paused with one hand on the knob and looked back.

"I like you, Colter. I always did. If you ever do get tired of the straight life, you come see me."

Colter grinned then, crookedly. "I'll do that, Sherwood."

Summer stared at the door after it had closed.

"What a . . . strange man," she murmured.

"He's different, all right." Colter shrugged, rather sheepishly. "And I have to admit, I kind of enjoyed going up against him. He's smart, shrewd and strong, and he doesn't make mistakes."

"What did he mean?"

"I'm not sure." Colter rubbed the back of his neck; he'd been much tenser during this confrontation than he'd shown. "But he's obviously not worried about my finding anything in his domain. Which means either he's sent the shooter to deep cover again or . . ."

As his voice trailed off, Summer's eyes widened. "Or the shooter's not . . . the shooter," she whispered.

Colter nodded slowly.

"But—"

"I know. That would make it a whole new ball game."

He got to his feet and walked to the window. The rain had stopped, and it was the crystalline kind of morning that made life in this frequently rainy place so special.

"He could have been driving the car," Colter mused. "I wouldn't put it past Sherwood."

Summer scrambled to her feet and joined him at the window. "Do you really think so?"

Colter sighed wearily. "I'm not sure what I think now." He chuckled grimly. "When I started beating the bushes, this is the last thing I expected to shake loose."

"'You should be checking your own backyard,'" she quoted softly.

"Yeah. Whatever the hell that means."

"Do you think he was telling the truth? That he didn't have anything to do with you getting hurt or...with Terry?"

"I don't know." Colter sighed. "He's always been pretty straight with me. Sounds crazy, I know, but since he knew I could never prove anything, he never bothered to lie much. He didn't have to."

"Colter?" she said suddenly, as something else came back to her.

"What?" He turned to face her as she looked up at him from beneath tangled bangs.

"When you said...Terry was the same kind of man..."

"I know. Sherwood as much as admitted I was right."

"But if he knows Terry was clean and if he was telling the truth that it wasn't his man..."

"Then we're really back to square one."

"But why now? Why didn't he come forward then if he didn't have anything to do with it?"

Colter ran a hand through his hair. "Hell, I don't know. Maybe he didn't want the heat just then. He could have had a big deal in the works. Or maybe he was involved, but not with Terry's murder." He sighed. "Or maybe the whole thing's just one big bluff."

"Do you really think so?"

"Honest? No. I'm not sure why, but no."

She nodded slowly, as if his words were confirmation enough. He stood looking down at her. This was not at all how he'd planned this morning. He'd wanted to wake her up slowly, with soft, sweet kisses all over her body. He'd wanted to make hot love to her until she came apart in his arms again. And then he'd wanted to tell her all the things he'd never said, make her see all the things she was, both to him and to herself.

But ugly reality had intruded on the peace of this morning, and he knew that all the things he wanted would have to wait. He smothered an inner sigh; he'd waited this long for her, he supposed he could wait a little longer.

It didn't surprise him that he thought of himself as still waiting, even after the passionate night they'd shared. It had never been just her body he'd wanted, even though it drove him mad, and last night had taught him things he'd never known were possible. He wanted her soul, her mind, that quick intelligence, that warm gentleness, that gallant spirit. He wanted all of her, and he wasn't going to settle for less. Somehow, he would get past the barriers, free them of the ghost that lingered between them.

And to do that, he'd better get to work. He had to figure out in a hurry what the hell Sherwood had meant. And if he'd been telling the truth. Because if he had been, it turned everything upside down. And that meant there was a whole lot of work to do—as soon as Colter figured out where to start.

The omelet Summer had fixed was delicious, full of cheese, ham and mushrooms, but Colter was having trouble doing it much justice. He made himself take another bite, savoring the flavor, but his mind was soon racing again, bouncing off all the different possibilities that Sherwood's visit had conjured up.

Summer was sitting across the table from him, pushing what was left of her own omelet around on the plate. She had said very little since Sherwood had gone, and Colter could have strangled the man for showing up at that particular time. They should have been able to spend this morning alone, together, in quiet discovery, answering all the personal questions that were hovering over them.

Instead, they were smothered in new questions, grim questions. All the things he wanted to tell her, all the things that were bursting to be said would have to wait; the tightness around her mouth told him this wasn't the time. He couldn't blame her. Their entire conception of what had happened to Terry had been shaken, and he was more than a little unsettled himself.

Colter set down his fork with a smothered sigh. He picked at the corner of the stack of papers on the table, the files he'd gone over so many times he had them nearly committed to memory. He felt as if the rug had been yanked from beneath him, and he didn't know where to begin.

Except, he thought wearily, to begin at the beginning. To start all over again. He flipped open the top folder. Maybe if he read it all again, from a new angle, with the assumption that the man Albert Webster had seen crouched over Terry's body had not been the actual triggerman...

He watched the pencil that had been tucked between the file and his scribbled notes roll away, only at the last second reaching out to catch it as it tumbled off the edge of the table. Quit putting it off, he ordered himself, twirling the pencil idly in his fingers.

He began to flip pages, wondering where to start. The original crime report, he supposed, and thumbed through the stack looking for it. When he found it and lifted it out, the copy of the artist's drawing, caught on a staple, came out with it, then drifted down to the table.

He stared at the face that had become so familiar, the face he'd spent endless hours looking for on the Seattle streets. The face that belonged to the man who'd killed his partner, his best friend. Or so he'd thought.

Tapping the pencil against the table, he made himself remember what Albert had told him the last time, rather than reread the transcript of his statement that was in the file. He remembered Albert talking about how he'd been walking home from his friend's tavern and had heard the commotion in the alley. He'd gone closer—gutsy for an old man,

Colter had always thought—and seen this man crouched over Terry's collapsed body.

"He ran for his car," Albert had said, "one of them fancy foreign jobs. It was still running, lights on and all. He skedaddled out of there like a bat out of hell. Pardon me, missy."

The last had been for Summer, who had given the old man an affectionate smile. Then Albert had gone on, saying that the man had, indeed, had a gun.

"Had it right there in his hand. I saw it, plain as day."

Colter remembered the day in the hearing room when Albert had been giving his deposition. He remembered the senior officer on the panel asking how he could be so sure of what he'd seen in that dark alley. Albert had stared down the questioning officer with disdain.

"Like I said, sonny, that car of his had the lights on. Lit it up like a stage. Think you can remember that?"

They had been very careful after that not to offend the old man's touchy dignity.

Colter stared down at the drawing. Had this man not been the one, after all? Had that been what Sherwood meant? Had he been so casual about Colter poking around because he knew, when the truth was finally unearthed, it would have no connection to him? But then Colter was faced with the question Summer had raised: Why now? And if not this man, who?

In disgust, the fingers that held the pencil flexed over the drawing. He barely managed to restrain the urge to scribble over the image on the paper. And then he was scribbling on it, or rather, drawing. He was far from an artist and he knew it, but nevertheless, he kept on, adding to the portrait with short, straight lines.

At last he stopped, dropping the pencil to the table and lifting the paper. He stared at it. Then he picked the pencil up once more, reversing it this time, and erasing some of the lines he'd added. Then he held it up again.

Summer watched him curiously. She had thought it idle doodling, an outlet for the frustration he must be feeling. That is, until she saw him erase part of what he'd done and stare at what was left intently. But before she could reach any new conclusion, he had glanced at his watch and gotten swiftly to his feet.

"Come on," he said peremptorily, folding the drawing up and slipping it into his pocket.

She looked startled. "Where are we going?"

"To see Albert."

She was puzzled, but he gave her no chance to mull it over. She wondered if part of his haste to get her out of here was so she wouldn't dwell on how easily Sherwood and his men had breached her sanctuary, but he didn't give her time to ponder that, either. And in fact, she didn't really care; at least he wasn't leaving her behind.

She was in the passenger seat, watching him as he deftly maneuvered the car out of the narrow drive. She remembered what Terry had once told her about Colter being an instructor in the pursuit-driving course for all law enforcement agencies in the state. His reputation had been such that, before he'd quit, agencies all over the country were sending their people to him.

He drove now with a steady competence that made the stories Terry had told her, stories that had become legends among cops throughout the northwest, seem difficult to believe. Colter could have, Terry had said, made a hell of a lot more money as a stunt driver in Hollywood.

She wondered, with a little touch of pain, if there was anything Colter attempted that he didn't excel at. Not like you, she thought tiredly, who just manages to struggle through. She smothered a sigh, already knowing the answer to her silent question: whatever Shane Colter did, he did well. Very well.

It was the use of his first name in her thoughts, along with the sudden realization of the double entendre her words could have been had she been fool enough to say them out loud, that made her admit to herself that she had been clinging to these thoughts to avoid those more urgent, nagging ones that kept trying to rise up and batter her.

She turned her head to stare out the side window, afraid that if he looked at her, he couldn't help but read in her face the confused, muddled chaos of her emotions. Sweet, fiery memories of last night flooded her, making her blood heat and her breath quicken.

God, had she really been like that? Had she really been so wild, so frantic? Had she let him touch her in ways no one had, reveling in it? And had she truly, in the dark hours of the night, awakened him and begged him to begin again? Her cheeks flamed, her boldness seeming altogether too abandoned in the light of day. But he hadn't seemed to mind then.

Whatever she would have said to him this morning, or what he might have said to her she would never know. She felt as if the most important event in her life had been put on hold, as if it were hovering over her, undecided and unresolved.

Had it just been a matter of mutual need, happening to catch the both of them off guard at the same time? She'd been alone for so long. . . .

No, it wasn't just that, she thought. She'd had to fight an embarrassing response to him since the first time Terry had brought him home. She remembered that night as vividly as anything in her life. Terry had been working for him for only a month, although she had heard nothing but Colter this and Colter that for weeks before. She had built up an image in her mind of a hard-boiled, hard-nosed cop, and then in had walked this tall, leanly muscled man with a crooked grin that did crazy things to her insides and the most incredible pair of eyes she'd ever seen.

She had immediately smothered her instant response and had refused in the months that followed to even acknowledge its existence. Just the thought of him somehow guessing humiliated her; how Shane Colter would laugh, thinking that Terry's little mouse of a wife found him attractive. She had succeeded in suppressing it until that day on the island when, as they watched a pod of cavorting whales, he had held her in his arms. And she had realized that Colter would never, ever laugh at her.

She'd never felt a warmth like she'd felt that day, never known anything like his silent but solid support. She'd had to acknowledge it then, but she had done it with a silent determination never to let it show. And she never had.

She doubted if she could do that now. Not when she knew the true extent of what she felt for him. Not when she knew what his touch could do to her. Not when he had shown her what it meant to be a woman, just as surely as he had shown her the true capacity of a man to be gentle and tender yet still take her soaring higher than she'd ever thought herself capable of going.

But what had it meant to him? Her eyes slid sideways to study his strong profile as he drove. Had it been as stunningly special to him as it had to her, or had it just been an encounter to relieve the pressure of a long-endured celibacy?

She swore, the oath no less furious for being silent. Of all days, why did Sherwood have to show up today? Why did he have to bring this cloud that now hung over them?

She jerked her head away with a sudden, shocked movement. When had this happened? When had her focus shifted so completely to where the need to vindicate Terry had taken a back seat to her feelings for Colter?

She had fought off the shock of realization, trying to think, to remember. It had started, she thought, when she had begun to realize what coming back here had done to him. When she had begun to see the relaxed, contented man she had found under a palm tree in the Florida sun turn once more into the wiredrawn, tightly wound cop he'd once been.

And now she knew that nothing mattered as much as what she'd unintentionally done to him. Nothing was more important because, somehow, he had become the most important thing in her life.

The flush that had colored her face faded before the chill that suddenly swept her. Oh, God, she thought, I've really done it. Her throat tightened and she swallowed heavily. I love him. God help me, I love him. What on earth do I do now?

"Summer?"

She looked up to see that they had pulled up in front of the shelter. She tried desperately to control her expression, and she avoided his eyes, knowing her discovery must show in hers.

"Are you all right?"

He sounded strained, a little awkward, as if he didn't feel comfortable talking to her anymore. Her heart quailed. Was he regretting it already? Had the passion-filled night that meant so much to her meant so little to him?

"Fine," she managed to get out.

"Summer—"

"I'm fine." She reached for the door handle and hastily yanked at it. "Let's find Mr. Webster."

They found Tim, the young attendant, first. He told them Mr. Webster had gone for a walk.

"He should be back soon, though. He's been feeling really good lately. Since about the time you started coming to see him, as a matter of fact." He eyed Summer meaningfully. "Of course, I can understand that."

Colter barely managed to hold back a snarling comment. His eyes narrowed as he glared at the younger man.

"Er, I've got to get going," Tim said hastily, taking a step back. "Got a family that just arrived I've got to get set up. See you later."

He turned and walked rapidly away, glancing back over his shoulder warily. His expression jerked Colter into an awareness that the jolt of anger that had shot through him had been jealousy and that it had shown. All the kid had done was look at Summer, make a teasingly flirtatious remark, and Colter had come off the wall at the man. He'd never done anything like that in his life. But he'd never had Summer to be jealous about before. And she was looking at him rather oddly, with an expression he couldn't quite figure out.

Ten minutes passed before Albert, his cheeks reddened and his eyes bright, returned from his walk. He greeted them effusively, and any trace of the vague, crotchety old man Colter had seen the first time he'd come here had vanished.

"You two are gettin' to be regulars here, aren't you?"

"It's your magnetic personality," Summer teased him gently. The old man scoffed, but looked pleased. After an exchange of greetings, he turned to Colter with a glint in his eyes.

"Now, what is it that I can do for you this time?"

Colter guessed that this feeling of being useful more than anything else had contributed to the older man's sudden resurgence of health and vigor. Summer had said something like that once before when they had been on their way here, about how awful it must be to feel as though you had no purpose in life anymore. She'd been right, Colter thought. She had, with the warmth and perception so inherent in her, understood and acknowledged what many people preferred to ignore.

"We need your help again," he said quietly, seeing the truth of his thoughts in the gleam in the lively eyes opposite him.

"You find that joker yet?"

An odd grimace crossed Colter's face. Then he reached into his pocket and drew out the drawing. He unfolded it and held it out to Albert.

"I don't know," he said softly, "did I?"

The older man studied the drawing. Summer moved to look over his shoulder, only then seeing what Colter had done to it. He had sketched in a rough, short beard and a full, flowing handlebar mustache. After a minute, Albert nodded.

"That's him, all right. Just what he used to look like. Beard kinda scraggly on the sides, but a real beaut of a 'stache."

Colter's jaw clenched and his eyes closed as if in pain. Then he whirled away from them, stalked over to the porch railing and slammed his fist down on it.

"Damn. Damn, damn, damn!"

Summer followed, her eyes wide with anxious distress. "Colter?"

"You know what I am?" he spat out. "An idiot." He slammed his fist down again. "A—" he spat out another curse, a word she'd never heard him use before "—idiot. It was right in front of my face all the time and I was too damned stupid to see it."

Summer stared at him. "What is it?"

He turned then, a bitter look on his face that she hadn't seen since the days after Terry's death.

"Him," he snapped, handing her the drawing that was crumpled from his fist.

She looked from it to his face, not understanding. "What about him?"

His eyes were bleak as he looked at her. "I know him."

Chapter 12

Summer stared at him in wide-eyed shock.

"What?"

"I arrested him once. Six, seven years ago. His name's Jimmy Ellis. He was running a shipment in for Sherwood." Colter swore again, violently. "Great. Just great, A damned beard and a stupid mustache, and I can't see past them."

Rage radiated off him, a fury so intense, Summer could feel it, and when she realized it was all directed at himself, it frightened her.

"Stop it," she said. "You couldn't have—"

"I damned well should have," he snapped. "I'm supposed to be a trained observer, remember?" He expelled a breath that was more snarl than anything else. "So trained, I can't see past the end of my own stupid nose."

"But he looks so different."

Colter turned back to the rail and slammed it again. "The eyes are the same. And the shape of his head and the nose. And I should have been looking for something like this, especially the beard to hide that off-center jaw of his." He laughed hollowly. "I carried that damn picture around for months, showed it to everybody I saw. But I never saw it myself.''

Hesitantly, Summer put a hand on his arm. It was rigid with tension. ''Maybe...you were too close to it. You wanted to find him so badly—''

''I was a cop!'' he said, cutting her off sharply, and jerked away from her. ''I was supposed to be uninvolved.''

Summer dropped her arm to her side. ''But Terry...he was your friend.'' Her voice was shaky in the face of Colter's wrath.

''And I spend all that time looking for a man I should have already known and then, when it might not matter anymore, I recognize him,'' Colter said bitterly.

''Why don't you just blow your brains out and get it over with?''

At the quiet, unexpected words, both of them whirled to face Albert Webster.

''What?'' Colter said, gaping at the old man who was looking at him with an expression of disgust.

''Makes as much sense as takin' it out on that little girl,'' Albert said, nodding toward Summer.

Colter's head snapped toward her. Her expression, the pain and worry in her wide green eyes, told him that he had been doing exactly that. Guilt flooded him, drowning his fury.

''God, Summer, I'm sorry.''

''It's all right.''

''No, it's not. I had no right to yell at you.''

''You weren't. You were yelling at yourself.''

He opened his mouth, then shut it again as he lowered his head in half-sheepish acknowledgment of the accuracy of her statement.

''I feel so damned stupid.''

''Even if you had recognized him, would it have mattered? You said Sherwood had probably sent him out of town until things cooled down. You couldn't have found him anyway.''

''Maybe not.''

''So,'' she said gently, ''if you want to chew yourself out for not recognizing him, fine, but don't add thinking you could have caught him on top of it. Especially since . . . he might not be the one anyway."

Colter stared at her, seeing the soft warmth in her eyes and hearing it in her voice. He lifted his hands to gently clasp her shoulders.

"You're incredible," he whispered.

"That's more like it," Albert said in satisfaction.

Summer blushed, and Colter cast the older man a crooked grin.

"Now, then," Albert began, eyeing Colter with interest, "what was that about him maybe not being the one?"

Colter hesitated, but decided the man had earned an explanation. Especially, he thought, considering what he was going to ask Albert to do. So he explained quickly, being careful to indicate that no one doubted what Albert had seen, but only the interpretation of it.

"Possible," the old man nodded when Colter had finished. "I didn't see the officer actually go down—sorry, missy—" This to Summer, who nodded steadily enough. "Only the man crouched over him. But with that gun . . ."

"I know," Colter said. "And he may be the one. This might just be a smoke screen."

Albert grinned suddenly. "You rattle some cages, boy?"

"So it seems," Colter admitted with an answering grin.

"Good," Albert said briskly. "Now, what's next?"

It was going to be easier than he'd thought, Colter observed silently, his smile widening. "That depends on whether or not you'll help again."

The lively, bright eyes lit up. "Well, I just might be persuaded."

"Good. Feel like going for a ride?"

"You bet, boy. Where to?"

Colter had been worried about Summer, but she seemed to be handling the situation well enough. He'd asked if she wanted to go home while he and Albert came here, but she'd quietly said no. He didn't think she'd ever been to this place, couldn't imagine her ever wanting to come here. He certainly didn't; the place made chills ripple up and down his spine.

In the days after Terry's death, he had come back here compulsively, staring at the bleak, dank walls rising around him, at the spot on the grimy pavement where Terry's life had leaked away, as if they could give him the answer to all the questions, as if they could tell him what had happened.

He glanced back at Summer. When they had pulled up at the curb, she had stared for a moment into the alley that was in shadow even on this bright afternoon. She had worn an expectant expression, as if she, too, had felt that this place had answers they'd been unable to find. Then she had let out a breath and had gotten out of the car.

She leaned against the fender close to the car door, managing deftly to make it seem as if she was there because she needed the support, not in case Albert needed help getting out of the back seat. She was more than incredible, Colter thought. She was...she was...she was Summer, he thought, and that said it all.

He watched Albert as he walked briskly, looking like the man Colter had known five years ago.

"This far enough?" he asked when he'd gotten almost to the corner. Colter nodded. He was aware of the odd looks they were getting, but ignored them.

"Just do exactly what you did that night," he called out to the old man. With a nod, Albert began to walk again, toward them this time. Colter had parked blocking the entrance to the alley, giving him a clear view of both the sidewalk and the alley itself. He lounged next to Summer against the fender of the car, his arms crossed casually, but he watched Albert intently.

"It was right here," Albert said, "when I heard the noise. I remember because of the grate." He gestured downward, where an iron grating extended across most of the sidewalk.

Colter nodded. "Then what?"

"I kept going. When I got to here—" Albert paused just short of the center of the alley entrance "—I looked. That's when I saw the car and the man with the gun." His eyes flicked to Summer, who was still leaning impassively against the fender of the rental car. "And missy's husband," Albert finished softly.

"How far down were they?" Colter's voice was matter-of-fact, helping to ease the tension.

"Just a ways. About by that Dumpster thing there." Albert pointed at the large metal container. "The car was parked facing out, lights shining right on them."

Colter nodded slowly. That was where Terry had been when he'd gotten there. The Dumpster screened a small part of the alley from view, but otherwise, it was wide open. He studied the scene for a moment, remembering that night with cruel vividness. He suppressed a shudder. It was as if it had just happened. Terry lying in his arms, choking his life away, his last thoughts for Summer.

Summer. His beloved wife. For Terry had loved her, Colter knew that, even if he had been a little lax about showing it sometimes. He remembered the moment when Terry had tried to talk, tried to say her name, although it came out painfully strangled. And he remembered the sickening moment when he realized that Terry had known how Colter felt about her. The image of Terry dying in the arms of the man he expected to go after his wife the moment he was buried rose up to beat at Colter.

And he'd done it. He'd waited five years, true, but did that really make it any different? Terry had died, and he'd moved in on Summer. She was alone and vulnerable, and he'd moved in like a vulture.

His stomach began to churn. How had he managed to forget? Hell, he knew how. He'd wanted her so badly, nothing else mattered. He'd ached for her for so long that he'd lost control like an infatuated kid. He'd forgotten everything except for his need of her. He'd been utterly, totally selfish, taking something that belonged to a man who couldn't defend it anymore. A man he'd once called friend.

Colter shook a head that was throbbing with a sudden, fierce ache. He'd expected this place to affect her, but instead, he was the one falling apart. All the reasons why he'd left, why he'd stayed away, had come rushing back, engulfing him in a tide of guilt and contrition that left him spinning.

He consciously tightened every muscle in his body, striving desperately for equilibrium. Think about what you're doing, damn it, he ordered himself fiercely. Use that cop instinct everybody was always saying you had.

He knew, as he tried to concentrate, that there was more to it than just words. It had developed somewhere along about his third year in law enforcement, that instinct that sometimes suggested, sometimes ordered and sometimes took him by the ear and dragged him kicking and screaming wherever it was that it wanted to go and he didn't. And it was usually, annoyingly right. Except, he thought sourly, when I should have been recognizing that clown.

"Come on, Colter, think," he muttered under his breath.

"What was that?" Albert asked from where he stood in the middle of the driveway that led to the alley.

In the middle.

Colter straightened up, covering the distance between them in two long strides.

"Why here, Albert?"

The old man looked puzzled. "What?"

"You said you came to this point before you looked down the alley. Why?"

"So I could see, of course."

Colter lifted his head. Then he walked to where the sidewalk met the asphalt of the alley and turned back so he was facing the same direction Albert had been. Then he turned toward the alley. And was greeted with a clear, unobstructed view. He looked back at Albert.

"It's a clear shot from here," he said slowly.

"Well, of course it is, now," Albert said in exasperation. "But with that big boat of a car parked there, you couldn't see a darned thing until you got to here."

"What car, Albert?" It was almost a whisper.

"Why, I just told you. There was this big, long, white car there, one of them Lincolns or Cadillacs or something. Had to walk around the front of the darn thing, it stuck out so far."

Colter stared at the older man. "You never said anything about it. Not at the hearing, not in your deposition."

"I told that first guy about it," Albert protested. "He said it wasn't important. That all they wanted to hear about was what went on back there." He gestured down the alley.

Summer was standing up straight now, staring at Colter as he walked over to Albert. A sudden tautness was evident in every stride, a tension so strong, she could sense it even from where she stood a few feet away.

"Albert," Colter said carefully, intently, "tell me exactly what you saw when you looked down there."

"I told you—"

"I mean *exactly*." He took the older man's elbow and guided him into the alley. The tension had spread to Summer as she moved to follow them.

"Where were they?"

Albert studied the place for a moment, then pointed to a spot just clear of the Dumpster. Colter's face tightened.

"That's not where . . . they found Terry."

Colter heard the tiny sound Summer made, but he didn't dare look away from Albert.

"I know," the old man explained patiently. "I moved him."

Colter sucked in a harsh breath. "You what?"

"I told that sergeant fella, I went to call for help, then I came back. The other man was gone then, and the officer was all twisted and his head was almost under that trash thing." Belatedly, Albert flashed an apologetic glance at Summer. "Seemed a shame just to leave him like that."

"So you . . . moved him?"

"Well," Albert began defensively, "I figured he'd been shot, so I didn't think it would hurt him any more. Them medical fellas would have had to move him, anyway."

Colter tried to regain his equanimity. After a moment, calmly enough in view of the inner chaos Albert's words had set off, he said, "That isn't in the statement, either."

Albert bristled. "I tried to tell that fella, but he wasn't interested." He snorted. "Not my fault all you fine young cops haven't got the time of day for a 'senile old man.' Think because a fella takes a drink now and again, he can't see what's in front of him."

Colter winced but didn't rationalize; Albert was right and Colter knew it. "No," he said, "it's not. It's our fault. And our loss."

Albert appeared mollified, and after a moment, Colter went on. "Albert, was the white car still here when you came back?"

The gray eyebrows furrowed. "Why, no. No, it wasn't. Funny, I never thought of that. Whoever moved it couldn't have helped but see..."

Colter risked a glance at Summer; she was pale, but seemed steady enough. "Albert, this is very important. Exactly how did you find him? Which way was he lying?"

"Why, this way. With his feet that way." He pointed toward the sunlit street.

"You're sure?"

"Sure I'm sure. I moved him, didn't I? Just pulled him around—" The gray brows creased at Colter's expression. "I do something wrong?"

"It doesn't matter," Colter said tightly. "When you first saw him, what was the man with the gun doing?"

Albert looked a little testy. "I told you, he was crouched down—"

"Like this?"

Colter went into a crouch, staring down at the pavement where Terry had lain. Albert studied him for a moment.

"More that way." He gestured, and Colter shifted. "Yeah. That's it. Just like that. 'Cept he was looking up, of course."

"Up?" Colter twisted his head to look back at the gray-haired man.

"Well, not up, like this," Albert said, jabbing a thumb toward the sky, "but like this."

He lowered the thumb to his own eye level. Colter moved his head, looking straight ahead and up to about the level Albert had indicated. And found himself looking into the shadows behind the big, metal trash bin.

"Damn."

"Colter?"

Summer's voice was soft and questioning. He rose slowly, turning to face her. And knew from her tiny gasp that he looked as sick as he felt.

Summer paced anxiously, stopping occasionally to peer out into the dark. More than once she'd thought she heard a car, only to race to the window to peer out into the unrelenting blackness. She was, she realized, following the same path Colter had worn across the small room. Before he'd gone, before he'd said the words that had chilled her soul and walked out.

He'd been so agitated, she'd been worried. She felt a little stupid in addition because she didn't understand the implications of what they'd learned. She'd sat in silence, watching him, afraid to disturb what seemed to be his fragile control. Finally, as if he couldn't hold them back any longer, the words began to spill out.

"We made a big, big mistake," he'd said grimly. "We all did. We took Albert's description of the man and ignored Albert from then on. None of us dug any further. None of us did our damned jobs."

He was pacing the living room almost in a frenzy, and Summer doubted if he was even aware of his own movement. He'd been rigidly silent ever since that moment in the alley, barely remembering to thank Albert when they dropped him off. She had kept up a steady stream of chatter to cover it, but the tension had been obvious.

"We never asked if he'd seen anything else. Albert Webster was just a useless old man, probably senile when he wasn't drunk. 'No point in asking him anything, he's probably just confused anyway.'" He laughed mirthlessly. "No wonder he never volunteered any information. We treated him like a doddering idiot."

"You didn't know. If—" Summer began, trying to defend him. Colter winced at the immediate protest that reminded him of too many things he was delaying thinking about.

"We should have known better," he said sharply. "But we didn't." He slammed a fist into his open palm. "We got the positioning of the body from the paramedics and took it as gospel.''

Summer winced at the flat, graphic words. "Does it . . . matter?''

He let out an explosive, bitter chuckle. "Yeah," he muttered. "Yeah, it matters. It means the angle of trajectory was wrong. It means the direction of fire was wrong. It means the positions of the principals were wrong.''

He realized she was staring at him and made himself stop as he passed the window seat for the fifth time.

"I'm sorry," he said. "I shouldn't be saying this in front of you. I didn't mean to upset you.''

"I'm not upset. I just don't understand.''

He let out a long breath. "Sorry," he said again. "I was . . . talking about it like a cop. Like it wasn't Terry.'' He turned and stared out the window. "It's the only way I can handle it," he said, his voice tight.

"Oh, Colter," she said softly, going to him, reaching out to touch him. He didn't pull away, but he didn't put his arms around her as she'd hoped, either. She drew back, confused. It stung, but after a moment of hurt, she decided he was just wound too tightly to slow down. Congratulations, O'Neil, she said to herself miserably, you've turned him into a full-blown cop again. Then he went on, as if she'd never moved, never touched him.

"The entire investigation was based on the premise that where he was found was where he fell. But if he went down where and how Albert said . . .''

"What?''

"Then the shot came from the opposite direction.''

Summer gasped. "Then Sherwood wasn't lying! His man didn't do it!''

Colter nodded. "He would have been behind him.''

"But then who—''

"Whoever was behind that Dumpster. And probably whoever belonged to that car. The man Albert never saw.''

Stunned, Summer sank down on the cushions of the window seat. "My God," she breathed. "All this time—''

"Yeah," Colter bit out. "All this time, chasing a guy I should have known, and all for nothing.''

"Don't be so hard on yourself—"

"Stop it!" He whirled on her. "Quit trying to justify my stupidity! This is Terry's killer, damn it! Or don't you care about that anymore?"

Summer gasped, stiffening. Contrition flashed in the turquoise eyes, but Colter didn't speak.

"Of course, I do," she whispered, shaken.

As if he couldn't bear to look at her shocked face, Colter spun on his heel and strode across the room to pick up his jacket from the back of a chair. Summer stood up shakily.

"Where—" Her voice cracked, and she had to swallow before she tried again. "Where are you going?"

"Out."

"Colter..."

She couldn't help the pleading tone that had come into her voice. She didn't understand what was wrong. She knew he was agitated over this new, unexpected knowledge, but she didn't know why he was acting so strangely, why he had been ever since they'd left that grim alley where Terry had died.

She'd thought he wasn't going to stop, but at the last minute, his hand on the knob of the door he'd just yanked open, he looked back at her. When he spoke, his words were short and clipped, as if he was trying to suppress them.

"There's only one man who saw who was in that alley. It's time I found him. Past time."

"When... will you be back?"

"I don't know."

The words were flat, cold, and they sounded more like "Never."

Summer didn't want to say it, didn't want to say anything in the face of his inexplicable, implacable coolness, but couldn't seem to help it. She took two faltering steps toward him. "Colter... last night..."

His face went wooden, his jaw rigid. "Last night was a mistake. It should never have happened. It won't again."

All the color drained from her face. Colter cringed inside at the stunned look of pure agony that twisted her delicate features. It was tearing him apart, but the guilt that had swept him in that grim alley was stronger. He made himself move on.

"I have to go. The sooner I wind this up, the sooner I can...get out of here."

She made a small whimpering sound, as if he'd struck her. It chilled him to his soul, and it took every last bit of the resolution that had come back to him in the alley to make him walk out the door.

Summer had very nearly sunk down to the floor right where she stood. Her legs could barely hold her up as she stumbled the three feet back to the window seat. She was trembling violently as she sagged down onto the cushions.

A long time passed before the shaking had stopped. Only the gradually creeping chill had roused her from the sea of pain his words had cast her into. She had made herself get up, had forced herself, through the numbness that had overtaken her, to move. She had gone through the motions of fixing a meal she didn't eat, staring at the open pages of a book she didn't read and finally gazing blankly at a television screen she didn't see.

She didn't know when her pain had become worry. She only knew that as the hours went by and he didn't come back, the old ache faded a little before the new one. And no matter how much she berated herself, no matter how many times she told herself she was a fool for caring, she couldn't conquer the fear. And it was that fear that kept her pacing now, racing to the window at every sound.

She didn't understand. She'd never felt this way before, when Terry had been late. But then, she'd been a naive little fool, she told herself bitterly, with no idea of the reality of his work. Now she knew it all too well, and she was terrified.

She even believed it, almost. The naive part had been true, she realized, but the rest was just kidding herself. She hadn't felt this way before because she'd never felt this way about Terry. She'd loved him, she had since she'd been a child, but not as she loved Colter. She saw now the truth of the doubts Fiona had had about her and Terry. The woman who'd been like a mother to her had always told her that someday she'd know the difference between what she felt for

Terry and the kind of love that took your mind and body, heart and soul. The kind of love that was for a lifetime.

Well, she knew now. She knew it as well as she knew this would, indeed, last that lifetime. Even when he left, she would still love Shane Colter. She would love him until the day she died, whether he was with her or a continent away.

It was a frightening realization, especially when he'd made it quite clear he couldn't wait to get out of here. Couldn't wait to get away from her. A mistake. That's what it had been to him, that glorious night that had set her heart free.

But as the hours crept by, even that ceased to matter. Please, God, she murmured over and over, let him be all right. I can't lose him, too. She didn't care if he didn't want her, didn't care if he got on the first plane out, as long as he was all right.

She swore, if he came back, she wasn't going to break down. She wasn't going to let show how worried she'd been. And above all, she wasn't going to let him see how badly he'd hurt her.

She was concentrating so intently on everything she wasn't going to do that she didn't hear the car she'd been waiting for all night. She gave a smothered little gasp as the door opened and she saw him silhouetted against the porch light.

His shoulders were slumped wearily, bending the usually tall, straight line of his body. He lifted his head, and at the hollow, exhausted look of his eyes, all her fine warnings, all her self-admonitions vanished. She loved him, and she couldn't find it in her to hate him for not loving her back. She took one look at him and did what she'd vowed not to do. She ran to him, tears glistening on her cheeks, and threw her arms around him.

"God, I was so worried—"

"Summer—"

"I know, I know. I know you don't want to hear it, you don't want me, but I don't care. I don't care about anything except that you're all right."

"God, Summer . . . what I said—"

"It doesn't matter. I understand."

"No. No, you don't."

"Colter, it doesn't matter. I don't expect anything from you, I—"

"Summer, stop!"

The sharpness of his voice interrupted the rapid flow of her words. Only then did she realize that his arms had come around her, that he was holding her. It was the last thing she'd expected after how he'd left. She stared up at him, confused and trembling.

"Oh, God, Summer," he whispered harshly, tightening his arms around her. She sagged against him, bewildered. He felt her go slack and bent to slip his arm behind her knees and lift her into his arms. Little tremors went through her as he sat down on the window seat, holding her carefully. He swung his feet up, raising his knees and cradling her gently in the curve of his body. He pulled the worn drawing out of his pocket.

"I've been walking most of the night," he said, his voice low and hoarse. "I told myself it was to find him—" he nodded at the drawing "—but I'd put out the word everywhere I could in a few hours."

Summer stared at Colter through a haze of bewildered tears. His eyes were red rimmed and weary, weary with more than just physical exhaustion. But they were also warm, as they had been in the flickering firelight when he had—

Stop it, she told herself fiercely, quashing the soaring leap of hope that shot through her. Don't be more of a fool than you already have been. She kept silent, waiting for him to go on.

"But I kept walking. I went by the station and stood around outside for a while. I went to the coffee shop we used to go to. I even went by McRory's."

His eyes were lowered, and Summer stared at the sweep of thick, gold-tipped lashes as she wondered what he was trying to say.

"After a while, I went to the cemetery." Summer's breath caught in her throat. "I sat by his grave for a long time. But he wasn't there."

She understood what he meant; during the months after he'd died, Terry had seemed close in the oddest places; the

ball park where they used to play as children or the room
that had been his in the house that had been Fiona's. What
she didn't understand was why Colter had been seeking that
sense of presence. But she was afraid to ask, afraid to say
anything for fear of seeing that icy coldness in his eyes
again.

"Finally, I went back to the alley. That's where it hit me
this afternoon." His voice had changed, had become taut
with remembered pain. "I sat there where I'd held him...."
He stopped, shaking his head.

"Why?" Summer finally whispered.

He shuddered. "God, I felt so guilty. So damned guilty,
I couldn't stand it anymore."

Guilty? Summer's eyes widened.

"I wanted to... talk to him, to tell him that I... couldn't
help it—"

"Colter, it wasn't your fault. You were doing him a favor,
trading the late stakeout shift with him so he could get home
earlier—"

"That's not what I felt guilty about."

Her brow creased. "Then what—"

"You."

She nearly gasped. She drew back a little, staring at him.
"Why?"

His eyes lifted to hers then; the turquoise depths were full
of the hard-won calm of a person who had come a very great
distance in a short time.

"Because I... took what was his. Because I was alive to
be with you while he was dead. Because I had taken advantage of your vulnerability—" He lifted a hand when she
started to protest, and she lapsed back into silence. "But
most of all, because...I couldn't help it." He said the words
again tightly. "I tried, but I couldn't help it."

"Help...what?"

He looked at her, the turquoise eyes studying her intently
as if he were trying to gauge her reaction to words he hadn't
spoken yet.

"Loving you," he whispered. "Like I've always loved
you."

Summer stared at him, her lips parted as she struggled for the breath his calm avowal had knocked from her as surely as a blow.

"You loved...me?"

"I've loved you since the first time I saw you."

"I..." She was too stunned to go on.

"I remember Terry talking about you. He used to kid about what a...sweet little thing you were. He never told me you were the most beautiful woman...." Colter dropped his gaze as his voice faltered. "Then I saw you. When I walked into your house and saw you talking to that silly plant, I never had a chance."

"It wasn't a silly plant," she protested automatically, her mind still struggling to deal with what he'd said. His gaze came up again, a soft smile spreading across his face.

"It was beautiful. Like you."

A slow flush of color was rising in her cheeks. Colter had loved her then? But he couldn't have, she thought. All that time he'd been around, he'd treated her only as a friend. True, he'd been perhaps nicer than she might have expected to just his partner's wife, but never had she guessed...

"I didn't know.... You never said..."

"God, Summer, how could I? You were married to my partner. And my best friend." He took a deep breath. "You don't know how much I hated myself. Falling in love with your best friend's wife is not a recipe for peace," he said wryly.

She shook her head in slow wonder. "I—I never knew."

He sighed, his mouth twisting ruefully. "You weren't supposed to. Lord knows I did my damnedest to hide it. And when I couldn't anymore, I just...stayed away."

Astonished realization widened her eyes. "The day we saw the whales..."

He nodded. "That's when I knew...I couldn't be around you anymore."

"That's why I never saw you again...until that night?"

"I didn't dare. And it...hurt too much to see you. You were always so...damned nice to me, and I knew it was only because of Terry, and there I was aching for you, knowing you'd be...disgusted if you knew.... It just hurt too much," he said again. "So I started to avoid you."

She looked stunned, disbelieving. "Me? You stayed away because of—of me?"

He smiled, a small, rueful, reminiscent smile. "I've lived with a lot of things, Summer. I couldn't have lived with what I would have done if I'd kept putting myself in temptation's way. And believe me, you were one hell of a temptation."

"I... It never... I never imagined..."

She looked so stunned, so utterly shocked, that he knew it truly had never occurred to her. She had been such an innocent, she had never guessed the reason behind his frequent presence or his sudden disappearance. And it told him that, about this at least, Terry had been right; she was completely unaware of her own appeal, of the quiet, seductive charm that had pulled him to her since the first instant he had found that the picture on Terry's desk hadn't lied.

And then he told her all things he'd wanted to tell her before, all the things she didn't know, the brave, beautiful things she didn't see in herself. He told her how proud he was of her, of how she'd handled what a suddenly vindictive life had thrown at her and of how she'd grown, changed, matured into the woman he'd always known she could be. She blushed deeply, shaking her head in mute denial.

"I mean it. I'm so damned sorry I wasn't here for you...but you didn't need me, did you? You did what you had to do and never complained. You're a hell of a woman, Summer O'Neil. And don't you ever forget it, not anymore."

A tiny quiver shook her. She could almost see it now, looking back, she thought. Or was it this new, shocking knowledge coloring her memories? Making her think now that he had always treated her carefully, almost tenderly.

No, she thought in sudden realization. He *had* treated her differently, differently than Joyce or any of the other women he'd come in contact with while she was around. In her innocence, she'd assumed it was because of some exalted status he'd conferred upon her as Terry's wife; never had she supposed it was for her alone. Not from Shane Colter, not for her. She felt like an utter, blind fool. Another quiver rippled through her.

He felt it, pulled her close, pressing her head to his chest, hugging her. "I didn't know about... the way things went so horribly wrong for you. I thought everything was all right, that it was all taken care of, or I never would have gone."

She didn't question that he knew just what had gone wrong, had known and hadn't said anything. She gathered courage from the strength of his arms around her. Somehow, in that precious shelter, she didn't feel foolish anymore for not having seen the truth all those years ago.

"Why... did you go? Afterward, I mean."

The fingers of the hand resting on his upraised knee curled into a fist.

"I had to. I couldn't stay. I wanted you too much, and with Terry just... I felt like a damned vulture." His jaw clenched, making his words sound tight and forced. "And I felt so damned guilty.... God, Summer, I envied Terry so much. I used to think about him going home to you, and it about killed me. Then when he died, I felt like it was my fault, somehow, because I'd begrudged him you, like somehow I'd... wished it on him."

"Oh, Colter..."

He shrugged. "So I ran."

"Why didn't you ever... come back?"

He took a deep breath. "Because I didn't think you'd ever get over him. I didn't think you'd ever love anyone but him. You'd been together so long...."

Summer straightened up, bracing herself with a hand on the shoulder where her head had lain. She was loath to surrender the comforting warmth of him, but this was something that had to be said.

"I loved Terry," she said quietly. "I really did."

"I know that."

"I loved him. But he wasn't perfect. And being dead doesn't make him that way. If saying that makes me a rotten person, then I guess that's what I am."

"You're not. You wouldn't know how to be." Colter struggled to find the right words. "Terry was a good partner. And a good friend. That doesn't mean he didn't have faults."

"Yes, he did." Summer sighed. "But you know what really hurts? Right before...he had finally admitted that he had a problem with alcohol. He was thinking about... getting help."

"I know."

She stared at him. "You do?"

"He...talked to me about it." Colter shrugged. "I guess he figured if anybody would understand, I would."

"Why?"

His fist uncurled, his fingers stretching over his knee. After a moment, his head came up and he met her curious gaze.

"My father is an alcoholic."

Her eyes widened. "But...you always said he didn't drink!"

"That's why. He quit when I was twelve." He looked at her steadily. "After he broke my arm in a drunken rage."

Her face was suddenly white against the darkness, and Colter heard her sharp little intake of breath. "I—I'm sorry. I never knew."

"Don't feel sorry for me. He did what he had to do." His voice changed, became softer, warmer. "I'm pretty damned proud of him. If he ever fell off the wagon, I never knew about it."

"That's why you're always so careful about how much you drink, isn't it?"

"I had a hell of an example, growing up." His mouth twisted. "But so did Terry. His father was nearly as bad as mine."

And that, Summer thought suddenly, was the difference between the two men. Both with the same negative factor in their backgrounds, one had gone down the same path, and one had fought it. And won.

She felt the slight stirring of guilt, as if she was somehow betraying Terry by her thoughts. It was an old and familiar feeling, one she had come to terms with. It had taken her a long time to conquer the self-hatred she'd felt when, after the initial grief had faded, she had first begun to look at her dead husband as the human being he'd been, without the veil of perfection death conferred on people.

"Maybe Terry really would have quit," she said at last. "Maybe we could have worked it all out. We never had the chance to find out." She sighed. "But maybe we just would have found out Fiona was right. That we shouldn't have gotten married, that we were too much like brother and sister after practically growing up together."

"I didn't know," Colter whispered, barely aware of speaking out loud. "I always thought . . ."

"I loved Terry." Her voice had taken on a tone of gentle finality. "I still do. But now I love him like I always did, perhaps like I always should have. As a dear friend, as a brother. I'm just sorry that we tried to make it something else. Something it wasn't meant to be."

"I never knew," Colter said again, numbly.

And what if you had? he thought. What would you have done then? Gone after her? Broken up your best friend's marriage? You felt guilty enough when Terry died, how would you have felt then?

"But it wouldn't have mattered if you had known, would it?" she said softly. "You're an honorable man, Colter."

He grimaced, rolling his eyes.

"Maybe it's an old-fashioned word. But I don't think it's an old-fashioned idea. I'm glad, Colter. But I still wish I'd known."

"And now that you do?" His voice held an odd, almost quivering note that set up an answering quiver in her heart.

"I remember that day you came to the house, too. I was expecting some grim, hardheaded old cop, and then you walked in." She lowered her eyes shyly. "I couldn't figure out why the room got so warm all of a sudden."

He stared at her bowed head, at the golden gleam of her hair. God, had she felt it, too, even then? "Summer?"

Her head came up. "You always made me feel that way. It scared me because I didn't know what to do." The full line of her mouth twisted ruefully. "I didn't even know what it meant then. I just knew it was dangerous. But you made me feel...supported, too. Like there was someone who believed in me, didn't think I was just a mouse."

"You're not. Not anymore. Sherwood was right about that, wildcat."

She blushed furiously, but she held his gaze. There was something else she had to ask, had to know. It took her a moment's struggle to get the words out.

"When you left last night..." she began, but stopped at the look of misery that flickered over his face.

"God, I'm so sorry about that. I know I hurt you." He shook his head in slow pain. "The one thing I never meant to do. But all I could think of was that I was...betraying Terry somehow...."

She nodded, and her voice was low, quiet. "I've felt it, too. But we've got to let him go."

"I know. That's what I realized tonight. There in the alley. It was as if he really were there."

He didn't tell her about the other thought that had come to him then, that odd sense of certainty that Terry's dying nod had been one of more than just understanding; it had been one of sanction. He only said, gently, "And all of a sudden, I knew it was time to...let him rest."

"Yes," she whispered. "He wouldn't begrudge us. He wasn't that kind of man."

"I know, but..." Colter's words trailed off, that odd tremor back in his voice.

"What?"

"I was afraid you didn't really...want me. That you'd just been...alone so long...."

"I was," she whispered, "but it was by choice. I wanted it that way. I just didn't realize why until you came back."

Slowly, deliberately, she leaned forward to press a soft, tender kiss on his lips. His arms came around her and he growled her name low in his throat. He returned her kiss hungrily, fiercely. She stroked his lips gently, tentatively with her tongue, the movement a combination of eagerness and shyness that fired his blood, and in one smooth, strong motion, he gathered her in his arms and stood up. With long, swift strides, he carried her toward the bedroom.

Chapter 13

It was slower this time, less hungry, but no less sweet. He undressed her with slow care, kissing every silken inch as he exposed it, then laid her on the big four-poster bed with exquisite gentleness. He swiftly shed his own clothes, then turned back to the bed.

"Wait," she whispered huskily, her eyes eagerly taking in every hard, muscled line of him. "I didn't . . . I was too nervous before. . . ."

Her face was flaming, but she didn't take her eyes from him. When he realized what she meant, he felt his own face heat. But he stood still, letting her look, the innocent eagerness in her eyes making his heart begin to hammer heavily in his chest. Then, as her glance slid down his body, he felt the muscles deep in his belly ripple convulsively before a wave of chill and heat combined. She made a tiny sound deep in her throat at the movement.

"I'm used to it by now," he said hoarsely. "It happens to me every time I'm around you, every time I think about you. It always has."

She gave a tiny cry and held out her arms to him. He went down to her in one controlled movement, stretching his naked length along hers, echoes of that quivering in his belly now rippling through his entire body as she touched him, running her hands over him as if she wanted to trace with her hands every taut, muscled line she'd seen with her eyes.

"Tell me," she whispered, "please. Tell me what to do, how to make you feel like I do when you touch me."

He shuddered, burying his face in the curve of her neck, and he didn't know if it was from her words or from the feel of her hands sliding over his chest.

"It doesn't seem to matter." His voice was thick with both pleasure and amazement. "Wherever you touch me, it's like—"

Words failed him as her searching fingers found his nipples and stroked gently. He gasped as fire shot from beneath her fingers to that aching thrust between his legs, and a shivery finger raced down his spine, every muscle in his back rippling as it passed.

"Like what?" Her voice was soft, coaxing as she teased the flat nubs of flesh with increased pressure.

"Fire. And ice. Together. I—"

Her hands had moved, sliding down his chest to the ridged hardness of his belly. He held himself tensely still, barely aware he was also holding his breath. She kept her palms flat against his flesh for a long moment, then slid them down a scant inch. It was then he realized she, too, was holding her breath, and why.

"Please," he rasped out. "I've been waiting seven years for your hands on me."

A little quiver of pleasure darted through her, and she moved her hands to clasp him gently, tentatively. He gasped and bucked so sharply, she thought she'd hurt him and jerked her hands away.

"No!"

He grabbed her hands and dragged them back down his body to his heated, throbbing flesh. He arched to meet her fingers, and when they closed around him once more, he made sure she knew what the convulsive jerk of his hips that he couldn't control meant.

"Yes," he hissed out. "Summer, if you only knew how often I've dreamed of this!"

Her fingers trembled around him at the words, at the realization that he had dreamed, longed, just as she had. She stroked, caressed, until, with a sudden, sharp movement, he grasped her hands and stilled them.

"Summer," he gasped, "I can't take any more."

Her hands left him to clutch at his back, her nails digging into his flesh. He barely noticed the bruises; her fingers were sending signals much stronger than pain. He was able to beat back the tide that had been threatening under her direct caresses, but the innocent sensuality of her response to his touch did nothing to relieve the incessant, expanding pressure. Then her hands slid down to cup the taut curve of his buttocks, and he knew he'd lost the battle.

"Summer," he groaned against the soft flesh of her breast, "I can't stand it. I thought I could wait, but when you touch me like that . . ."

"Like this?"

Her question was shyly soft, but there was nothing shy about her hands as they gripped his lean hips and pulled him to her, pressing his hot, aroused length against the silk of her stomach. A hoarse groan broke from him, and he shuddered with the effort not to push her legs apart and bury himself in her with one desperate thrust.

And then she parted her thighs for him, letting his weight slide down between them before she raised her legs to enclose him. It was a wordlessly eloquent invitation, and he didn't have the strength to deny it.

His mouth took hers fiercely. His fingers tugged at the taut, tingling peaks of her breasts, and in the same moment, his hips jerked forward, hard and fast, driving him deep inside her.

His kiss smothered the cry of joy that rose from her, but he felt her pleasure in the convulsive bucking of her body. She moved in an undulating wave, first her legs locking

tighter around him, then her hips rising to drive his hardness even deeper inside her, her back arching to thrust her
breasts into his hands, and then her mouth lifting to meet
the plunging stroke of his tongue.

Summer had never felt anything like this, even in the
heated frenzy of their first joining. His hands, his mouth,
his body seemed to be everywhere, touching her everywhere, turning her into a mindless mass of feeling and sensation whose only thought was a brief, unfocused regret that
it had taken so long for her to know this glory was possible.

He was touching her as if he'd been making love to her for
years, as if he knew every special, secret place. Suddenly, she
knew that it was true, that in his mind, in his imagination,
he had made love to her a thousand times. He had wanted
this, and she had never known. He had kept it hidden because of that innate sense of honor that made her love him
so. It was this that she had sensed, that made her feel so
safe, so secure, so treasured the first time they had made
love.

And then she had no room in her thoughts for anything
except the wonderful hardness plunging into her, filling her,
the exquisite tugging at her nipples and the hot, sweet taste
of his mouth.

He let out a guttural cry as she writhed beneath him. He
thrust forward again and again, unable to believe how deep
she was taking him, how her wet heat was clasping him,
stroking him, until it was all he could do to hold back. Yet
still he wanted more, wanted to drive deeper, with all his
strength.

"Oh, Shane!"

The sound of his name echoed sweetly, and he erupted
into furious motion. The sweet, hot friction grew, the slap-
ping of eager, straining flesh matching the pounding rhythm
of two racing hearts.

Summer looked up at him from beneath eyelids that were
oddly heavy. He was so beautiful, she thought as she
watched his golden body flex above her, his face drawn taut
with pleasure and need. And when he answered her plea and

drove himself into her very depths, she felt a gasping moment of pure, feminine wonder that she was able to take this proud, magnificent flesh so deeply inside her.

And then he was rising sharply over her, grinding his hips hard against hers, as if he were trying to climb inside her.

"Summer," he grated out, "I'm unraveling, I can't stop...."

Just the thought that she, the little mouse, could bring this fiercely strong man to this brought her to the edge. Then he shuddered violently, her name ripping from his throat as his body pulsed within her. He held her as if his life depended on it, as if he would never let her go. And knowing she was safe there in his arms, she let herself hurtle after him, crying out his name as the world ruptured into spinning, dancing heat and light.

She could hear the harsh, gasping pants of his breath as he sagged against her, his hands clutching at her shoulders. She felt the little quivers that shook him and knew they were the same echoes of that incredible explosion of sensation that she was feeling. She heard him murmur and felt an exquisite dart of pleasure when she recognized her name spoken in an awed tone over and over, like a litany.

When he spoke at last, it was to answer something she'd said a lifetime ago, it seemed.

"You had to be 'Terry's wife' to me. I had to think of you as connected to him. I had to..." His voice trailed off, and he shook his head, at a loss to explain.

She looked up at him, her eyes still a little blurry as the golden haze of pleasure lingered. "I think I understand," she whispered. "You made me feel things I shouldn't have felt, made me wonder about things I was missing. Maybe that's why you were always 'Colter' to me. I didn't dare let you get any closer."

His eyes heated suddenly. "You called me Shane a minute ago."

She colored, lowering her eyes as she gave an embarrassed little laugh. "Better than calling you George or Sam or something."

"Damn right," he said in mock severity. Then he chuckled ruefully.

Summer looked at him curiously, but he only shrugged.

"What?" she persisted.

"I was just . . . thinking."

"About what?"

"Remembering, mostly." He eyed her hesitantly for a moment, then went on. "About how you almost got me killed once."

She gaped at him. "What?"

"Well, maybe not killed, but at least . . . unmanned."

She shifted beneath him, staring. He slid to his side, taking her with him carefully.

"It was in New Orleans," he said, a wry grin tugging at the corners of his mouth. "One of the few times I tried . . . seeing someone."

He paused, as if he was afraid that hearing he'd been with another woman would hurt her. Summer remembered once more her first glimpse of him in all his naked, male glory, and couldn't blame any woman for wanting him.

"And?" she asked mildly.

"The lady had a hot temper. She came after me with a razor. I think she had mayhem in mind. A very personal kind of mayhem."

Summer gasped. "Why?"

"I called her by your name. At a very . . . inopportune moment."

Her cheeks flushed, and Summer lowered her eyes again, embarrassed at the rather vindictive feeling of pleasure that flooded her. When he spoke again, it was in the low, silky tones of a caress.

"I was pretending it was true. I always did. I had to. It was the only way I could . . . finish what I started. But after that, I just gave up. If I couldn't have the real thing . . ."

He moved to kiss her gently. "It's a good thing I didn't know that the real thing would be like this. My dreams were hot enough. This would have killed me."

"Your dreams were . . . hot?" She couldn't believe she'd said it, and she knew that nothing could be hotter than her cheeks right now.

"Oh, yes," he said huskily. And when he pulled her close to whisper into her ear, she found that words could be as powerfully erotic as a touch when they came from the right man. By the time he was done, she was breathing in quick little gasps and her blood was racing, pounding in her veins.

When he rolled onto his back and pulled her on top of him, holding her above him with strong, muscled arms as he lifted his head to nuzzle her suspended breasts, she knew with a sudden thrill exactly which of his heated fantasies he was fulfilling. And she knew what he wanted her to do next, and with a little shock at her own abandon, she moved to do it, straddling his lean hips, reaching to slide him into the soft, caressing heat that was crying out for him again already. She gasped in pleasure as he filled her; he groaned as his rigid flesh slid home. Home at last.

When they once more drifted to earth, Colter pulled the covers up over them with one arm while he held her close with the other. In the dawning light of morning, deep, sated, dreamless sleep claimed them both, each savoring the warmth and security of the other's arms.

The phone jangled harshly and Colter came abruptly awake. He wondered who was calling so early until he glanced at the clock and saw that it was nearly noon. Summer roused more slowly, blinking against the flood of sunlight that filled the room. She glanced at him, a soft smile curving her lips before the jarring ring came again. With a smothered sigh, she reached for the phone.

Colter looked startled when, after a brief exchange, she handed him the receiver.

"It's Dave," she explained.

He glanced down at their naked bodies pressed together, legs entwined, then back at the phone. Suddenly, she realized the reason for his hesitation and smiled at him, a warm, loving smile that made his insides turn over in the way he'd never known until he'd seen her for the first time.

"I'd like to shout it to the world," she said softly, "so I certainly don't care if Dave knows."

He kissed her swiftly, then took the receiver.

"Did I wake you?" Dave asked archly.

"I was out late," Colter snapped.

"Don't take my head off," Dave said with a laugh. "If you two finally got it together, I'm glad to hear it."

Colter stared at the receiver. "Finally?"

"You think we're all blind or what?"

Great, Colter muttered to himself. "Did you call just to be a nuisance, or did you have something to say?"

"Yeah," Dave said good-naturedly. "An old friend of yours called this morning. Said he heard you were looking for him."

Summer watched with concern as Colter snapped upright. He listened for a moment longer, then thanked Dave and hung up. Then he swung out of bed.

"Colter?" She couldn't help the fear in her voice; was he running from her again?

"Ellis called."

"Ellis? You mean the man in the picture?" Colter nodded. "He called for you?"

"He wants to meet."

"But why?"

"I put it out on the street that I knew he wasn't the shooter. That I just wanted to talk."

"Is Dave going with you?"

He hesitated, then shook his head.

"Colter—"

"It'll be fine, Summer. He's not the shooter, we know that."

"That doesn't make him an altar boy."

His mouth quirked. "Neither am I."

She didn't like it, but grudgingly subsided when she realized he was adamant.

"I want this finished," he said flatly.

His mind had little time to spare for the upcoming meeting with the man he'd searched for for so long; it was too full of hot, sweet memories of Summer. Of her open responsiveness to him, of her growing boldness, of the way she touched him, caressed him—

Knock it off, Colter, he snapped silently, before you drive off the damned road. Think about something else. Think about winding this mess up so you can concentrate on the future instead of the past. A future with Summer.

Someday, he was going to have a quiet, lazy morning with her, he promised himself. A morning in which they could talk, could ask all the questions, make all the plans they needed to make. A morning in which he could just hold her, savor the sweetness of having her in his arms, marvel at the unexpected reality of what had once been an impossible dream.

Sighing, he tore his mind away from the tempting, luring thoughts of his golden-haired wildcat. He made himself think of the present, made himself go over it all again, needing the distraction to divert his attention from a body too easily rousing to the thought of her.

They had blown it from the getgo, he thought grimly. Ignoring what Albert could have told them about the car, the actions of the man they'd assumed was the shooter and the position of the body. Things that changed the entire case. Things that were imperative and had never made the reports.

All the pieces tumbled around in his head, caroming off each other and shaking loose other thoughts that seemed unrelated but kept floating around nevertheless. Colter shook his head as if that would clear them away, but it didn't work. They lingered, stubbornly, demanding to be looked at.

That old instinct might be rusty, he thought, and need a little dusting off, but it was still working. So he looked. And suddenly the thoughts didn't seem so unrelated. Unconsciously, he slowed the car as the pieces began to fall together, forming an incredible, unbelievable pattern.

Halfway there, the drive, and the meeting, became academic. He knew who had killed Terry.

He was still stunned as he walked out of the dingy bar, sadly crowded even at this early hour of the afternoon. He pushed his way through the narrow entryway, past the three already-tipsy men coming in and the man who stood at the phone. Colter barely noticed how the man with the receiver in his hand turned his back to the door, seeming to huddle in a heavy coat that seemed oddly bulky for the warmth of the day. All he could think of was the horrible truth he'd finally discovered, the truth the man he'd searched for so hard had just confirmed.

It made him sick, and he didn't know what to do. He needed time to try and digest the impossibility of it, needed time to think, needed to sort out the options. He needed Summer, he thought. Needed her warmth and care and support. And her thoughts. She had more right than anyone to decide what was to be done.

He drove numbly, doing all the necessary things reflexively, automatically, while his mind cringed away from a reality he didn't want to concede, decisions he didn't want to make. He felt like such a blind, stumbling fool because it had been there in front of him all the time.

He drove faster as he neared her house, anxious to see her. He went much too fast for the narrow lane she lived on, and the tires squealed a little as he turned into the drive. He got out of the car, pocketed the keys and started toward the house. He cleared the steps to the porch in one bound and reached for the knob.

She was sitting in the chair closest to the door. He started toward her eagerly, then stopped dead as he realized she hadn't moved. She sat stiffly in the chair, her feet oddly wide apart, her eyes fastened on the space behind the door he'd left open in his hurry to go to her. She never said a word, but her every muscle screamed a warning by their rigidness. Her eyes flicked to his, wide and fearful, then went back to that spot.

He uncoiled with the speed of a striking snake. He slammed one shoulder against the open door. He drove it back hard, and a gasping shout echoed through the room. The door rebounded, the knob catching him hard across his thigh. Colter staggered slightly. The man behind the door careened into the room as Summer shouted a warning.

"Colter, he's got a gun!"

Colter heard her, but he was already moving. He came in low and fast and took the man around the knees. Summer screamed another warning as she saw the hand holding the snub-nosed revolver come down in a sweeping arc. Colter was pinned by the man's considerable bulk. He twisted but couldn't get clear, and she heard him grunt as the lethal chunk of metal rapped against his skull.

"No!"

She'd seen the pudgy hand pull back the hammer and train the barrel on Colter's dazed form. Her cry distracted the man for a moment.

"Shut up, bitch!" he snarled.

Past him, she saw Colter shake his head sharply and start to move. Something must have shown in her eyes because the man sidestepped, rather easily for all his bulk, and came up beside her chair.

When his hazy vision cleared, Colter wished it hadn't. The sight of Terry's murderer with a gun to Summer's head sent a chill through him unlike anything he'd ever felt before, even that night in the alley.

"Freeze, Colter. Right there."

He sank back on his heels. His head and his leg, where the door had caught him, ached, but nothing mattered except the fury that was boiling in him. He saw now the bruise that marked the side of her face, and knew the bastard had hit her. And he realized why she was sitting so strangely; she'd been tied to the chair with a thin nylon cord around her waist, and each ankle had been bound to a leg of the chair. The sight of that livid mark and the cord digging into the tender flesh above her slim ankles enraged him; unconsciously, his body tensed, ready to spring.

"Don't try it. She'll be dead before you take a step."

Colter knew it was true. The man had killed a cop; he wouldn't hesitate to kill again. Colter made himself drop back on one knee, but kept that foot braced under him. It was a posture that, although it looked relaxed, would enable him to spring to his feet at the first glimmering of a chance.

"Good boy. We wouldn't want anything to happen to the poor widow, now, would we?"

"You hurt her and there's no place in the world far enough for you to go, no hole deep enough for you to hide." Colter's voice was cool, steady.

"My, my, such gallantry. But then you always were a noble bastard, weren't you?" The words were scornful. "That's all I ever heard about. Colter's the best cop. The best man. The toughest, the fastest, the smartest." A laugh came, a cold, harsh sound that was chilling in its malevolence. "But it doesn't look that way now, does it?"

"Give it up, man. It's all over."

"Oh, no, it's not. I'm finally on my way, and if you think I'm going to let you stop me now, you're crazy."

"You're crazy if you think you're on your way anywhere but straight to hell."

"You got in my way before, Colter, with all your big arrests, your heroics, all the crap that kept forcing them to notice you. But not now. You're gone and you're going to stay gone. Permanently."

Colter stared at the man who had once been his boss, wondering what had brought the man to this. Grissom had never been a great cop, never even a very good one, but a cop was a cop...or so Colter had thought.

"He was one of your own," Colter said softly. "Don't you feel anything?"

"Yes!" The word came out as a furious hiss. "It should have been you!"

Understanding sparked in the turquoise eyes. "You thought it *was* me, didn't you? It was supposed to be me, except Terry and I traded shifts." Colter heard Summer's gasp but never took his eyes off the man with the gun. "But you didn't know that because we didn't write it down anywhere. Terry got shot because you thought he was me."

"It should have been you," the man spat out again.

"You hate me that much? Even enough to change my file after I'd gone even though it didn't matter anymore?"

"Smarts, doesn't it," Grissom said smugly, "knowing that all the official records say you left before they came after you?"

"That's where Billy got the idea. And you let Sherwood's man take the heat for Terry's murder...that's what he meant about being used."

Fear flickered in flat brown eyes. Colter didn't miss it.

"Oh, yes, your association with Sherwood is over now." With calculated coolness, Colter began his attack. "He sent word through Ellis. He said you've outlived your usefulness."

"He didn't. He needs me." Grissom didn't sound certain.

"Like lice." Colter snorted. "Did you really think you could get away with it forever? That nobody would notice that all those 'big busts' you made were really penny-ante? That there was no money and less dope? Or that they all were out the next day on bail? Bail that came from Sherwood? How much was he paying you to lay off his big runners? How many little ones did he throw to you?"

"Nobody helped me—"

"Was it all part of your deal? He throws you enough to get you a promotion so you'll be more useful to him? And how many of our guys did you sell out? How many good cases got blown because of you? How many hours of work went down the tubes because you warned Sherwood?"

"You can't prove I had anything to do—"

"With what? Locking up Sherwood's file the day after I got here? Or with omitting crucial evidence in a murder investigation?" Colter laughed harshly. "I should have known when you insisted on handling all the interviews yourself. You never handled anything tougher than a petty theft." He shook his head ruefully. "That's what messed me up. I thought you'd just been your usual stupid self and bungled the investigation. That you were just too dumb to understand how important that car was or even that Terry had been moved."

"You arrogant—"

"That's why you kept pushing the composite, saying it was the only thing worth using from Albert. You knew it would throw us off. And I'll bet you knew about whatever Sherwood had coming down the pipe that made him send Ellis to deep cover even though he wasn't the shooter. He was stalling for time, wasn't he?"

"Shut up—"

"How about your bank account? Bet that'll be interesting reading when it's subpoenaed." Colter was inching forward, praying that Grissom wouldn't notice. He kept talking to distract the man. "What kind of personal car do you drive, Grissom? A white Cadillac, maybe?"

"He drove up in it."

It was the first thing Summer had said since her shouted protest. Grissom nearly jumped at the soft sound of her voice.

Edgy, Colter thought. Good. Then he risked a glance at her and knew she'd seen what he was doing, that she had spoken intentionally to add to the confusion. She was amazing, he thought, and he gained at least three inches as she added carefully, "It's exactly as Albert described."

"Damned old bastard," Grissom snarled at her. "I should have gotten him out of the way a long time ago."

"It's over, Grissom," Colter said flatly. "All of it." His voice went low and ugly. "The only thing lower than a killer is a cop killer. Or a crooked cop. And you're all three."

"Shut up—"

"You murdered Terry." He sensed rather than saw Summer move, her arm reaching down over the side of the chair. He went on without a pause, covering whatever she was doing. "Then you planted your own payoff money on him.

And you used his death to build your own career on because you didn't have what it takes to make it."

"You've got it all figured out, haven't you?"

"I didn't have to once I remembered. Terry told me."

The fleshy face paled a little. "He didn't. He couldn't have."

"He did. I just didn't realize it until all the other pieces came together. I thought he was asking me to look out for Summer when he said 'Sum.' But he was trying to say Gris-*som*, wasn't he? He was telling me who killed him."

"Too bad you won't live to tell anybody."

"But I already have." Colter fought to keep his expression even, not to let his eyes flick to Summer. He was running a big bluff, and as much as he wanted to look at her, to let her know what he was doing, he didn't dare.

Fear darted across Grissom's pudgy face, then disbelief. "You just met with Ellis. You didn't have time."

"I told you he got a call this morning," Summer said as coolly as if she was discussing the weather. "It was Dave Stanley."

Colter gained another precious stretch of floor as the man gaped at her. God, I love her, Colter thought. His eyes went to hers then, a brief, warm flick of salute before he said casually, "Who do you think told me Ellis wanted to see me? I wasn't even looking for him anymore since I already knew you were the one. And I told Dave everything when he called."

I only wish I'd been that smart, he thought sourly. But right now, the only thing that mattered was that Grissom believe him. The muddy brown eyes were doubtful, but they held fear as well, and flicked from Colter to Summer nervously. Colter saw her shift suddenly, as if to hide something in the cushions of the chair, but Grissom didn't seem to notice.

"He would have done something. I saw him in the office when Billy called me."

A sudden, shadowy memory of a man at the phone in the bar where he'd met Ellis came to Colter. So that's how he'd known. He must have come straight here, knowing Summer would be alone. Anger flared in Colter again.

"He had to wait to see the Captain. But they'll be looking for you by now." He lifted his wrist to look at his watch, praying that Grissom would instinctively do the same. The pudgy arm began to raise, the barrel of the gun wavered and Colter tensed.

Suddenly, Summer moved, something glinting in her hand, and with a little thud of shock, Colter realized what she had picked up. Her arm flashed up and back and Grissom howled in sudden shock and pain as the knitting needle she held dug into his corpulent flesh.

Colter launched himself, taking Grissom full in the chest. They crashed to the floor, then rolled back toward the door.

With trembling fingers, Summer plucked futilely at the nylon cord that held her. Then she bent and yanked furiously at the knitting basket beside the chair and pulled free the scissors.

She heard the sounds of struggle behind her. She sawed furiously at her bonds. She heard a grunt, then the whoosh of air leaving lungs under duress. She sawed harder. The cord at her waist finally gave way. Then she bent to the restraints at her ankles.

She heard a crash and her head jerked around. Still locked together, the men had come up hard against the table in the entry. Colter was undeniably stronger and more fit, but Grissom, though several inches shorter, outweighed him by at least forty pounds. And right now, that gave him the advantage. He was holding Colter down with his full weight. One forearm was lodged against Colter's throat, cutting off his breath. She could see him struggling against that killing pressure. Her sawing became frantic.

There was a heavy thud as at last Colter got leverage and forced Grissom to give way. They rolled again, Colter on top now. She heard a muttered oath and the dull thumps of flailing feet striking the floor. The last cord separated and she leapt to her feet.

Just as she began to turn, she heard a muffled explosion. Fear froze her to the spot and she stared at the two men. The struggle had stopped, but neither of them moved. Then Colter slid to one side, flopping on his back with a terrifying slackness. The moment stretched out for what seemed a lifetime. No, her mind screamed, no, not again!

And then she saw his chest rise and fall with a ragged breath. His eyes fluttered open and with a little cry, she ran to him, dropping down on her knees.

"God, I thought it was you," she sobbed.

He reached for her, pulling her down against him. He had to drag in another gasping breath before he could speak.

"It's all right," he soothed, lifting one hand to stroke her hair and press her head to his shoulder. She was trembling violently, and he thought how like her it was. She held up so gallantly, fought so courageously during the worst of it, only letting down now that it was done.

"It's all right, Summer. It's over. It's all over, now."

He lifted his head to press a soft kiss against her hair, then pulled her close against his side as she wept in long-awaited relief.

Epilogue

"You okay, Summer?"

She looked up at Dave Stanley and nodded. Her gaze strayed once more to the group clustered near the unmarked police car and the grimly labeled coroner's vehicle. Colter was surrounded by a group of men firing questions. She wished they would leave him alone; he looked so tired.

Dave followed the direction of her gaze. "They offered him his job back, you know," he said casually.

Summer looked at Dave, startled. She tried to control the sudden pounding of her heart. Would Colter take it? Deep down, did he miss the job, the highs, the chase? Now that he'd had a taste of it again, did he want it back? Had she ended his chance of leaving it behind forever by bringing him back here? She didn't want to think about it, about how she might feel if he did become a cop again.

"They did?" she asked finally.

He nodded. "Practically promised him a sergeant's position if he did. They'd like to make a little hay out of rewarding the man who uncovered a crooked cop. Cleans up the image."

She didn't want to ask what Colter had said, wasn't sure she wanted to hear the answer. As it turned out, she didn't have to ask; with an odd glint in his eye, Dave told her.

"He told them not a chance. That he had better things to do."

She couldn't hide the relief that flooded her. "It's their loss," she said fervently. "Colter's a hell of a cop."

"Colter?" Dave looked at her with raised eyebrows, then said teasingly, "Somehow, I got the idea you two were . . . a little closer than that."

Pink tinged her cheeks, but her voice was steady enough. "Closer than what?"

"Than calling him Colter."

"Oh, she calls me Shane." Summer hadn't heard him come up behind her and she nearly jumped. He slipped his arms around her as he added one more teasing word. "Sometimes."

Her face flamed as she remembered in vivid detail the times when she had called him by his given name. Dave grinned widely before he spoke again.

"Hey, before I forget, did you call that guy I told you about?"

"Yes. I think it'll work out."

"Good." Dave eyed the way Colter was holding Summer so closely. "Well, I'd better get moving. Give me a call before you leave, okay?" He left them hastily.

Leave? Something cold and hard grabbed at Summer's heart. She twisted in Colter's arms. She stared up at him as he intently watched the police cars begin to head out of the drive.

"Leave?" Her voice was tight.

"Umm-hmm," he said vaguely, his eyes never leaving the departing unit that held his former boss.

"I—"

Her voice caught and the tiny sound snapped him out of his contemplation. He looked at her, his eyebrows lowering at her look of confusion.

"What's wrong?"

She looked down, studying a button on his shirt. "Dave said they offered you your job back...and you said not a chance."

"Of course not. I still feel the same way about it. This didn't change that."

"So...you're leaving...?" Her voice was tiny.

"In the morning. I have to go—" he began before the sound of her voice registered. He gripped her shoulders and held her away from him so he could see her face.

"You thought I was leaving? Leaving you?"

"I—"

She lowered her eyes, but he'd seen enough. He pulled her back to him a little roughly.

"How could you think that?" he asked incredulously.

She lifted her head then, slowly, but at the look on his face, the words came out in a rush.

"I guess it was...the mouse doing the thinking again."

"God, you don't still believe that, do you?"

She looked down, studying that shirt button again.

"Summer, you're not that little mouse you're convinced you are. You never were. You've got more pure courage than anybody I've ever known."

Her head moved slightly, a tiny, protesting disclaimer of his words.

"You do," he insisted. "Summer, could a mouse cope with her family dying and her whole life falling apart? With having to give up her hopes, her dreams? Could a mouse face the realities you've had to face alone and keep going?"

He cupped her face in his hands and tilted her head back, forcing her to meet his gaze. "My God, Summer, could a mouse go after a killer with a damned knitting needle?"

She blushed and tried to lower her eyes, but he tightened his grip and made her look at him.

"No more, Summer. It's time you saw yourself for what you are. And I'll keep telling you until you believe it."

Her color deepened, but she held his gaze with worried eyes. "If that's true," she said slowly, "you don't have to...quit on my account."

He took a breath. "Summer, I love you. That's one of the reasons I turned down reinstatement. I would never put you through that. But it's not the only reason. I don't want to go back. Ever."

She sighed, the last flitting little doubt vanquished. She hugged him, snuggling up to the heat of him. "You love me," she said wonderingly. "Mmm, say it again. It sounds so wonderful."

"I wouldn't know."

His wry tone made her pull back and look up at him. "What?"

"I wouldn't know how it sounds." His mouth twisted into a slightly off-center smile. "You never said it."

Her eyes widened in shock. "I—I thought you knew. I never would have—"

She broke off, her cheeks flaming. Colter's smile widened. "No, you never would have slept with me, would you? You'd be incapable of making love with someone you didn't love. I know that." His smile became a little sheepish. "I guess I was waiting to hear it."

"I love you."

She said it suddenly, fiercely, then repeated it. Colter felt his heart give a funny, soaring leap in his chest. His throat tightened and to his embarrassment, he felt an intense stinging in his eyes. He swallowed, blinking rapidly, then sucked in a deep breath.

"You're right. It sounds wonderful." He let out the breath on a long sigh. "I could never leave you, Summer. When I said I was going, I meant to see that guy Dave mentioned. He's an ex-cop. He runs a training school out near Renton for corporate bodyguards, teaching them how to protect clients from kidnap attempts, terrorists, that kind of thing. He's been looking for someone to teach them offensive driving techniques. Evasion, pursuit—"

"What you did at the academy," she breathed in sudden understanding.

He nodded, grinning crookedly. "For once, my reputation was a help instead of a nuisance. When I called, he said the job was mine if I wanted it. I was only going out to meet him and look over the setup.''

''You won't miss Florida? You were . . . happy there. . . .''

''What I was in Florida,'' Colter said wryly, ''was kidding myself. I used to sit there chuckling at all the tourists who came to escape their futile little lives for a while. And all the time it was me escaping, trying to live without living. It's about time I woke up.''

''Oh, Colter.'' She hugged him fiercely. Then she tilted her head back and, with two spots of color staining her cheeks, said shyly, ''Or should it be Shane, like Dave said?''

He laughed huskily. ''No, I'd much rather you kept that for . . . special moments.''

Her blush deepened, but she never relaxed her hearty embrace. He returned it, crushing her to him.

''Marry me, Summer. I want a lifetime of those special moments. I want to wake up with you slowly and not have the world come crashing in. I want—''

''Yes.''

''Yes?'' He stared at her, willing her to repeat it.

''To all of it. To you.'' She lowered her eyes. ''To all those . . . special moments.''

His arms trembled as he held her. ''I love you,'' he murmured against her hair. ''I love you.''

''I love you, too.''

He held her for a long time before he said quietly, ''I want you to go back to school, Summer. I want you to go back to the Aquarium, do all the things you wanted to do.''

She made a small sound of repudiation. ''It's too late.''

He kissed the tousled blond hair again. ''Maybe for a mouse. Not for a wildcat.''

She raised her head, and the warmth and support she saw in those eyes that had always tumbled her insides took her breath away. She hugged him again, burying her face against his chest. Maybe, she thought. Just maybe it isn't too late.

After a moment, her head came up. ''Colter?''

''Hmm?''

''Would you . . . like to hear your first name?''

Puzzlement flashed across his face for a split second. Then a joyous, exultant expression took its place as he laughed delightedly. He swept her up into his arms, whispering into her ear exactly what he planned to do to make sure he heard that name often, for the rest of their lives.

*   *   *   *   *

SILHOUETTE·INTIMATE·MOMENTS®

IT'S TIME TO MEET
THE MARSHALLS!

In 1986, bestselling author Kristin James wrote A VERY SPECIAL FAVOR for the Silhouette Intimate Moments line. Hero Adam Marshall quickly became a reader favorite, and ever since then, readers have been asking for the stories of his two brothers, Tag and James. At last your prayers have been answered!

In August, look for THE LETTER OF THE LAW (IM #393), James Marshall's story. If you missed youngest brother Tag's story, SALT OF THE EARTH (IM #385), you can order it by following the directions below. And, as our very special favor to you, we'll be reprinting A VERY SPECIAL FAVOR this September. Look for it in special displays wherever you buy books.

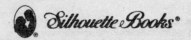

Silhouette Books®

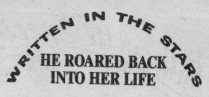

Silhouette Special Edition

presents

SONNY'S GIRLS

by Emilie Richards, Celeste Hamilton and Erica Spindler

They had been Sonny's girls, irresistibly drawn to the charismatic high school football hero. Ten years later, none could forget the night that changed their lives forever.

In July—
ALL THOSE YEARS AGO by Emilie Richards (SSE #684)
Meredith Robbins had left town in shame. Could she ever banish the past and reach for love again?

In August—
DON'T LOOK BACK by Celeste Hamilton (SSE #690)
Cyndi Saint was Sonny's steady. Ten years later, she remembered only his hurtful parting words....

In September—
LONGER THAN... by Erica Spindler (SSE #696)
Bubbly Jennifer Joyce was everybody's friend. But nobody knew the secret longings she felt for bad boy Ryder Hayes....

SSESG-1

MILLION DOLLAR JACKPOT
SWEEPSTAKES RULES & REGULATIONS
NO PURCHASE NECESSARY TO ENTER OR RECEIVE A PRIZE

1 Alternate means of entry: Print your name and address on a 3″ ×5″ piece of plain paper and send to the appropriate address below.

In the U.S.	In Canada
MILLION DOLLAR JACKPOT	MILLION DOLLAR JACKPOT
P.O. Box 1867	P.O. Box 609
3010 Walden Avenue	Fort Erie, Ontario
Buffalo, NY 14269-1867	L2A 5X3

2. To enter the Sweepstakes and join the Reader Service, affix the Four Free Books and Free Gifts sticker along with both of your other Sweepstakes stickers to the Sweepstakes Entry Form. If you do not wish to take advantage of our Reader Service, but wish to enter the Sweepstakes only, do not affix the Four Free Books and Free Gifts sticker; affix only the Sweepstakes stickers to the Sweepstakes Entry Form. Incomplete or inaccurate entries are ineligible for that section or sections of prizes. Torstar Corp. and its affiliates are not responsible for mutilated or unreadable entries or inadvertent printing errors. Mechanically reproduced entries are null and void.

3. Whether you take advantage of this offer or not, on or about April 30, 1992, at the offices of D.L. Blair, Inc., Blair, NE, your sweepstakes numbers will be compared against the list of winning numbers generated at random by the computer. However, prizes will only be awarded to individuals who have entered the Sweepstakes. In the event that all prizes are not claimed, a random drawing will be held from all qualified entries received from March 30, 1990 to March 31, 1992, to award all unclaimed prizes. All cash prizes (Grand to Sixth) will be mailed to winners and are payable by check in U.S. funds. Seventh prize will be shipped to winners via third-class mail. These prizes are in addition to any free, surprise or mystery gifts that might be offered. Versions of this Sweepstakes with different prizes of approximate equal value may appear at retail outlets or in other mailings by Torstar Corp. and its affiliates.

4. PRIZES: (1) *Grand Prize $1,000,000.00 Annuity; (1) First Prize $25,000.00; (1) Second Prize $10,000.00; (5) Third Prize $5,000.00; (10) Fourth Prize $1,000.00; (100) Fifth Prize $250.00; (2,500) Sixth Prize $10.00; (6,000) **Seventh Prize $12.95 ARV.

*This presentation offers a Grand Prize of a $1,000,000.00 annuity. Winner will receive $33,333.33 a year for 30 years without interest totalling $1,000,000.00.

**Seventh Prize: A fully illustrated hardcover book, published by Torstar Corp. Approximate Retail Value of the book is $12.95.

Entrants may cancel the Reader Service at any time without cost or obligation (see details in Center Insert Card).

5. Extra Bonus! This presentation offers an Extra Bonus Prize valued at $33,000.00 to be awarded in a random drawing from all qualified entries received by March 31, 1992. No purchase necessary to enter or receive a prize. To qualify, see instructions in Center Insert Card. Winner will have the choice of any of the merchandise offered or a $33,000.00 check payable in U.S. funds. All other published rules and regulations apply.

6. This Sweepstakes is being conducted under the supervision of D.L. Blair, Inc. By entering the Sweepstakes, each entrant accepts and agrees to be bound by these rules and the decisions of the judges, which shall be final and binding. Odds of winning the random drawing are dependent upon the number of entries received. Taxes, if any, are the sole responsibility of the winners. Prizes are nontransferable. All entries must be received at the address on the detachable Business Reply Card and must be postmarked no later than 12:00 MIDNIGHT on March 31, 1992. The drawing for all unclaimed Sweepstakes prizes and for the Extra Bonus Prize will take place on May 30, 1992, at 12:00 NOON at the offices of D.L. Blair, Inc., Blair, NE.

7. This offer is open to residents of the U.S., United Kingdom, France and Canada, 18 years or older, except employees and immediate family members of Torstar Corp., its affiliates, subsidiaries and all other agencies, entities and persons connected with the use, marketing or conduct of this Sweepstakes. All Federal, State, Provincial, Municipal and local laws apply. Void wherever prohibited or restricted by law. Any litigation within the Province of Quebec respecting the conduct and awarding of a prize in this publicity contest must be submitted to the Régie des Loteries et Courses du Québec.

8. Winners will be notified by mail and may be required to execute an affidavit of eligibility and release, which must be returned within 14 days after notification or an alternate winner may be selected. Canadian winners will be required to correctly answer an arithmetical, skill-testing question administered by mail, which must be returned within a limited time. Winners consent to the use of their name, photograph and/or likeness for advertising and publicity in conjunction with this and similar promotions without additional compensation.

9. For a list of our major prize winners, send a stamped, self-addressed envelope to: MILLION DOLLAR WINNERS LIST, P.O. Box 4510, Blair, NE 68009. Winners Lists will be supplied after the May 30, 1992 drawing date.

Offer limited to one per household.

LTY-S791